CHRISTOPHE DUFOSSÉ

School's Out

TRANSLATED BY
Shaun Whiteside

Published by Vintage 2007

2 4 6 8 10 9 7 5 3 1

French edition copyright © Editions Denoël, 2002
English translation copyright © Shaun Whiteside, 2006

First published in French under the title *L'Heure de la Sortie* by
Editions Denoël 2002

Christophe Dufossé has asserted his right under the Copyright,
Designs and Patents Act, 1988 to be identified as the author
of this work

First published in Great Britain in 2006 by
William Heinemann

Vintage
Random House, 20 Vauxhall Bridge Road,
London SW1V 2SA

www.randomhouse.co.uk

Addresses for companies within The Random House Group Limited
can be found at: www.randomhouse.co.uk/offices.htm

The Random House Group Limited Reg. No. 954009

A CIP catalogue record for this book
is available from the British Library

ISBN 9780099466727

Th   to
ensu   ees
th
cred   :an

For A.

'There is no question here of suspicion or innocence. Please say no more about it. We are strangers to each other, our acquaintance is no older than the church steps are high. Where would we end up if we immediately started talking about our innocence?'

Franz Kafka, *Description of a Struggle*

'This is really a good time,' Vern said simply, and he didn't just mean being off-limits inside the dump, or fudging our folks, or going on a hike up the railroad tracks into Harlow; he meant those things but it seems to me now that there was more, and that we all knew it. Everything was there and around us. We knew exactly who we were and exactly where we were going. It was grand.'

Stephen King, 'The Body'

1

Éric Capadis died in the Accident and Emergency department of the Trousseau Hospital at five p.m. on Monday, 19 February, 1995.

During the short time that he spent in classroom number 109 of the middle school he must, on a number of occasions over the course of the school year, have looked through the window – the window from which he could not, in the end, keep himself from jumping – at the chestnut tree by whose base his body would eventually crash. It had happened at about half past one, shortly after the second bell, as his year nines waited outside the classroom door to be allowed in. Later, in their statements to the police, they would say that when they heard no sound from inside, they concluded that their teacher was absent.

Groups of children were still crowding around the body a quarter of an hour later, when I tried to push my way through. Their tense faces, their ghostly stillness, accentuated by the police-car headlights which were switched on in broad daylight, made them look like the stunned survivors of an environmental disaster. Christine Cazin, who had been in charge of Capadis's training, clung to the arm of the PE teacher. She stood apart from the rest, beneath the flashing lights of the ambulance that had just pulled in to the school playground. She was a fair-haired woman in her early thirties, and Capadis had been engaged in an inconsequential power struggle with her from the moment of his arrival. When the deputy headmaster leaned over the body at the same time as she did, Christine Cazin raised a trembling hand to her mouth as though she were about to vomit.

A chubby-faced young policeman took some notes, indifferent to the hubbub beyond his notebook. He pressed his pen so hard on the paper that the muscles in his forearm tensed and relaxed in turn. Then he asked the disciplinary counsellor to round up some members of staff to move the pupils away from the accident zone. The supervisors brought in as reinforcements immediately formed a cordon sanitaire around the body, their fingers touching tip to tip. They looked like a ring of militants frozen in silent protest, lending the scene the impassivity of a comedy film. Events seemed to be unfolding at a glacial rate, as though the participants in the tragedy were running in all directions, but only in their minds.

The two ambulance crew, a man and a woman wearing cut-off jeans, got out of their vehicle and made their way towards the body with an air of weary competence, an easy gait that suggested a familiarity with violent death. The man must have been about forty. His face quivered with nervous tics. He screwed up his right eye and then, a quarter of a second later, pushed out his lips to create an effect of incongruous asymmetry. The woman, a few years older, raised her eyes towards me and frowned when she saw that I had my arms folded over my chest. I glanced away from her towards the school matron, who was eating an apple, and hesitated between lifting the collar of my jacket or running my hand over my unshaven cheeks to achieve an air of composure.

Exchanging a nod of agreement, the two ambulance crew crouched by the body and tried to arrange it in a straight line. Then they checked its pulse and pupillary reaction, and the woman opened its shirt and listened with a stethoscope. It was then that the man stood up and headed for the ambulance. He tried to open the back to fetch the stretcher, but the lock wouldn't open. Striking the door panel with the flat of his hand, he finally attracted the attention of his colleague, who stood up in turn to come to his assistance. With a gesture both supple and ironic, she held out the key to the door. No one dared to smile.

I screwed up my eyes against a shaft of winter light, and felt my face grimace with tension. The headmaster glanced at me with annoyance and slid back his glasses with his little finger, but it was administrative annoyance, a pale and casual glint in his eye, nothing more than that. He remained utterly motionless, an anxious line tugging at the corner of his mouth. Finally he lowered his eyes as though to rejoin the rest of the teaching body who had gathered around him.

It was the first time that I had seen someone die. It seemed clear to the little group of teachers bent over him that Éric Capadis would not survive his fall. I saw him struggling to open his eyes every now and again. Bright scarlet foam pulsed from his ears and his mouth. I felt as though I were watching him through badly focused

3

binoculars. He looked at the faces with what appeared to be a mixture of surprise and embarrassment, as though he didn't really understand what he was doing there, lying at our feet with his blood draining away, when he had always been so standoffish in his dealings with other people.

The blue of the police car's revolving light passed over his body, followed by the yellow. One of Capadis's legs, broken, stuck out at an unbearable angle. However courageous we might like to consider ourselves, an anxious dread insists on taking hold of us in the presence of the dying. Could it be the life still in them that alarms us? Before the ambulance crew finally removed him from our sight, I remember wondering to myself how I would have reacted in his position.

Éric Capadis had just turned twenty-five. He had arrived as a student teacher in the last week of September, after taking his teacher's exam in history at Créteil, where he had done most of his studies. The Paris teacher-training colleges had filled up very quickly, so for some unknown reason at the end of August the ministry had decided to send him to the Academy at Tours-Orléans for teacher training, a requirement if he was to graduate.

To the great displeasure of the headmaster, he did not start the new academic year at the same time as his future colleagues. The education authority had accidentally sent his file to another office, prompting the usual comments about the inanity of the system by which teaching staff were assigned. Someone even suggested that the whole matter be raised at a subsequent union meeting. A number of people were outraged that such obstacles should continue to exist between the various different departments, even at the turn of the new century. The suggestion was put forward with the best of intentions, and immediately forgotten. This brought it into line with the most significant daily plans, conceived out of habit and structured in such a way that they went precisely nowhere.

Éric Capadis taught six classes a week. He very rarely came to the staffroom, and this made his character both mysterious and thoroughly disagreeable to the rest of the staff, who interpreted his absence as lofty disdain. Once his classes were over, he dropped off his attendance sheet at the supervisors' office, handed in the key to his classroom to the school office, and then set off on his stork-like legs towards the teachers' entrance. Everyone at the Clerval College saw him as something of a stowaway.

He and I never tried to form any kind of friendship. He seemed to avoid conversations of any kind, especially those of a professional nature. He never talked about his training modules, he never expressed an opinion on the reforms that were then under way. He was not a union member, and neither was he affiliated to any teaching body. Worst of all, he refused to take part in disciplinary discussions.

I have few memories of him, but I do recall that his height seemed to be a nuisance to him, as though the gap between his head and his feet were a source of concern that he refused to acknowledge. Like all men who live at a distance from their own bodies, he appeared to consider his own actions with an oblique and doubtful eye. It was his eyelids, more than anything else, that drew attention to his face. They were thick, wrinkled, almost too large for his face. There was something captive about the eyes beneath. He had black, quite full hair, run through with

5

silvery threads despite his relative youth. His hair was receding on either side of his brow.

On two or three occasions he had been obliged to talk to me about trivial matters, in that hesitant voice he had. On each occasion I had been fascinated by his milky complexion, his thin neck and the bleak jiggle of his Adam's apple. I was reminded of the poignant solitariness of giraffes.

And of George Sanders, too.

The nurse, an Arab girl the colour of weak tea, strode down the corridor towards me clutching a temperature chart, and told me in a voice devoid of emotion, 'It's over, I'm sorry.'

Her first name, Nora, was written on her badge, like that of a waitress in a fast-food restaurant. Her glasses, attached to a cord, dangled on her chest. Raising my eyes, I noticed the uneasy overlap of her lower and upper lips.

'Are you family?'

'Not really, no.'

'What do you mean, "Not really, no"?'

The harshness of her tone left me disoriented for a few seconds. I started to speak again, attempting to summon her attention by putting as much pathos as possible into my facial expression.

'We worked at the same place.'

'So you're a teacher.'

I nodded.

All of a sudden she relaxed. A pair of crescent-shaped dimples curved along her olive cheeks. I've always been troubled by the fact that the mere mention of my profession is enough to put people at their ease. I felt, for no particular reason, that I could have taken advantage of this opportunity to establish a more direct current of affection between Nora and myself, but I have never been attracted to girls who work in medicine. I'm quite convinced that hospitals are swarming with people with a secret grudge against humanity.

'Would you like a cup of coffee?' she asked. 'There's a coffee machine near the front entrance.'

A young man in white overalls, jeans and trainers, who looked like a final-year pharmacology student, had been staring at me from the wall across the corridor as soon as Nora had started talking to me. Probably an admirer of hers, I thought. He wore glasses with very thick lenses. They were the prettiest thing about his greasy, ashen face, doubtless drained by nights labouring over books in tiny print. He had the look of a person who had for years taken his meals on the kitchen table, with a specialist journal resting open against a bottle of red wine, the kind of person who switched on the radio or the television the minute he came home from work.

'Thanks, I've got to go. I have to break the news to his family.'

'I can take care of that. In this line of work it's something you get used to.'

'Again I'll have to say no. I don't wish to call your expertise into question, but' – for fear of mumbling, I finished my sentence in a rush – 'it's something I'd like to experience myself.'

'What, exactly?'

'Going to an unfamiliar town, sitting on a sofa that belongs to some people I've never seen before, and talking to them about the loss of their son.'

7

'I see.'

She gave me a disapproving look. Her liquid eyes hardened, casting a mineral blue glow. I flinched involuntarily. I'd got her wrong once again; Nora was clearly a balanced person with a positive, rational mindset, intolerant of any kind of equivocation. I suspected, above all, that she must be the kind of person who particularly valued straightforward conviviality, utter devotion and situations free of grey areas.

'I'll give you their address and phone number. You should tell them you're coming beforehand.'

She began searching in the right-hand pocket of her blouse. The weirdo hadn't stopped staring at us. When he saw that Nora was scribbling in her spiral notebook, his shoulders peeled away from the wall he had been leaning against, trying to give an impression of ease belied by his facial expression. When she tore out the page and handed it to me, he abruptly started walking straight towards us, veering away at the last instant like a bullfighter. There was a brief feeling of awkwardness between the young woman and myself. Nora lowered her head, furtively watching the student disappear. Her face was pale, gleaming with sweat.

'Is that your boyfriend?' I asked.

'No, just someone I went out with a very long time ago.'

Her answer was delivered in a functional, impersonal voice that sounded as though it had been constructed syllable by syllable in an electronics laboratory. She raised her eyes towards me without blinking, her lips tight, as though she were retreating from the note she had just handed to me. She took my right hand in hers for a

8

moment that felt endless. The nails of her tanned and delicate hands were bitten to the quick and the sight of those little swollen pads at the end of her ravaged fingers almost made me feel sick. 'Good luck!' she said finally, then slipped away, holding the temperature chart rolled up in her right hand like a telescope.

I remained motionless in the middle of the corridor for a moment, my mind empty. From time to time a door opened some way away, a nurse came out and headed for another corridor. The sounds of the town, a few floors below, were very faint. I wondered, as I emerged from my torpor, how Nora could have got hold of Capadis's parents' phone number. I immediately thought of the school, but the school administrators didn't keep the next-of-kin details of state employees on file. It could only be the police. By now they would have done their report and classified the case: deliberate fall from third-floor history and geography classroom.

The swing doors of the treatment room clattered open and a male nurse appeared, pushing a trolley covered with a blanket, as he whistled a military march. One of his legs seemed to be shorter than the other, giving him a very lithe and mobile gait, and subjecting his body to an unstable equilibrium of asymmetrical and compensatory motions. He passed in front of me, ignoring me, as though he were pushing a shopping trolley towards a supermarket cash-desk. I had just begun to follow him, hoping to catch up with him, when he glanced over his left shoulder and noticed me. He stopped dead and smiled at me, revealing a row of tobacco-yellowed teeth. There were large sweat-stains at the armpits of his overalls. His breathing was irregular, and I got close enough to him to feel his breath against my cheek.

'Excuse me!'

'How can I help you?'

'Is that Monsieur Capadis?' I asked him, indicating the shape beneath the spotless shroud.

'It was.'

'Where are you taking him?'

'To the toilet.'

'And after that?'

'To the fridge.'

'Can I come with you?'

'If you like . . . but I warn you, he's not much to look at. You'd really be better off if you didn't . . .'

I leaned my head to one side in a gesture of assent. Those last words had been spoken in a very pleasant, almost protective tone. We headed towards the lift. I pressed the call button first. We waited in silence, avoiding each other's eyes. To distract myself, I looked over at the trolleys lined up in single file outside the secretary's office. The leather on them was cracked in various places, and patched with long strips of latex insulating tape.

When the lift doors opened, he gave the trolley a shove, and it immediately plunged inside the metal box, with the rattle that oars make in rowlocks. The slight gap between the level of the lift and that of the second floor of the hospital had the effect of shaking the trolley, and slightly disturbing the position of the body.

Entering the lift and casting an involuntary glance into the mirror opposite me, I noticed that Éric Capadis's right hand, palm upwards as though in a post-mortem gesture of supination, was dangling from the side of the trolley.

Because the nurse was standing on the other side of it he hadn't noticed this, and continued to smile with an expression of confident beatitude.

'I'm going to the basement. I'll drop you off on the ground floor, ok?' he said, his hand hovering expectantly over the button.

'Aren't you going to take me down?'

'As I said, I'd rather not . . . we're used to it, you aren't. When you don't work here, it can come as a bit of a shock; it's not a place for normal people.'

'Press ground floor, then,' I murmured finally, wondering what sort of image of me he was alluding to when he placed me in the category of 'normal people'.

During the ten seconds or so of our descent, I tried as best I could to put the hand back under the blanket. I was concentrating my attention so completely on this act that I forgot the force that was propelling us downwards, so much so that when we were halfway down I felt as though my body was stretching downwards while my head had remained on the second floor. I mechanically massaged the bones at the back of my neck.

The male nurse was watching me thoughtfully, like a science teacher waiting patiently for a delicate and sensitive pupil to dissect the nerve of a toad on a dissecting table. Finally the cabin stabilised with a hiss of decompression, and the hand went on sliding down the right-hand edge of the trolley.

'You won't get it back on there,' said the man, his finger pressing the button to let me out. 'The body's starting to stiffen. Rigor mortis, they call it in the trade.'

I didn't reply.

I nodded at him, before abandoning Éric Capadis for

11

good to this man's fleshy, powerful hands, with their blue veins through which life undoubtedly pulsed with athletic immodesty. I looked for one last time at Capadis's hand stretched out towards me, and, before running off, took it in mine, as Nora had taken my hand a few moments before, and pressed it so tightly that it was only when I heard the cracking sound of the ligament between the scaphoid bone and the radius that I loosened my grip.

The analgesic effect of the torpor into which I had been plunged by being separated from my former colleague began to dissipate. I shut myself in the hospital toilets to wash my face. My mood lifted in the hospital lobby as I wondered where on earth I had parked my car. I so frequently forgot where my car was parked that I had consulted a neurologist to rule out early-onset Alzheimer's. Passing through the automatic doors, I headed for car park B. The hospital also had a car park A and a car park C, but in accordance with what I had always thought of as my happy-medium approach to life, B was the one I finally opted for .

An east wind shook the trees, driving sparse grey clouds past a setting sun. I was walking back up the central avenue when my attention was drawn by the appearance of a human figure whose features, indiscernible for a minute or so, became more threatening the closer I got. It was the bespectacled student from a few moments before. He was leaning casually against the driver's door of my car, arms folded under his armpits, legs parted. I felt a stiffening in my muscles and a throbbing ache in the pit of my stomach, sensations familiar to me whenever a potentially dangerous situation loomed.

Although I was about ten metres from him, he still hadn't noticed me; he stared straight ahead, rocking his head back and forth and mumbling to himself like someone in a state of catatonia. I walked towards him, slowing down lest I attract his attention. As I drew nearer, I realised that he was listening to an old Wham! song on a Walkman hidden inside his jacket ('Careless Whisper', for a long time the soundtrack to an advertisement for a brand of hypoallergenic shower gel). He had a lovely voice, slightly gloomy, and at the beginning of the saxophone break he stopped singing and abruptly raised his eyes towards me. For a moment he was too startled to react, and then he pressed the stop button on the black box fastened to his belt, his panicked fingers pulling the headphones from his ears. Then he tried to look nonchalant, one thumb hooked in his trouser pocket. He avoided meeting my eye, or rather he nervously scanned my face before lowering his eyes again.

'He-he-hello, I-I-I w-w-was w-w-waiting for you,' he said finally.

'You were waiting for me?'

'Yes, I-I-I w-w-wanted to t-t-talk to you.'

'Tonic or clonic stammer?'

'Cl-cl-clonic.'

The course that his delivery took was really quite striking. At the beginning of a sentence his eyes went blank, his jaw and neck tightened, sweat pearled at his temples, his chest trembled as he tried to catch his breath. Finally his head jerked back and sideways, his thorax was gripped by convulsions and his eyeballs rolled upwards, like changing slides projected on to a white wall. I decided to adopt an attitude of indifference, not wishing to try and gain a cheap advantage by completing his sentences for him.

'How did you know it was my car?'

'Oh, yeah, well, right! I-I-I'm the h-h-hospital security man. Yeah, I s-s-saw you arriving.'

'Why did you follow me to re-sus?'

'Right, you see I kn-kn-knew you were going to see N-n-nora.'

'And?'

'Oh, yeah, well, right! I've got to t-t-tell you that you're her t-t-type of guy.'

He studied the fragmenting cumulus clouds, and inspected the nails on his left hand, but he still couldn't bring himself to look at me. His eyes caught mine, then he turned his head as though speaking to someone standing next to him, or to an invisible creature perched on his shoulder. His verbal fluency was distinctly less impaired when he said emphatic words like 'well' or 'right'. The deployment of these monosyllables suggested that he used them like stones in a ford, resting on them to step across the flow of his own words. His attempts to master speech filled me with admiration.

Clearly I was dealing with a jealous man who had misinterpreted something that had happened. Was he going to smash my teeth in? It didn't seem likely. Was he intending to frighten me just in case I was thinking of seeing Nora again? I was more inclined towards that interpretation. Now I knew he worked as a security man, any idea that he might have been a science student had fled. He reminded me in turn of a computer programmer, a French cinema actor, and finally of Elvis Costello. His attitude was friendlier than it had been before, as though the time had come to seal a pact of manly complicity.

'Fine, right, well!' he started again, 'she likes guys like

you' (he was now speaking in the toneless voice of an automatic answering machine; there was something intimidating about the mechanical rhythm of his voice) '– tall, dark, something intellectual about them, an effeminate way of walking and the kind of face that draws people to you.'

'Are you suspicious of me?'

'Yes, particularly since you aren't wearing a wedding ring, and something about your manner suggests availability.'

'I'm gay.'

'I don't believe you, or you wouldn't have been in such a hurry to accept the note she gave you with her phone number on it. I saw ev-everything!'

I smiled despite his involuntary stumble over his last sentence. His emotional pain was so tangible that I hesitated to ask him for details of his relationship with Nora. I had to dispel the misunderstanding immediately. I took the piece of paper out of my pocket and held it out to him, trying to make my gesture pleasant and relaxed, to avoid any suspicion of sarcasm.

'It's only the address of the parents of a friend who's just died.'

He took the piece of paper and deciphered it with a great deal of concentration, before handing it back to me, trembling. For a moment he stared sheepishly at the toes of his trainers. Then, blocking his ears with his thumbs and covering his eyes with his fingers, he slid down the door into a crouching position, as though plunging into a sea that was slightly too cold. He started sobbing helplessly. His posture made me want to take him by the armpits and lift him up, but an instinctive embarrassment and my basic inability to console anyone at all prevented me from doing so. Finally he stood up.

15

He rummaged in the inside pocket of his jacket and took out what looked like a passport photograph. I looked at him quizzically, trying to establish the meaning of this gift. He repeated several times that he was sorry, that I mustn't be angry with him, and then he started sobbing again.

Leaving the hospital, I suddenly felt the need to go for a walk in the woods.

On the way back, responding to a very unfamiliar impulse, I picked up a girl hitch-hiker. Plumper than average, she couldn't have been more than eighteen years old. She had blond hair parted in the middle and pushed back over her ears. Her eyes, edged with long silky lashes, but outrageously over-made-up, tried desperately to conceal her small-town ennui. She was wearing a pair of washed-out jeans, a shirt with little fabric dice on it, an old brown leather jacket and cowboy boots.

'It's easier to get picked up if you're a twig,' she said with resignation once she'd got into the car. 'I've been waiting an hour!'

Why had I stopped?

Guilt, I had thought, or perhaps it was more that recent events had aroused in me an empathy for an abandoned fat girl, her thumb raised at the roadside, that kind of image within the unconscious that assumes the most painful level of identification imaginable in the right circumstances. It was only when I lowered the passenger seat window and heard the squeak of the glass against its rubber housing that I realised the rashness of what I had done. Having committed myself by my initial decision to stop in front of her, I couldn't simply ask her the time and set off again.

I had an insane desire to know where she was going, as if it could have had the slightest significance in the circumstances: I was sure that this teenager might have killed herself if she'd had to wait another five minutes.

'I'm going dancing.'

'On a Monday evening?'

'Why not?'

'The discos are closed.'

My suspicious questions met with a smile of commiseration. Her body bent forward, her hands resting on her knees, she was still framed by the window. A communion medal attached to a gilt chain peeped out from the neckline of her blouse, and with it came a moist smell of armpits perfumed with vetiver.

'We don't say discos, we say clubs. But I'm not going to a club, I'm going to a girlfriend's house and we're going to put on some music.'

'And where does your friend live?'

'In a small village, ten kilometres towards Saint-Ménars. It's on your way, there's only the one road.'

'Get in.'

'Thanks.'

The mystery of soft flesh, sturdy thighs, pink-striped rolls of fat. The whole impressive network of flabby fluidity that I surmised beneath her clothes led me for ten minutes or so from my usual devotion to more austere female forms. I almost forgot about the meeting I was having the next day.

'Do you want to listen to some music?'

She made a vague gesture of indifference, followed by a silence which she filled by tapping her right thigh with her sausage-like, be-ringed fingers. Then she studied the

17

nails of her right hand, with her fingers folded into the palm and her thumb stretched out.

'What do you do for a living?'

'I'm a French-teacher.'

'Which school?'

'In Clerval.'

'That new one?'

'Yes.'

'I knew the old one really well. It was like a borstal. I can't remember anything apart from the faces of some of the teachers. You look pretty normal for a teacher. I had to resit year eleven. Five years of my life in there.'

She sighed, and her body relaxed, drawing a dull creak from the seams of her leather jacket. Hearing that sound of subsidence gave me a feeling of well-being, and the currents of tension that had been passing through the small cabin of my car faded away.

'What about you?'

'This and that. I keep myself busy. Nothing very steady.'

'What kind of things?'

'Part-time waitress, mowing people's lawns, collecting pine cones for Parisians, cashier in a service station . . . The kind of job that means I don't have to travel far from where I live.'

'Are you planning to stay here for long?'

'I was born here. My family lives here, and my friends, and my boyfriend too. Why would I go anywhere else?'

'Absolutely.'

She adjusted a curl over her left ear, revealing a lovely leather bracelet bearing the name 'Luc'.

'Is Luc your boyfriend?'

'No, he's my dog, a beagle. A great hunting dog.'

I should have guessed. Monosyllabic names like Paul or Luc, or diminutives like Greg, Fred or Chris, all have the insulting brevity of dogs' names.

'My boyfriend's name is Daniel, but everyone calls him Dany.'

'Have you known him long?'

'Since I was sixteen. We were at school together, and at the end of year eleven, first time round, we went out with each other. I wasn't crazy about school, and it was about the only good thing that happened to me there. Do you want to see a picture of him?'

She didn't wait for me to nod before thrusting her hand into the inside pocket of her jacket. She looked so happy at the idea of showing a stranger a fragment of her life that I was almost angry with myself for not having agreed more quickly.

'You'll see, he's absolutely gorgeous . . . but that's not the most important thing as far as I'm concerned, what you need's a boy who'll be nice to you and keep his nose out of your business. You've got to keep a life of your own, don't you think?'

She started laughing, a laugh that didn't convey any particular gaiety, but served merely to underline what she had just said. She held out the photograph of a boy sitting on a small motorcycle, one hand clutching the handlebar, straight blond hair cut short on top and apparently thicker towards the neck. He was wearing a tee-shirt on which a team of white huskies stood out against a black background. There was a hint of moustache on his upper lip, a purple crescent swelled beneath his right eye. Wearing a mulish expression, he was busy staring at a point above the photographer, as though posing was a nuisance.

'Well?' she asked anxiously.

'He looks nice.'

'Do you mean that?'

A pause.

'Of course.'

'You're not just saying it to please me?'

'Why would I do that?'

'I don't know.'

Suddenly she turned her head to the right and in a panic-stricken voice yelled, 'There it is! Stop, stop the car!'

I slowed down, putting on my hazard lights so I could stop as quickly as possible. She opened the door while the car was still moving. Once it had come to a standstill she grabbed the picture from my hands, stuffed it feverishly into her wallet and then pointed at the farm where her friend was waiting.

'Sure you don't want to come in? It'd be cool . . .'

'No, I can't.'

'Are you sure?'

'Really, I've got to get home.'

'Well, I won't force you. Thanks anyway.'

She dragged herself out of the seat with considerable difficulty, giving me a little wave. I watched her disappear down a dusty lane lined with willow trees, and imagined her in ten years' time sitting on an unmade bed, a pink mohair dressing gown half-open over her heavy belly, her jaw becoming jowly, clutching her head between the palms of her hands in a gesture of infinite disbelief.

For three years I've lived in a sizeable three-bedroom flat of the kind known as 'council housing'. When colleagues come and visit, they always say that on my salary I could afford to live in more agreeable surroundings, the kind of place where professional people usually live. But I've always been horrified at the very idea of paying an exorbitant price for what is in the end a rather derisory surface area of one hundred square metres. Despite the fact that I haven't got much furniture, I prefer to sacrifice aesthetics for space. It's the only fixed moral concept that I'm willing to acknowledge.

Generally speaking, when I get home, I avoid paying too much attention to particular details, the way you steer clear of certain subjects when you're talking to your family. Most of the mailboxes are scratched, others bear picturesque inscriptions. None of them shut. There's no lift, the walls are painted battleship grey – the same colour as the Airfix models of my childhood, a utilitarian, collective colour that stands out against the pastel hues of the stairs. The stairwell is always filled with a lingering smell of vegetable soup, laundry and cigarettes.

In front of the block there are two rows of pollarded plane trees that look more like wooden beams than trees; a few tufts of pale grass give the tenants the illusion of being practically in the country. Porticos support seesaws and swings with hemp ropes so worn that families forbid their children to use them. The wretchedness of these abandoned playgrounds is indescribable.

Arriving home, I sat down in front of the television and channel-hopped for half an hour. I wasn't looking for any programme in particular, I just wanted to recover that feeling of calm that I always get from a flow of moving images disconnected from any kind of plot. Watching a continuous sequence would have required a level of involvement of which I didn't feel capable.

My sister called me in the middle of a documentary about the Vietnam War. Soldiers were marching in the mountains, smoking cigarettes. Squat helicopters ploughed the sky in swarms, their tails raised behind them like dragonflies. I told her of the day's events, stressing the fact that I had no connection with the desperate man, as my sister had always thought that suicide was essentially contagious. I went to bed after looking through my binoculars at the flats in the opposite block, a spectacle that never fails to disappoint.

I had a lot of trouble getting to sleep that night. I couldn't stop thinking about Éric Capadis, Nora, the amorous security man, the fat girl and the solemn speech that I would have to deliver to the parents the following day. When I closed my eyes, black dots started sliding about against a red background, before exploding in a myriad of dense clusters that finally intersected in the form of little snakes, tracing luminous ellipses in the darkness. To escape this phosphene phantasmagoria, I turned on the light and looked at Nora's slightly over-exposed face lying on my bedside table, until little transparent knots started to float diagonally across my eyes. Exhausted, I finally turned out the light and then went to sleep with her name in my head.

2

It was break-time.

In the staffroom, half the conversations began with the words, 'Do you know what one of my pupils has written?' Then quoted in offended tones the malapropisms, infelicities, barbarisms, in short the thousand offences committed against good style by pupils ignorant of the French language. I had recently reached the firm conclusion that if conversations based on grammatical transgressions and child psychology were banned with immediate effect, the means of staff communication in secondary schools would be reduced to pure mathematics.

Clearly Éric Capadis's death hadn't changed that. There was still the same administrative background hum focusing on various familiar topics: headmaster's notes, promotion, union information, accounts of extracurricular activities in the local newspaper, postcards announcing births or impressions of trips abroad, not forgetting the summary of the ministry's official report. Waking up that morning, I had thought that seeing my colleagues again would do me good, distract me, maybe help me tackle my anxiety about relationships (I've lived alone for three and a half years) and morality (I'm working half-time so that I can finish a thesis, for which I'm shamefully plagiarising various other works), but perhaps we always expect too much of our professional colleagues.

I had taken a seat in one of the armchairs, eight of them, arranged in a diamond shape, an arrangement thought to encourage conviviality. The spaces of the room seem to have been designed in such a way that the eye can circulate freely. This deliberate absence of barriers was awkward at first, but one quickly developed a taste for spying on one's colleagues without their noticing.

A physics teacher opposite me was enthusing about prefabricated window frames which allowed for simpler and faster installation than the traditional kind. The others nodded and stared into the distance. Their eyes lit up vaguely when he pursued the topic of the value added by such frames when it came to reselling your property.

Someone else started talking about the comparative costs of installing a heated 'geothermic' floor, and a floor heated by a circulating-water system. He even asked my advice. It was the first time since the end of the holidays that someone had consulted me on a practical matter. I replied that I didn't really have an opinion, and returned to my misery.

Barely twenty-four hours previously, a young teacher had thrown himself from a window, and any morbid contagion that might have passed through these walls, any allusion to intentional death, had been carefully eliminated by our collective. A kind of conspiracy of silence now impregnated the place. The concern for a neutral tone with which each spoke to his neighbour, the vitality that gleamed in everyone's eyes and gestures, these little local diversions seemed to contribute to the preservation of a sense of health in our little group.

I was reassured, in a way.

Not only had fear been banished from the establishment, not even such a remarkable event was able to upset the balance of our little world. That was the absolute proof of our invincibility.

We had become so used to living without the unexpected. The moment a dangerous breach opened up in the walls of our world, we turned in on ourselves without ever losing our sense of solidarity as a group, the better to rethink the 'incident'. Only by stripping it of its drama were we able to forget it in the short term, and restore a sense of continuity. Each of us returned to his own task, swathed in that very particular corporate radiation that immunised us against reality. For us teachers, it seemed that the only way of surviving was to rein in our own perspectives as far as possible, day after day, to live as close as we could to our centres.

I'm somewhat ashamed to admit it, but on many occasions I found myself feeling sorry for people who aren't teachers.

How did they cope?

The first voice that reached me was that of Françoise Morin, a craft teacher with a voice that contrived to be raucous and intimate at the same time. This quality gave a warm inflection to her insulting remarks. She was universally respected for her role as a shop steward and as a mediator between the staff and the headmaster. Her frankness and direct way of speaking embarrassed most of her colleagues. She was one of those people who have remained closely in contact with their childhood states of mind, and who always give other grown-ups the impression that they're only pretending. Between her yellowed fingers she held the remains of a cigarette butt with a shaggy fringe of tobacco strands. The flame of her Zippo lit a miniature bonfire that expired on her overalls, stained with the distinctive mauve of potassium permanganate.

Françoise Morin was in heated discussion with Butel, a tall, elderly-looking, spidery young man, his eyes always smugly creased into a fixed smile and his arms moving around in ways suggestive of benediction. I deduced, from the fact that she was blowing her smoke into his face and that he was drifting, barely perceptibly, towards the non-smoking area, that she was trying to get rid of him. Since her tactic did not appear to be effective, and Butel was not to be persuaded, Françoise tried her hysterical laugh. In this performance, which I knew by heart, her head was thrown back, her hands rested like claws on her chest, and a series of incoherent exclamations exploded from her larynx, designed to bring down a few notches her interlocutor's faith in the pertinence of the information he was communicating to her.

I secretly admired Françoise Morin, as I admired all those people who had successfully silenced within themselves both communal voices and the fear of incurable illnesses.

Butel finally headed for the toilets. Françoise stuffed her cigarette into an empty coke bottle, and then came towards me, taking me conspiratorially by the shoulder.

'I've finally managed to shake off that idiot. A piece of inside information for you. For your eyes only. But only

26

if you invite me to dinner in a flash country-house restaurant for women at a loose end, women with freckled hands, cigarette-holders and all that jazz . . . You know my weaknesses: Trotsky, young bachelors like yourself and binary arithmetic. What d'you say?'

'That would be a no.'

She spat out a thread of tobacco that was on the tip of her tongue.

'Ok. Tex-mex or McDonald's. You can introduce me as your mother.'

'Each of us only has one.'

'Mummy's boy!'

'What's the information?'

'Tsss, tsss! What's your answer?'

'Twenty-year age gap. Usually women your age just want to take me to tearooms.'

'You little fucker.'

'I'm not free this evening.'

'Yeah, sure. Try again!'

'You're too good for me. Your proletarian origins, your art-nouveau face and that boyish appearance of yours all hold me in thrall.'

'Shithead.'

'Come on, out with it!'

'The headmaster wants to see you as soon as possible.'

'Why?'

'Why do you think?'

'My progress review.'

'You're daft.' She burst out laughing with a throaty smoker's laugh like a flight of locusts in northern Madagascar.

'Capadis?'

27

'Get a move on, he's waiting for you in his office.'

Her tone had switched to the professional part of her character. Clearly she wanted advance knowledge of the gist of my meeting with Poncin, the controversial headmaster whose mistress she had been for a good ten years. I had no classes on Tuesday morning. I'd shown up during the mid-morning break to do some photocopying and fill in some forms. Françoise Morin must have spotted me at the beginning of break, passed the word to Poncin and set the gears in motion for our meeting.

I walked past my pigeonhole (a teacher's second home!) to reach Poncin's office, and glanced at it out of habit. Among the indescribable chaos of dog-eared exercise books, salary forms and coursenotes crammed into shapeless cardboard folders, I found a card showing a sad-looking kitten crouched in a tiny basket full of pink wool. It was a Hallmark card, the kind of kitsch little photograph that you send someone to remind them of your presence in the world in the gentlest possible way. There was no message on it. Without thinking, I slipped it into the pigeonhole of Ginette Balard, a fifty-year-old spinster who dressed like someone in a Victorian costume drama, and who had adopted, ten years previously, a little Asian girl whose family had been killed in a bombing raid. Her rectitude and honesty in her dealings with other people greatly impressed all her colleagues. Even her moral intransigence was a permanent reproach to the rest of us, and we needed her goodness to give a balance to our lives. I reckoned she deserved the card more than I did.

Poncin was absorbed in the local paper when I knocked on his office door. He folded it up with the false ease of a Calvinist banker feeling guilty about a moment's relaxation during the conduct of his earthly affairs. He invited me in, rubbing his hands together as though they were a pair of cymbals, and then indicated one of the two standard black leather armchairs facing his desk. There was a moment of hesitation. He stared at the parquet floor as though searching for something, and must have felt my eyes fixed on his lowered lids. His effort at concentration etched a fold between his brows, above which two flaps of hair twitched slightly.

What always struck me when I found myself in Poncin's presence was his manicured nails, testimony, in my view, to the excessive care he devoted to himself. Second was his smell: there was a Swiss-German smell about him, a smell of the good dry wood of a mountain chalet. That smell often set me thinking. I knew only two other people who smelled like that: an uncle from Bern whose second marriage had been to my aunt, and my sister, a teacher who added to it a whiff of artist's chalk.

I tried to catch his eye, but saw only the velvety skin of his lids. While he fiddled with the top of a Bic pen, I cleared my throat to remind him that I was there.

'Have you ever wondered why there's a hole in the end of the top?' he asked abruptly, without looking in my direction. 'People are always curious about details like that!'

It was his way of unsettling the person he was talking to, by asking him a question unrelated to the subject at hand. This question was all the more pernicious in that it included a number of different aspects that had to be distinguished on the spot: the content of the question (the top), the intention behind the question (why was he asking it?), the form of the question ('Have you ever wondered?' presupposes that the person facing you has indeed asked himself the same question, and that it is there that his actual power over you resides) and finally, to cap it all, its degree of absurdity, which never corresponded to anything one was psychologically prepared for.

'Yes,' I replied in a toneless voice, 'it first appeared in 1993, imposed by regulation ISO 11540. It's so that children continue breathing should they happen to get one caught in their windpipe.'

'Exactly,' he said, looking at me with interest for the first time. 'So the teachers' exam is coming up?'

'I'm not sitting it.'

'Weren't you the one who wanted to pass the head-teachers' exam?'

'No, really, no.'

I had stressed my denial in spite of myself, and without any clear intention of denigrating the job that he had been doing for ten years. He reflected for a long time, with a finger resting on his lower lip, and his shoulders hunched.

'Yes, that's right, I remember, you're writing a book.'

'No, I'm writing a postgraduate thesis.'

'What's the subject?'

'I'm trying to show, using photographs, that writers always resemble their writings. An essay in literary physiognomy, if you like.'

'What drew you to the topic?'

'I had no clear thoughts on the question, nor any evidence. Subjects you know nothing about are easier to deal with, you don't get bogged down in facts.'

'Is it interesting?'

'It can be.'

'Yes, things are like that . . . and between ourselves, *do* writers always look like their writings?'

'Without exception. Apart from two, perhaps . . .'

'Go on, tell me.'

'Walser and Hawthorne.'

'I don't know them.'

'It doesn't matter.'

'Could you tell me if my face fitted my job, for example?' he asked with a slight trace of anxiety.

'That's a question I'd have to think about, I can't just give you an answer off the top of my head.'

'I'm asking you for a personal opinion.'

'Personal opinions just make a whole lot of trouble.'

'You don't like getting your hands dirty!'

There was a long pause during which I tried to avoid looking him in the eye. It was, typically, the kind of awkward question that people are always asking.

'I sense a terrible inner loneliness in you.'

'That's not the question,' he said, half hiding his face with the palm of his right hand.

'It's the only answer that comes to mind.'

'Let's move on to the subject at hand . . . You know . . . I very much appreciate your going to the hospital for news of our colleague.'

'How did you know about that?'

'A nurse called the school at about six o'clock in the evening to tell us about the death of that poor chap Capadis, and told us that you'd been there. I also knew that you were planning to visit his parents. When there's a tragedy in an educational institution, you will be aware that the administration usually delegates a representative to go and express condolences to the family in the name of the body as a whole. I have no problem with you assuming that role.'

He rummaged in his desk drawer and took out a Manila envelope which he handed to me with the solemnity of a chamberlain.

'This is a letter that I have written personally for Capadis's parents. I'd like you to pass it on to them.'

He had stressed the word *personally* as though I were about to suggest that he had hired a speech writer to discharge his duty for him. I tried to evince a genuine interest, and I even took the trouble to try and tell him how happy I was to observe that he had a sense of compassion, not essential in a person of his stature.

He then sank into his thoughts. The chalky cliff of his forehead was creased with concentration. He had stretched out his legs in front of him, and his chair had slipped a good metre back from his desk on its castors. Then, with his head still bowed, he explained to me the difficulty that he had had *personally* in standing back from this whole suicide business, which he still regarded with disbelief. He added something about the trauma experienced by the year nines, as though he were appropriating it to himself.

Two secretaries looked as though they were exchanging insults in the next room, but they were just having a giggle, something about a fax that had got stuck in the machine. A heavy shower started falling, and the light darkened a shade or two. Poncin switched on an imitation Tiffany lamp, and for a moment the multicoloured squares of the lampshade gave our postures a frivolous appearance. He glanced over my shoulder, his expression frozen in a moment of geological sadness. Suddenly his voice emerged from the gloom.

'I have a favour to ask you before you go.'

'I'm listening.'

'You can always refuse.'

'Pure rhetoric. If you'd thought for a moment that I might refuse, you'd have presented it as an obligation.'

'I don't like your tone.'

'Sorry.'

'So do you accept?'

'I have no choice.'

'Fine. I've talked to the deputy head about possibly replacing Capadis with a supply teacher, but she would rather we fill the vacancy ourselves. It's February, halfway through the school year, and Mme Spoerri thought we should try to avoid a certain . . . how should I put it? . . . discontinuity by bringing in outsiders unfamiliar to the pupils. To put it more clearly, the arrival of some- one from outside our "little community",' and he gave a slight chuckle, 'could be a destabilising factor for our pupils. They're already psychologically unsettled, and such a disturbance is to be avoided. Do you under- stand?'

'Perfectly.'

'That's why I thought you were the man to replace Capadis, given the flexibility of your timetable and your personal qualities, which are so universally appreciated.'

'Thank you for your trust in me, but I teach French, not history and geography.'

'It doesn't really matter . . . just do what you can. History and literature, as you know, aren't so very distant. Mme Weber, the head of history, will lend you some textbooks.

I can guarantee that you won't be working any harder than you normally do.'

'If I understand you correctly, you want me to take on another six hours of teaching on top of the nine hours I'm doing already.'

'No, no, not at all,' he replied, holding out the palms of his hands, 'you'll divide up your six classes with Mlle Cazin, the history and geography teacher who was in charge of Monsieur Capadis's training.'

'In that case . . . all right.'

I felt an inexplicable melancholy as I heard myself accepting those additional three classes. I slumped in my chair, then thrust my body forward again. Raindrops hammered on the glass, lending an equatorial density to our conversation. Finally I put both my hands on my knees, having sat with my arms crossed over my chest throughout the entire conversation. All of a sudden I felt filled with a cool and calming sensation.

Poncin looked at his watch.

'Are you going to see Capadis's parents today?'

'Yes, this evening. They're expecting me at seven. I phoned them this morning,' I replied, recalling Capadis's father's gruff voice on the phone.

'The evening's better, in fact. Today's Tuesday, which means you'll be starting with the year nines on Thursday afternoon. Is that going to be all right?'

'It'll be fine.'

'One last suggestion about that class: never so much as mention your predecessor. I don't think I have to explain why.'

'What are you worried about?' I asked.

'Contrary to what most people think at this school, I'm

a very simple person, and fear is far too complex a feeling for me. I'd be quite grateful to you if you'd pass the message on.'

He broke off as though he'd just registered after an hour of uninterrupted monologue with a deaf-mute that the other person could hear and speak perfectly well.

'I'm willing to bet that you're a Capricorn,' he said, shaking my hand. 'According to my own statistics, most teachers are Leo or Taurus, the signs that are linked with self-esteem, rootedness in reality, allergy to pain and grief. Tell me if I'm wrong?'

'I'm Scorpio with Cancer in the ascendant. Limited inner life, lack of involvement with the prevailing social organisation, excessive fatalism and self-pity, hypochondria, self-hatred, a negative and cerebral attitude . . . it's true that I do get on very well with Capricorns. What about you?'

'Try and guess . . . see if I look like my star sign.'

'Gemini?'

'How did you guess?'

'I read my horoscope in today's paper. It said that a Gemini was going to drop something annoying into my schedule.'

Capadis's parents lived in a whitewashed brick house with wisteria running along the roof of the veranda and above the front door. The bars of the railings were covered with honeysuckle. Once past the gate, a gravel drive curved up between two rows of cypress trees. On the inside of the curve stood a knurled oak tree, surrounded by a wooden bench hideously disfigured by woodworm clearly greedy for extreme sensations.

35

Night had fallen a long time ago, but the garden was lit by four spotlights. The front door emitted a pale, almost ghostly light. The ancient porch that hung over it looked like a bat's wing or a Chinese pagoda, depending on where you looked at it from.

As I moved towards the front door, I thought I could hear the sound of running water; I stopped and tried to work out where it was coming from, apparently somewhere on my right. I set off down a little path that I hadn't been able to see until then in the gloom. I climbed the few steps of a stone staircase and walked around a cypress. Here, the narrow strip of sandy earth passed beneath a jumble of trellis which resembled the knot of a shroud. I pushed my way beneath the arch of foliage, my muscles tense with the cold that grew more and more piercing, and stood still, waiting for my eyes to get accustomed to the dark.

The first thing I made out was a fallen plaster statuette representing a chubby, smiling little god. Suddenly a noise behind me attracted my attention. It was the sound of leaves being trodden on, or swept in front of someone. I remained rooted to the spot, my spine stiff and tingling, the nape of my neck bent, my stomach so tense it was about to explode with fear. Sweat trickled down my right cheek, and then ran along my neck. It was finally absorbed by the wool of my polo neck. I thought in turn of a nocturnal bird, a provincial reptile, an insect with elephantiasis, a squirrel in its death throes and finally the ridiculousness of my situation.

In the end I turned my head three-quarters of the way round to try and see whatever it was that was moving behind me. I had barely turned my head when a dark mass came panting over and stood beside me. As I remained motionless, the dark mass stood in front of me and, without warning, placed two paws on my hips and tried to plunge its head into the hollow of my groin.

I rang the bell. The labrador was still by my side.

'Pépito helped you find the way, then,' said a small lady clad in a beige velvet suit, as she opened the door.

She was as dry as a mouthful of salt. Her face was almost entirely covered with wrinkles. Folds and puckers, little furrows scattered above her mouth. Her hands were old, long and worn, with translucent blue veins lacing their tired joints.

'I took a little stroll, you have a lovely garden,' I said, leaning forward. 'Pépito and I met down by the arbour.'

'I hope he didn't get you dirty with his feet. He's always very affectionate with visitors. Please, do come in. You didn't tell me your name on the telephone, you're Monsieur . . .?'

'Hoffman, Pierre Hoffman.'

'Hoffman, Hoffman,' she said with a finger at the corner of her lips. 'Are you Jewish?'

'Not to my knowledge, no. My parents were from Alsace . . . an old Lutheran family. Perhaps on my mother's side . . .'

'Come in, Monsieur Hoffman, it's very nice of you to have come all this way. Poor Éric . . .'

She didn't finish her sentence, but stood back behind the door to let me pass. The brighter, more garish light enabled me to ascertain, with a glance at my jacket, that the woman was very well acquainted with her dog's habits. The noise of a television set – as well as an underlying scent of pipe tobacco, damp leather and disinfectant – hovered between us. The wall-lights emitted a glare that forced me to narrow my eyes for a few seconds.

'My husband's really going to have to put forty-watt bulbs in those,' she said as she closed the door. 'Don't go thinking that we want to dazzle our visitors!'

They were the kind of old-fashioned lamp that you could still get from mail-order catalogues – the bulb fittings had fake candle wax running down the sides. Because the light forced me to look towards the floor, I noticed that the granite tiles had been meticulously cleaned, suggesting a certain level of expectation or at least a sense of duty far beyond the requirements of the situation. Various tourist snaps in cheap frames were lined up in a row, leading, with a slight gap on the right-hand side, to a little wooden staircase with marine rope as a banister, which must have ascended to two or three rooms overlooking the courtyard.

'Watch the two steps as you come out of the hall,' said Mme Capadis, closing the door.

I let her pass.

She walked with her back slightly bent, and because of my height she was forced to look at me from below, with a hesitant smile. The atmosphere of the place was exactly as I had imagined: Capadis's parents must have been self-contained pensioners, awkward when it came to having a conversation unrelated to their daily life. The habit of keeping to strict timetables, the lack of contact with other people, the constant presence of each other: I imagined that those three factors must have made them rather impatient with the outside world.

I followed her through a reception room that must have

been a study, to judge by the desk, covered with greenish fabric, that stood by a French window. Dead flies the size of haricot beans lay behind the velvet curtains, and the wallpaper was peeling at the corners. The décor was sober: a fireplace set back from the room and a Hungarian parquet floor. The beams and joists visible in the ceiling gave the place a touch of rustic charm, almost making the deafening noise of the television seem out of place.

Mme Capadis opened a heavy oak door, unleashing the booming voice of a game-show host. I followed her into a vast dining room from where I could not at first locate the television. Opposite the door there was a cherrywood buffet-table. A tarnished mirror above the fireplace reflected a dresser with a central niche containing old plates and earthenware pots. The weighty furniture, along with the chocolate-brown wallpaper and the dark hexagonal floor tiles, made the place prematurely receptive to the falling dusk. The room's texture seemed to be closing in on itself.

Stepping further in, I noticed a spinning-wheel, a rustic bread box, a number of chests and two card tables along the walls. In the middle of the room a large white wooden table with baluster feet and a crosspiece in the shape of an elongated H attracted the eye with its massive, austere presence. All of this furniture seemed sunk in thick, black, velvety shadow. There was something remarkable about this diverse collection, allied to the fixity of life, a life that had accepted its own limitations. I took another few steps forward. A large coal-black television turned its back on the rest of the room as though it had felt a technological contempt for its older companions since its arrival. The glow from the screen, the only source of light in the room, flickered in the glass eyes of the stags whose stuffed heads decorated the walls.

'Georges,' Mme Capadis called gently, cupping her hand around her mouth, 'Monsieur Hoffman is here . . . could you switch off that television, please?'

She gave me a submissive look, the equivalent of someone clearing their throat in an administrative context. The colour had faded from her face, and a hint of remorse was suggested by one of the wrinkles around her mouth. She went and stood in front of her husband, an ageless man huddled on the sofa, apparently hypnotised by the screen. For a moment she seemed to be angry with him, in a strangely personal way, as though ironically apologising for being a vague form that interfered with his solitude.

'He's a little hard of hearing,' she said, turning towards me.

She waited for a few seconds for him to look in our direction, and then went and resolutely turned off the television. Her husband glanced up at her, keeping his head absolutely straight, his mouth pinched as though he were suffering an absolute injustice. He was wearing a lorry driver's pullover, a pair of green work trousers with a patch pocket that had a folded metre-rule sticking out of it, and a stout pair of boots. He was a vigorous man of about sixty with quite a full head of white hair. His face looked fairly affable as long as you didn't notice the venomous jowls and the ferocious, bushy eyebrows. In his deportment he affected the manners of a young man, but there was discouragement in his grey eyes. Glassy pouches had formed inexorably beneath his lower eyelids. When he registered my presence, he assumed a pompous pose, with his elbow jutting out and his hand held open. His wife went off to the kitchen and returned with a chair which she set down opposite the sofa.

'Do sit down,' she said to me, pointing to the chair. 'Excuse the mess.'

She went and sat down next to her husband, taking care to leave a space between them, apparently according to long-observed rules. I had expected to be confronted with a replica of David Hockney's painting *My Parents*, that kind of lazy stereotype that you can sometimes have of the middle classes. Their existence was not at all unlike the painting: they led a calm and organised life, devoid of passion, but they only had to sit down side by side to look good-natured, almost indolent, like animals at rest.

'Can I get you something, a drink, some coffee?' asked Georges in a voice more guttural than I had expected.

'Thanks, I won't disturb you for very long.'

They didn't even utter a word of polite denial; they left the phrase floating above the low table. They remained sitting side by side, their hands clasped under their knees, their backs quite perpendicular to their legs, and they didn't so much as blink when my eye came to rest on them. There was something insulting about their apathy. I had a sense that they only tolerated me because they guessed that I wasn't going to stay after half past eight, the threshold beyond which I might have compromised their chances of watching the evening film. At the very worst they would miss the ads.

'Did you know him well?' asked Mme Capadis, lingering over the words with a trace of intense weariness.

'No, not really, but well enough.'

'Enough?' the man asked brutally. 'What do you mean, "enough"?'

I allowed a few seconds to pass, staring over their heads at a collection of little porcelain thimbles inscribed with the names of towns, assembled on a glass tray. This intimate geography made me think of a life that they must have lived in a far-distant past, and which they sometimes remembered as scraps of a more responsible reality that they had progressively abandoned as they grew older.

'Just enough to come here.'

'You knew him better than we did, then,' said the lady as fatalistically as one might view a flood.

'Didn't he ever come and see you?'

'He came twice in five years,' the man replied harshly, 'and each time it was to collect some of his things . . . his old model ships or his dog posters, never for a birthday. He never phoned, never wrote. We didn't even know if he was married, if he was living with someone. Can you imagine that?'

'I don't know. My parents have passed away.'

I lied on purpose, not wishing to side against a dead man about whom I still knew nothing.

'Capadis, that's a Greek name, isn't it?' I asked to change the subject.

'Quite so. We came to France when Éric was born, in 1970. We lived in Paris first, before coming here. Éric was always cross with us for leaving Paris. He felt very isolated in the countryside. It was different for us, we knew the way of life. We both came from farming families.'

And then their son had been a success. Constantly misunderstood, the school reports full of good grades, eulogies that distanced him more and more each day from the history of the country, from his origins, from the family romance. His parents would look at all those A-pluses and

A-double pluses crammed together with the same air of distress, the same dark shadows around their eyes, haunted by their offspring's betrayal. The wide world, which began just beyond their neighbour's field, had seized hold of him, making him unfamiliar and offhand, forcing them to live on a low heat, with the lid closed. Over time their sense of loss had turned into resentment at the world in general. Their view of things, remote and melancholy, was that of those who have withdrawn from the world one step at a time, turning away from any kind of contact with other people. The accumulation of objects must have had a compensatory function, to console them for having lost their direct contact with life, the massive and reassuring presence of their son which might have halted the slow-motion catastrophe of existential ennui. The longer I looked at the objects, the more I felt that there was something taciturn about them, like a life refusing any kind of description because that would have meant losing all conviction, all density of meaning.

'I've got to go.'

'Don't be angry with us . . . there are a lot of things that we won't mention, and which wouldn't be of interest to anyone. It's better that way.' (Silence.) 'Éric is dead, it's sad, but there's nothing we can do about it. He wanted to know, to know more and more, and, well . . . even as a child he couldn't even spend more than half an hour in his room, he always had to go and see what was happening outside! It was always more interesting than anything that was going on at home. That was a terrible torment to my husband, he never said anything, but I'm sure that deep inside he'd have loved to teach him more. Because he knew a lot of things that are only ever passed on within

43

families, you know, secrets that aren't in books but only in real life. Éric never wanted to learn anything from us. My husband was hurt . . .' (loaded look towards Georges, who lowered his head) '. . . sometimes I tell myself that by keeping those things to himself he must have ended up forgetting them.'

'I'm not angry with you,' I replied after waiting for a few seconds for fear of interrupting her.

How could I have been angry with them? I had come to talk the language of mourning, sadness, compassion, and feel that dark pleasure, that false empathy you have with passing strangers. The sense of an imperative duty, eating and drinking with human beings, talking with them about their loss, had, in my eyes, represented the kind of gratifying lack of commitment that kept me away from any kind of group psychotherapy involving girls wearing leather sandals and boys with dandruff on their jacket collars. In return, I had encountered resistance and unexpected confusion. I had been met with the language of abandonment and ingratitude.

It was time to go.

'We'll come with you. Are you going to the funeral on Friday?'

'I don't know yet.'

'It's being held in the village cemetery, at three o'clock. The procession starts at the church at two.'

'I don't know yet.'

'Won't you stay a little, have a bite to eat before you leave?'

The man had just asked the question with an intensity that fell away with his final words. Man and wife had risen to their feet at the same time and stood where they were for a few seconds, hesitating about the next step to take, the next word to utter.

'No . . . really, thanks, I'm a bit tired. I know the way. You stay where you are, you'll catch cold. Will you let me drop in . . . another day . . . just to say hello?'

Their cheeks turned purple with surprise; nodding their heads, they held out their hands almost simultaneously, which eased the sense of awkwardness that followed.

'Safe home,' said Georges. 'If you're passing by, drop in. You're very unlikely to disturb us. I'd hurry, though, if I were you.'

I promised.

From the garden gate I looked down an asphalt boulevard lit by streetlights leading right to the centre of the village where I had parked my car. About 300 metres away you could see, if you focused your eyes on the last two oak trees of the double row that punctuated each side of the road, the indigo oblong of the town hall with its green bench in front of it. I walked slowly down the boulevard. The moon was the colour of madder orange, and a chill breeze lifted scraps of alfalfa grass like a bundle of amaranth and deposited them in the bramble-covered ditch.

I thought of my parents, whom I hadn't seen for two years, and the phone call I'd been promising them for two months. It was only as I passed by the tufa wall of the cemetery at right-angles to the road that I thought once again about Capadis, the child and the teenager that he must have been, and the fact that he had chosen to be a teacher. There must have been some connection, but I stopped thinking about it as I left the village, concentrating only on the speed of my driving.

3

Running through class 9F's coursebook for the fifth or sixth time in a row, I discovered that Éric Capadis had finished three-quarters of the history and geography curriculum on Friday, 16 February, the date of his final class. I had been sitting in my office for two hours, trying to formulate a coherent plan for the rest of the year. There was no particular urgency, since the first class was an introduction, the second, on Friday morning, had been cancelled to allow the class to go to the funeral, and the February holidays began that evening and would last a fortnight.

But at my first class, the following day, I had to present a bi-annual report designed to maintain a reassuring sense of community for the pupils. It was half past five on Wednesday afternoon, and between that moment and the idea of my future performance a zone of utter incomprehension was beginning to settle. I had even phoned Christine Cazin for some information. After mentioning the fact that her one-and-a-half-year-old son had mumps, and spending half an hour criticising the egocentric and superior character of her former student, she excused herself, saying she had some urgent shopping to do, and effectively hung up on me.

I was impressed by the fact that Capadis had managed, in the course of a term and a half, to cover modern Europe in the seventeenth and eighteenth centuries, absolute monarchy in France, the questioning of absolutism, the major phases of the French revolutionary period from 1789 until 1815, and, by way of conclusion, the various transformations of Europe after 1815. This didactic foundation worried me. It wasn't its regularity or the fact that it hammered out an intangible rhythm, but the way he had hurried through his syllabus as though he were racing against the clock, as though he had had a tragic prescience of events to come since the start of the school year.

He had, of course, arrived a fortnight late, but I was sure that that discrepancy wasn't enough on its own to explain his accomplishment. He had raced through the course 'at breakneck speed', and in spite of my inclination to be suspicious of metaphors, particularly in view of their limitless power, I found that expression so suggestive that I lost the little concentration I still had left.

As the afternoon stretched off into total inertia, and I consulted the various subjects studied since the 25th of September, the beauty of Capadis's prose style continued to exert a great attraction upon my flagging attention. It was a curious mixture of precision and fatalistic emphasis, as though he had wished to defy the abrupt and systematic tendencies of administrative officialese.

The entry for 15.02 read as follows:

After a two-hour session, a comparison between the situation in Europe at the end of the eighteenth century and the situation in

47

1815 effected with the help of documents of different kinds (a page of the Civil Code, a map of the French départements, David's Coronation of Napoleon, etc.) led the pupils to highlight the transformations wrought at every level of the political structures of society, as well as the aspirations born of new ideas and utopian visions which have never been satisfied since that era.

I was also struck, in another entry, by a final rhetorical flourish which bore a certain resemblance to some Golden Age book of manners:

Using maps, we highlighted Europe's political, economic, social, cultural and religious contrasts. In the field of art, the study of the baroque and classicism, taking as our starting-point examples from painting and literature, enabled us to show that a dichotomy also existed within the heart of man: on the one hand, a pronounced attraction to changing forms, violent passions and inconstancy; on the other, a powerful need for stability acquired through restrictive regulations, the desire to escape that 'deceptive power' of the imagination.

This account of his activities, pointless and anonymous though it might have seemed (he didn't even take the trouble to sign it), convinced me that I was reading the Work of Capadis, as opposed to his life, which he must have felt to be deficient in both language and meaning. He seemed always to have moved within the same habitat, and to have become aware very early on of its meagreness and lack of prospects. I imagined his attempts to populate it with an imaginary crowd, his spectral guests, always the same, moving endlessly around in the same sitting room.

★

The sky was white, and colours faded in the saturated light. A few isolated clouds had assumed a faint coloured lining. I became aware of a yearning for snow, a climatic appetite for whiteness and withdrawal. When I reached the motorway exit that I took regularly to get to school, five police cars and fire trucks were arranged in a quincunx around a car that had crashed through the safety barrier and finished up facing the wrong way.

I slowed down. A crowd of people was starting to form around what remained of a metal crash barrier which bore an unsettling indentation, cavities and pointed gashes. The few people who had come to gawp were already down at the scene, talking to each other as though in the balcony of a theatre. Putting my car into neutral, I noticed that some people had brought binoculars and some of them let them dangle over their bellies as they discussed the spectacle with their neighbours. A man knocked on my window. He had a gap-toothed smile that almost made me jump, and asked me in a sibilant voice if I could give him a cigarette. When I replied that I didn't smoke, he looked at me in dismay, as though he were sincerely sorry for me for having lived half my life without filling my lungs up with filth even once.

A gust of wind suddenly brought the irregular rattle of a pneumatic drill. I edged my car forward to try and reach the end of the slip road. The front part of the vehicle that had been hit was completely crushed, and crumpled upwards towards the windscreen. The driver's side gaped like a toothless mouth. The firemen had just forced off the doors with hydraulic jacks. The crowd of onlookers grew more and more dense as the minutes passed, and it looked increasingly less likely that the driver would be

49

saved, the warped metal looked so much more like a piece of avant-garde art than a car.

Some motorcycle cops emerged from further up the motorway where the traffic was still flowing quietly, and forced the crowd – not to disperse as one might have imagined – but to clear the road by pressing themselves against the barrier so that any new arrivals could witness the closing minutes of the drama.

I was ten minutes late for school. The school gates always reminded me of the entry to a crematorium. But beyond the low cream-coloured walls and the well-tended geranium beds, the huge lawns and the clumps of poplars gave a sense of being on the campus of a teacher-training establishment or a Jesuit college. The only insult to good taste lay in the bits of twisted metal that rose two or three metres into the sky, like a spherical astrolabe by Giacometti suffering from delirium tremens.

The children of 9F were grouped in orderly pairs behind a chalk line marked with the number 109. As I walked towards them through the playground I heard a muffled sound, a host of indefinable sensations that began to tremble around the pupils. Out of the group there emerged a tawny-coloured face covered with freckles, a boy standing almost to attention, his wall-eyes staring straight ahead with the intensity of a horseguard.

A girl with a cold, bony face and black hair that looked as though it was drawn in India ink, wearing a fake buckskin jacket, jodhpurs and a 'Girl Power' tee-shirt, stood next to him with her hands on her hips and her shoulders thrown back in an attitude of mute defiance. I took it that she was the class delegate, since her pose identified her as the group leader, and made it clear that all communication would pass via her.

'9F, hello!'

'Hello,' they echoed faintly.

They merely stared at me, as if waiting for some kind of signal.

'Sorry I'm so late,' I told them, keeping my eyes on the girl with the black hair.

She didn't blink.

I had a key-ring that hung from one of the belt loops of my jeans by a little snap clasp, one of those 'youthful' accessories whose covert purpose is to establish an immediate rapport between the thirty-year-old teacher and his target pupils. I detached it and held my car key out to her, its crenellations pointing towards my chin.

'Could I ask you to move my car? . . . It's not hard to recognise, it's a small car, the kind you don't actually need a licence to drive, red with white dots and a little nodding dog in the rear window.'

There was muffled laughter.

'I can't drive toy cars . . .'

There was a dead silence, punctuated by voices droning through the half-open windows around the playground.

'. . . but I'm happy to have a go,' she said finally, letting her fingers, with their black varnished nails, fall on the key. Her smile formed a mocking and contemptuous arch in the corners of her mouth. The other pupils still hadn't moved. They seemed to be waiting with vague interest to see what happened next. She took a step forward, turning her back on the group, and held out the palm of her right hand to return the keys to me.

'You're playing a funny sort of game, but if I disappeared with everything . . . you'd have a hell of a lot of trouble getting the class started. Having said that, you've got quite a sense of humour!'

'Thanks. You're miss . . .'

'Botella. Sandrine Botella.'

'Are you the class delegate?'

'Well, no . . . the delegate's this little kid behind me,' she answered without turning round.

A yellowish-looking girl with a brown bob raised her head slightly in my direction and looked at me from below her fringe with an attitude of defeat. She was wearing a mottled grey jacket tailored to look like a greatcoat, matching trousers, and a pale grey shirt with stripes across her chest. Her apparent sophistication, timeless and allusive, contrasted with the substantial and practical presence of her colleague.

'Could you go and fetch the register from the headmaster's office?' I asked her.

She nodded ambiguously. Just as she was about to leave the others, a boy's voice came from the group.

'I've got it, sir!'

The delegate fell back on her feet with a sigh of relief.

'Let's go!'

They followed me in close ranks like a disciplined troop. I sensed that they had developed these disciplines all on their own, establishing voluntary limits a long way from school codes and adult decisions. My initial impression was that they were neither a class, nor a group, but a gang.

Having reached the door of the classroom, they lined up against the wall, waiting for my invitation to go in. I opened the door and went inside, looking to right and left as though watching like a hawk, and put down my bag on the first table of the middle row with a gesture that was supposed to be both generous and relaxed.

It was vital, I thought, to catch the tune of the group and show no sign of nerves. My usual technique for adapting to a new environment was to develop, as a matter of urgency, a precise course of action in order to create a space of unthreatening relations. The great problem with this strategy was that I seldom got beyond the idea that I had formed of people, remaining firmly attached to my initial impression. I had always been convinced that the structure of my personality depended on the maintenance of this attitude (I'm afraid that only people who lack boundless confidence in life will understand what I'm talking about).

I couldn't help glancing towards the window from which Capadis had thrown himself. It was a pivoting window with a superimposed frame, which was opened by being rotated around a horizontal axis. There were three such windows per class, all on the same white standard pvc model which gave any administrative building the healthy, uniform appearance of a clinic of palliative care. There were no bits of paper on the floor and the chairs were tilted forwards, their backs resting against the desks, in perfect harmony. My wastepaper basket had been emptied and the blackboard wiped with a sponge, not a common-or-garden rag that might have left traces of chalk. I found it hard to believe that they'd spent all morning in the room. I took my time settling in, stretching my legs out in a straight line with the rest of my body so as not to obstruct the circulation of the blood. A luminous globe stood on the top right-hand corner of my desk. Some slides, designed for an overhead projector that looked rather neglected in the map corner, lay on the desk-top like a film of translucent jelly. There was an indefinable smell in the classroom, based around some sort of floor-cleaning product and cheap perfume with a strong musky base. No compass or Stanley knife had disfigured the desks, which had the smooth and immaculate appearance of furniture in a room that might have been used as the seasonal setting for a seminar of financial analysts.

It might have been an assertion of austerity, a minimalist conception of school work. Instead it suggested something more unsettling to the visitor, there was something about it that told me that when they returned to this room, *their* room, everything I might have predicted or imagined about them would melt away along with the vague meanings that accrue for most people on the margins of normal life.

As the pupils passed through the classroom door I was aware first of all of a swarming of maleness, a concentration of masculine energy. The sensations of femininity only came afterwards, once the class had taken up their positions beside their chairs without a murmur, staring at me with faces free of expression. The last time I had seen pupils waiting for a teacher to give them permission to sit down was at the Protestant college which I myself had attended, and for a second I had a vivid mental image of the portrait of Luther above the blackboard. I often thought of the practice of standing to attention in the civilian context an old custom that had fallen into desuetude, a tangibly unsettling fragment of the past. If some pupils continued to show their respect in this way,

54

it seemed to me that they were asserting a sophisticated attitude connected with the exercise of some obscure power.

'Sit down!'

There was barely a sound, barely a scrape of chair against floor. The room contracted with sudden violence, and the fluorescent lights that had just been switched on somehow shifted the still and wintry context in which I was to speak. I studiously avoided staring at any one pupil in particular, and only by taking advantage of the initiation rite of the register was I able to observe each of them as casually as possible. Eleven girls, thirteen boys (apparent respect for conventions), and an evident diversity of social origin.

I took some questionnaires out of my bag and asked Sandrine Botella to hand them out. To my great surprise, she got to her feet without demur, and silently acquitted herself of the formality, licking her fingers to separate the copies. She handed me the leftover sheets with a smile that clearly told me I would be dealing with two different personalities: the one inside the walls and the one outside them. I nodded my thanks ('message received') and tried to lower my voice an octave to adopt the serious tone expected by my job and my age. I even decided to change the tempo (*andante moderato*) in order to introduce myself and explain the purpose of the questions they'd been presented with.

'My name is Monsieur Hoffman. My first name is Pierre. I come from a nearby town whose *lycée* you will probably attend in due course. I arrived in the region two years ago.'

'Where are you from originally, sir?' asked a tall boy

with cropped fair hair and thick glasses, raising his finger very high.

'Strasbourg. I'm from Alsace.'

I heard some muffled giggling. One pupil was using his thumb and index finger to make a silhouette that was supposed to imitate a stork, the symbol of the region.

'How old are you?' a girl asked, her hands deep in the pockets of a pair of denim dungarees, without raising her finger. Typical question for a girl.

'Thirty-two.'

'Are you married?' (Same girl. Same remark applies.)

'No.'

'Children?' (A different one.)

'No.'

I felt a wind of perplexity wafting around the class-room. Generally speaking, a positive answer concerning marriage or paternity closed off the field of imaginary possibilities for the rest of the year, while a negative reply encouraged fantasies about the existence of a secret life. In the hit parade of reasons for wanting to stay on one's own at what was really quite an advanced age, the number one slot was occupied by womanising bachelorhood (the solution favoured by the boys), then came homosexuality (distinctly privileged by the girls), and finally the impos-sibility of finding a soul-mate (a touching and 'human' solution that appealed equally to both).

I went on.

'On the sheet that has just been handed out to you you'll find questions concerning not only your everyday situation, but also, and more particularly, your cultural prac-tices.' (Pause for scrutiny.) 'You may be surprised by the questions concerning your tastes in music, cinema and books, and you would be right to be. You are under no obligation to answer them. I'd just like you to formulate a coherent and well-argued reply to the last question: what do you expect to get out of your history and geography class?'

'Can we put sports down?'

'Television programmes?'

'Shortcomings? Positive qualities?'

'Optimistic? Pessimistic?'

'Open? Closed?'

'Hot? Cold?'

'Heavy? Light?'

'Standing up? Lying down?'

Each table started voicing its own little dichotomy with the rather exhausting delight that the act of writing lists so often occasions. I sensed that if I didn't intervene soon, I would be subjected to the whole range of contemporary dialectic.

'Just stick to the questions on the page.'

Startled by my tone of voice, they looked at each other as they took a sheet from their ring binders. It was only when I heard their fountain pens scratching the paper, and was certain that their thoughts were entirely focused upon their answers, that my sense of being in a real-life situation began to fade. My muscles relaxed, my head felt lighter, and a post-prandial drowsiness detached my brain from the confused energy of the group.

I had a sudden memory of being the same age as my year nine pupils. It had been in 1976, the year that saw the emergence of the punk movement that was to see my first real introduction to the world. My sister, who was four years older than I was, read *Libération* like the grown-ups, and in that paper I remember reading a phrase that continually haunted me all through that year: '1976 will be a great year for rock'n'roll because it's the only authentic music, the only medium that really responds to young people's aspirations, the only way of really kicking out the jams.'

Did I have any aspirations? I don't think so. Had I ever, even in a confused way, felt any desire to make something of myself? I can't remember. It seems to me that in retrospect it was the adjective 'authentic' as applied to the term 'music' that had grabbed me; I wanted to get to know 'the only authentic music' when its appearance on the scene had only just been announced. As a child, I had always been frustrated by things appearing and then vanishing again before they'd really got going. I had even wondered if it hadn't had something to do with the fact that my childhood had been played out between the end of the sixties and the beginning of the seventies. Throughout the whole of that period, I had desperately wanted to join in with events, to be in tune with them, but I had a sense that they moved forward so quickly that I only ever grasped their surface appearances. To put it another way, their 'authentic' content evaporated as they were emerging, and this gave my childish existence a spectral quality that haunted me for a long time.

The guitarist of the Who, Pete Townshend, declared one day, as though to confirm my impression: 'When you listen to the Sex Pistols, "Anarchy in the UK", "Bodies" and tracks like that, what immediately strikes you is that *this is actually happening*. This is a bloke, with a brain on his shoulders, who is really saying something he *sincerely* believes is happening to the world, and saying it with real venom, and real passion. It touches you, and it scares you – it makes you feel uncomfortable.'

It's true that 1975 hadn't been an outstanding year for 'young people's aspirations' in France: Gérard Lenorman sang 'The Ballad of the Lucky Ones', Michel Sardou sang 'France', and Nestor (the ventriloquist David Michel's little penguin) sang 'Mussel-fishing'. In the cinema, Claude Lelouch had made *The Good and the Bad*, and J. D. Simon the immortal *It Always Rains Where It's Wet*. You can understand why, given the urgency of the situation, people all over the country had joined bands, and after only three days of rehearsals, without having ever touched an instrument before, they were already going up on stage in ripped-up clothes adorned with a clanking mixture of large safety pins, swastikas and badges bearing aggressive slogans.

These days no one remembers how ugly the first punks were. They were anorexic, they had pock-marked, acne-covered faces, they stammered, they were sick, scarred, damaged, and what their revolting decorations emphasised was the failure already etched on their faces. Their very acts were ugly. Some fans, more extreme than others who were content with spitting, stuck their fingers down their throats to make themselves vomit. Then they picked up the vomit in their hands and blew on it, yelling, to spread it to the people on stage like a contagious disease.

I also remember the shop Harry Cover in the very middle of Les Halles, where you could pick up tee-shirts emblazoned with pictures of these new groups. The shop distributed the magazine *Rock News*, a dogmatic and condensed version of this self-proclaimed underground.

The articles were outrageously aggressive, and created the comical impression that the barbarians were at the gates of every village. And I can never remember that period without thinking of the excitement I got from anticipating the execution of jazz fans and disco lovers, anglers and psycho-sociologists, which was, according to the leaders of the movement, to take place the very next day.

Of all the many groups that appeared around this time, my favourites were the Ramones. Four guys in jeans, sneakers and leather jackets with improbable haircuts, proud to be old schoolmates who were still together at the age of twenty-two. Minimal text, basic music, two chords repeated over one minute forty-five. All they did was sing about their culture: sex, television, violence, and I shouldn't imagine they'd ever got beyond the first chapter of a Dickens novel. There were two fake brothers, Joey and Dee-Dee, two utter cretins who couldn't string two sentences together in an interview. But what struck me as particularly romantic about them was the fact that they stuck with music that was as repetitive as the railway timetable, just so that they could avoid ever leaving childhood behind. To my timorous child's eyes, they represented one of the last forms of contemporary resistance to the adult world, as represented by the Beach Boys, the Carpenters or the Everly Brothers. As regards the Ramones, they just kept on yelling out the same childish babble that they had used in the sandpit, and spurned the developed syntax of successful people with a colossal candour which always represented, in my eyes, the very essence of rock'n'roll.

Like the Situationists, whose inheritors they might reasonably have been considered to be, the punks had, with a remarkable lack of method, set about destroying all the values, knocking down all the walls that made story-telling possible. The anarchy that they called for was a destruction of the origin rather than a return to it ... unlike the hippies, to whom they were, in a sense, 'clever' successors. It would have to be acknowledged that this scorched-earth policy was about to open up an era of unprecedented cynicism and paranoia, in which everyone became convinced that *he alone* was right.

In retrospect, the punk phase seems to me to have been the final jump before the dive into the world of social communication. After the first failures of the system, many experts claimed that we were witnessing a bad realisation of utopia. At the time we didn't know that we were, on the contrary, experiencing the realisation of utopia plain and simple, that delicious moment when it begins to collide with reality.

Late in 1976 my parents, my sister and I were living about forty kilometres north of the capital. My father had just changed jobs, and we had left Strasbourg, without regret, for the Valois, a region that my mother considered to be ultra-Catholic. In December, the local community arts centre had organised a punk festival. It wasn't the first one. In July, there had been a festival in Mont-de-Marsan, and another one at La Borde in Félix Guattari's 'anti-psychiatric' clinic. The organisers' over-riding obsession seemed to be the desire to create punk Woodstocks all over France.

On the bill were Atomic Booze, Pain Face and Angelic Disease, groups that vanished long ago, and are to a large extent forgotten. My sister, who had passed her driving test, suggested that we go there with her then boyfriend, Mathias, a boy with a healthy-looking face and large, distracted brown eyes. His hair stuck straight up in a threatening way, and he later admitted to me that he used wood glue to keep it like that. I assume he's totally bald these days.

The venue, with its vaguely communitarian, boy-scout ideal, wasn't entirely attuned to the event. The posters spoke of pottery sessions and macramé lessons, as well as non-verbal expression workshops. Slogans like 'Youth is culture, and culture is youth' stood alongside advertisements for summer camps in Lozère and exhortations to show solidarity with certain Third World countries. The corridors leading to the concert stage had an indefinable smell of aftershave and goodwill.

In the hall itself, the audience was clearly divided. On the one side there were the punks who had come from Paris, and who were proud of their distinctive clothing – their dad's suit bristling with badges, and ties with knots not much bigger than a pin-head, their pointed shoes and their dark glasses. And on the other you had the locals, who looked at once easy-going and slightly alarmed.

When the first group began its set with a real blitzkrieg of noise, I noticed a couple in their fifties at the back of the hall demonstrating their incomprehension of the musical business by plugging their ears and looking to one side with an air of forlorn world-weariness that seemed to say, 'What do you expect? It's from Paris!'

The punks gesticulated in front of the stage, doing an improvised kind of Situationist cha-cha. They raised their knees to their chins in cadence, throwing their legs around in front of them without the slightest concern that they might hurt anyone. They hurled themselves against each other with rictus grins that quivered with mischief and hatred. Later it would be called *slam dancing* and *pit diving*, names for brutality like any others. Girls with multi-coloured hair, studded leather jackets and dog-collars around their necks provoked the long-haired teenagers with obscene gestures and openly sexual invitations. The boys seemed more concerned with the musical technique of the group on the stage.

When Atomic Booze got up on stage, they were welcomed by a shower of spittle, one of many testimonies of friendship among the punks. In reply, they raised their middle fingers to the members of the audience in an almost Pavlovian gesture of thanks. Even before they'd played a single note, the lead guitar and the bass were partly covered with saliva. It didn't reach the drums, which were at a discouraging distance from the edge of the stage. The guitarist, a wiry, old-looking boy with a lock of hair covering the right-hand side of his face, affected a contemptuous smile when he wasn't turning his back on the audience to adjust the volume controls of his amplifier. The one pupil that he did reveal was of such pale blue that it seemed in some mysterious way to have leached into the white of his eye. The girl singer started the set with a yell of 'Hi, wankers!', which unleashed a Dionysian frenzy. 'This one's called "Horror Typist"!' bellowed the drummer, who started hammering out a deafening roll on the snare before the girl at the mic started up with the usual 'One, two, three!', the magic triplet that tended to launch hostilities.

My sister, Mathias and I stayed close to the bar along with the locals. Mathias's face was growing more and more uneasy as the evening wore on. He seemed finally to have noticed that the flow of negative energy was oscillating dangerously as a result of the ingestion of bad beer and exchanged glances. His horror reached its climax when some punks who were a bit drunker than the others started smashing bottles on the floor and rolling about in the splinters, which glittered like menacing grains of quartz.

Later, my sister explained her then boyfriend's relationship with punk. According to her, Mathias had only ever encountered the movement in the form of badly recorded tapes and the special dossier that a monthly music magazine had cobbled together for fear of missing out on the nascent phenomenon. His private revolt did not seem fierce enough to bear what he later analysed as a characteristic form of self-loathing.

At the beginning of the third song, poetically entitled 'Die, Fuckers!', my sister took him by the hand, and they threw themselves into the tumult with the courage and self-denial of the early Christians. Léonore (and I only give her that first name as a guide because my sister had many nicknames, which relegated her real name to the rank of an administrative commodity) had always had the gift, whatever situation she found herself in, of practising a dangerous form of hedonism which sometimes led her into ill-considered actions, just so as 'not to miss out on her evening'.

Holding Mathias by the hand, she pushed her way into the middle of the melee of arms and legs. The punks were so surprised to see anyone joining them from the back of the hall that their immediate reaction was to link elbows in a kind of round-dance. Emboldened by what they took to be a welcoming ceremony, my sister and Mathias felt obliged to show that they were a match for the gesture, and after being jolted violently to the centre of the circle, they started hurling themselves against the punks.

From where I was standing, I wondered with some concern when the circle was going to become a pincer movement (I already had no time for anything that didn't resemble a book or a record). This performance lasted almost a minute and a half, the duration of a song. When the music stopped, the punks stood on the spot waiting for the next onslaught. The singer stood there, hands on hips, gazing out at her audience with a lascivious air that at first provoked a murmur of incomprehension. As the punks prepared to shift up a gear, the musicians started making animal noises that were supposed to simulate the sounds of coitus, while the singer simulated fellatio with the foam tip of the mic.

Mathias and my sister were still at the centre of the circle, arms dangling, sweat-drenched hair stuck to their faces, which bore an expression of terribly anxious inquiry. A couplet repeated *a cappella* and amplified by an echo chamber resonated around all the corners of the hall at a pitch that was almost physically painful. The interference of the instruments suddenly ripped through the atmosphere, already heavy with expectation, and unleashed a deafening shock wave. The musicians settled into a slow, muggy tempo, and the singer dropped to her knees, her peroxided hair sweeping the stage with the regularity of a metronome.

As expected, the circle closed around Mathias and my sister, who rolled frightened eyes at the sight of the mute faces approaching them like sleep-walking zombies. One big guy was lifting his arms up and down, top to bottom, fingers outstretched, as though he had just turned himself into a pair of human secateurs. The others immediately imitated him, and advanced on the central duo, bending their legs like Sumo wrestlers.

Taking advantage of a moment of respite in the barbarian advance, Mathias said something into my sister's ear, and she nodded back. The punks made for the centre once more. The singer started screeching like a woman possessed, rolling on the stage which was stained with pools of beer and crushed cigarette butts. Gripped by this musical form of the St Bartholomew's Day massacre, I held my breath, hoping I wouldn't have to go for help.

To universal amazement, the two of them bent down simultaneously, passed like goblins between the legs of the malicious punks and hurled themselves laughing, hand in hand, towards the exit. Their lightness, the grace that suddenly animated them, that aura that can only come from an act that is gratifying in your lover's eyes, caused me an unendurable shame that was to pursue me throughout the whole of my adolescence. Since that day, I have always sworn to intervene in any potential conflicts that threaten my loved ones.

For ten minutes or so I leaned on the bar, studying the various liqueur bottles that made the place feel like a hotel lounge, and waited for them to come back. I didn't dare look towards the stage, which was now quiet once more. The barman, a man in early middle age with arched eyebrows and a shaggy beard that covered the whole of his face, chewed on a pencil while trying to find a solution in a grease-spotted crossword.

'Eruption of gas, four letters,' he murmured without raising his head.

'Fart.'

'Thanks.'

When the thirsty punks started converging on the bar, I made for the exit. A gibbous moon illuminated a park with large numbers of trees and tiny patches of grass. In the darkness, in the distance, the oak trees seemed to be crowding one another in a continuous network of branches. The ground was scattered with Guinness bottles, crushed cigarette packets, a yellow plastic toy, the scattered remnants of a local newspaper and a pair of broken sunglasses. One cloud of smoke, followed by several others, rose from a bush like a series of strips of milky gauze, and I went over to it. Muffled laughter could be heard at regular intervals.

As I drew closer, I saw some hippies sitting in a circle either making or smoking joints the size of megaphones. Once my eyes had become accustomed to the darkness, I could make out the faces of my sister and Mathias, suddenly lit by the glow of a nearby cone. Pressed close against one another, they were looking beatifically at the fragments of moon that resembled little stains of ochre-coloured wax. Mathias's hair was plastered over his fore-head, and my sister looked as she always did.

The strident ringing of the bell dragged me from my daydream.

The pupils were already getting their belongings together for the next class. They had all put their questionnaires on the top right-hand corner of their desks, in the place where the hole for the inkpot had always been, right through until the 1970s. I cast my eyes over their faces for one last time before they left. There was not the merest hint of self-hatred to be seen, no inner conflict, no transgression of the laws of social gravity. On the contrary, what I had in front of me was what we are obliged to call 'citizens', children aware of their place in the world, possibly litigious and manipulative when their own interests are threatened. I envied them their reconciliation with this world, which earlier generations had sometimes thought worth confronting. I felt sorry for psychoanalysts and anyone else who dealt professionally with mental illness: an era of unprecedented unemployment was about to open up for them.

'Can we go, sir?'

'Please do.'

After all, this was their place.

4

On the screen, a young woman was hugging a much older one. If you looked very carefully, you could read expressions of almost incredulous happiness on their faces. From time to time the younger woman broke away and shook the older one by the shoulders. Was she a sort of apparition that had to be kept firmly on the ground if she was not to fly away? It was very hard to make out their conversation. A steady stream of music obscured their words. Then they walked side by side, gesturing with their hands and fingers. The music faded away, and a voiceover commented:

'Catherine and her daughter Éva are meeting up after years of separation. They are both deaf-mutes. Following a hang-gliding accident, Éva has lost her memory, and her mother, despite many clues as to her whereabouts, had lost trace of her. Thanks to this programme and the huge network of solidarity that you, the viewers, have helped to build, Catherine and Éva have been reunited. But let's listen to what they have to tell us . . .'

The subtitle appeared on the screen and vanished again like words on an autocue. The music started up once again. The mother and daughter were still walking side by side. The camera drew ever closer. You could now see them at three-quarter height, shot from a low angle. They went on talking with their dancing hands. Then they stopped again, and stood opposite one another. The camera rose to their faces, seen in profile. Sounds seem to be coming out of their mouths. It looked at first as though each was reading the other's lips, but if you looked more carefully, it became apparent that they were gazing into each other's eyes with a strange intensity. No one could have guessed what they were able to read there.

The film was followed by a debate presented by a man wearing a dark suit that was decorated with a little red ribbon. A very courteous, smiling man who seemed to have the common touch. This time the mother and daughter were sitting side by side, signing to an interpreter who translated their replies to the audience.

At that point I picked up the remote and zapped to Sternberg's *Blonde Venus*, a film that I knew by heart as I did all the films that Sternberg made with Marlene Dietrich. She was a nightclub singer, performing 'Hot Voodoo' in a monkey suit, and all of a sudden the grim rabbit hutch in which I had been persuaded to live for three years was transformed into somewhere actually quite pleasant.

There was always a moment when programmes featuring real people depressed me. Could it be that I didn't feel sure enough of myself to be receptive to someone else's story for very long? I thought it was entirely admirable for people to go into a television studio to tell their story, or talk about a particular moment in their lives. The novelistic dimension of real life always softened my heart, and gave me a sense of connection with others, an important illusion when you've been living on your own for a long time and the very idea of any kind of encounter assumes a terrifying potential for uncertainty. What inspired me from the titles onwards was a genuine visual impulse, a sense that I was finally going to be touching something like a real experience. That's probably why I never missed programmes under the pertinent rubric 'reality television'.

I was fascinated by that attempt to link up with other people, neighbours, parents, in order to reconstruct a life, externalising things in a studio just in order to give something of yourself; a kind of pure presence, utterly shameless. Sometimes I found myself wondering why I spent more time justifying the existence of these programmes than I did actually watching them. There was a contradiction there, a kind of absurdity that I was powerless to understand.

The endtitles came up on the screen. For fear of being seduced by the next programme – a documentary about the transplant of animal organs into humans – I pressed the stop button on the remote with my hand, which was wet with the condensation from a little bottle of tonic water.

I spent ten minutes in the dark listening to the noises in the street, the gurgling of the pipes. It was a break that I allowed myself each evening before going to bed, a way of excavating secret passages through the block of flats where I lived discreetly. Buildings have their own sound archive of creaks and clicks, generally caused by variations in temperature. I was like a researcher sitting in a little cubicle in a vast library, clicking on different sensory zones, mentally separating them out according to a premeditated plan. So sounds of intense conjugal relations generally developed at about half past ten, subsiding half an hour later to make way for a convivial chorus of snores that the plasterboard walls did their best to absorb. By eleven there was not a sound to be heard. The televisions, the radios, and then the human beings faded slowly into the silence of night.

The building was inhabited for the most part by a ghostly population of office-workers, a vast collection of people whose compliance with the dominant value system required them to get up early. During heatwaves that encouraged the opening of windows, the hushed whirr of video recorders revealed a surprisingly keen interest in a particular kind of programme, usually shown late at night during the week.

Violence was rare. In two years, leaving aside a few acts of vandalism committed in the basement and on vehicles parked in front of the building, the block had always been a haven of communitarian peace. Only one unemployed 45-year-old had caused something of a stir by hanging himself in his sitting room, from a hook that he himself had installed, in defiance of the express prohibition by the residents' association on drilling holes in the wall.

The man had been divorced for about ten years, and had no children. He was a quiet tenant with no record of misbehaviour; no one ever came to visit him, and he never went out. He had been dead for a month before the concierge, alerted by a dead-animal smell, thought of phoning the fire brigade. He had just scribbled a note, which was left out on the sitting-room table beside a magazine devoted to the lives of the rich and famous: 'All my remaining belongings I leave to my ex-wife.' This story had brought me back to my own solitude (any excuse, eh?): if I died now, who would notice? Who would find my corpse?

The desperate man had practically nothing left except a television and video player, an orange-patterned 1970s sofa, a drawing-room table decorated with stuck-on beer mats and a wall of pornographic video cassettes: his imaginary museum. I found myself imagining his wife's face when the lawyer called her in to receive her husband's legacy.

My fifth-floor neighbours and I formed a sort of clan that was respected by the other tenants in the building. Not only did we represent the middle of the building, which had nine floors (the idea that my body was the meeting point of the building's force-lines did nothing to appease my anxieties as a resident); we were also the only inhabitants to maintain any degree of contact with one another.

My neighbour on the left was a quiet 85-year-old pensioner whose sole ambition was to go on living for as long as possible, 'to piss off his offspring', as he put it himself. He was, according to my neighbour on the right, a 45-year-old hairdresser with a strong Mediterranean accent, 'stinking rich'. Most of his grandchildren were waiting for their inheritance so that they could pay off their second homes. In old age he had assumed a fanatically negative personality. I had never met anyone before who was so fervently 'opposed to life'. I was certain that the only thing keeping him alive was the pleasure that he derived from the visits of his heirs, when they came to assess the ravages of time. I imagined his insect eye resting on them, an eye that could grasp in a second the thousand facets of an issue or an object.

One day he told me, with the poker face that he had maintained for the past seventy years, that he had made up his mind from now on to keep only one chair in his kitchen, so that no one would be tempted to invite themselves in. Then he had given me a look out of the corner of his eye with the knowing air, the elegant understatement that was his personal trademark. I don't quite know why, but when I glanced at him unexpectedly he always made me think of a big toy monkey.

Like many old people, he could sometimes be wearing, but a guilt that I have always felt towards old people, and which I cannot explain, meant that I could listen to him talking for whole evenings at a stretch. Each time I left he insisted that I accept a banknote or two as though to compensate me for the time I had spent in his company. I think he must have known that I was as alone as he was, but that at my age it didn't matter. He reminded me from time to time, with polite insistence, that at the age of thirty-five he had been married with three children, but that it hadn't changed anything, and that you always ended up on your own sooner or later.

A cloudless sky, as motionless as the air in a freezer, hung over the concrete blocks of flats opposite mine. It was half past seven. The white sky seemed to shed some of its reality as I watched it, and began to look like a painted ceiling in a film set. At dawn, after a night of half-sleep, I had gone out on to the balcony to contemplate the silence of the city stretched out before me. Wrapped in a

74

claret dressing gown over a pair of pyjamas with a pattern of little embroidered teddy bears, I thought about the questionnaires that I had gone through before going to bed.

As far as their cultural pursuits were concerned, the pupils had read the same books (often given to them by the school), seen the same films, and listened to the same music. I thought about Adorno, that amusing German moralist who had predicted, in the short term, the large-scale standardisation of the products of the culture industry. He might have been interested in my questionnaires. It's easy to mock those who speak of the decline of civilisation, all those painful frowns, bitter grins and hands held firmly behind their backs. You listen to them, a little tired of their questions and their challenges, nodding away next to the coffee machines and praying for your plastic cup to fill.

That's why I like questionnaires. Their chief purpose is not to provide information about details known in advance, but to act as a reminder that the intellectually cosseted universe in which I have always tended to move was actually concealing the essential from me. For many people, Céline is and will always be the daughter of the man with the service station who lives in the next housing estate along, rather than the nihilistic novelist, Mahler is the name of the man who wrote the theme tune for a cheese spread commercial, and John Ford must surely be a brand of car.

This state of affairs has ceased to shock me, and the fact that it has occasionally worried me when I was on the brink of early middle age. Sometimes I saw, in my new, casual attitude, an implicit confession of a lack of firmness, like those old far-left militants who meet up again after twenty years and confess, heads bowed, that perhaps they'd overstated their case a little.

As far as my pupils' leisure activities were concerned, they practised one sport, or several. Most of the sports were violent ones that involved a loss of inhibitions, a good foundation course for life (and doubtless that was exactly what their parents thought). Some more original characters liked chess or card games. The girls liked dancing and mountain bikes, Nintendo and talking to their friends. The boys liked fishing and hunting, pets, watching television, playing table football and going out when they'd finished their homework.

I had complicated the questionnaire somewhat by asking them to select, after taking a brief look within themselves, the three adjectives that best described them. Without wishing to play the Jesuit and cultivate a manic interest in conscience, I was curious to know how introspective they were.

They denounced themselves as chatterboxes, as distracted, lazy, stubborn, aggrieved, whingeing, occasionally unfair towards their classmates. All of these small shortcomings were revealed so casually that I came to suspect a lack of interest in the question, thus confirming their account of their own qualities. They considered themselves to be good at concentrating, hard-working, 'cool', easy to live with and very open to others. I was at least reassured on one point: they were familiar with the use of antonyms.

Finally I asked them what sort of training they expected to go into, the issue of motivation being secondary. Most of them, both girls and boys, wanted to head towards a commercial career, expressed in mysterious circumlocutions such as 'marketing representative' or 'company director'. One boy called Maxime Horveneau had even spoken of being a 'CEO in charge of other people'.

I thought of the two year-seven classes that I had recently taken. If I correctly remembered their replies to a similar questionnaire, I had to confess that between the ages of eleven and fourteen some kind of shattering event took place which could not simply be understood with reference to puberty.

A thousand possible explanations came to mind. None of them was really satisfactory. For how was one to explain the fact that the aspirations of such a sizeable minority of the population had metamorphosed so radically in such a brief space of time? How, as a professional educationalist, could one account for the fact that a representative sample of French pupils had switched from the vocation of dolphin-trainer or 'explorer of secret caves' to the more aggressive calling of 'company director'?

I was missing something.

The funeral was to begin at two o'clock at the church in the town near to where Capadis's parents lived. I had only four hours to get ready. I showered, got dressed and then had a second cup of coffee, while reflecting upon what I imagined to be the dominant vision of the world. I was better at that kind of stylised thinking in the morning than at other times of day, but I couldn't take my mind off Capadis, sceptically imagining his lanky frame standing in front of the pupils, barely supported by the timbre of his frail voice. It was like that adolescent game in which, when no one has called you up to go out on a Saturday evening, you try to imagine the most unlikely couples making love. I had my favourite twosomes which, when I think of them today, are a fairly representative illustration of the mental shipwreck that is adolescence. Along similar lines, I found it difficult to conceive of the educational relationship between Capadis and his pupils in 9F.

A West-Coast arpeggio interrupted my reflections. The radio was playing 'California Dreamin'' by the Mamas and the Papas, a song which, inexplicably after so many years, still made me feel a twinge of melancholic terror every time I heard the first few bars. I got up to turn it off before the flute solo that had always had the same effect on me: I would burst into tears and want to die.

The tune reminded me of the flute that played the signature tune of *Good Night, Little Ones*, which, with its poignant sadness, rounded off my childhood television viewing at about eight o'clock every evening. I went to bed – along with thousands of children of my generation, I later realised – after the debonair teddy bear Nounours had thrown a handful of sand at my eyes to make me go to sleep. Long after I had abandoned the sunlit uplands of the pre-verbal age, I would still refuse to go to sleep before I had heard Nounours's little tune. My parents bought me the record of 'Good Night, Little Ones', and at eight o'clock on the dot the celestial teddy-music began to weigh down my eyelids and lull me into narcotic bliss. This habit, to my father's great regret, lasted longer than might have been expected. It ended in a way which those around me found strange, but which was telling from a psychoanalytical point of view.

One evening, when I had reached the ripe old age of thirteen, I leapt from my bed while the record was still playing. I took the lid of the record player and began to strike the turntable with increasing violence, as though a panel of doctors had just subjected me to the Ludovico treatment and I had to pulverise the black vinyl disc if I was to silence some dangerous voices from my childhood. After that, whenever I watched the eight o'clock news, I couldn't help thinking of the spangles of sand that had stippled the screen in times past, accompanied by a song that whispered the words, 'If only I were a fern' with the melancholy of an oceanic landscape after a cyclone has passed.

It is often said that the cult of objects is rooted in childhood, and that they enshrine the significant milestones in our lives, like a kind of personal metaphor. One day someone should retrace the anthropological importance of tunes and their place in family history. Recently I happened to hear someone talking about the flute-player of *Good Night, Little Ones*. His name is Antoine Berge, and he is seventy-one. At the Paris High Court he asked for 150,000 francs in back-paid royalties. In the end he was awarded 632.50.

All the cars but mine had a strip of black tulle tied to their aerials. Clouds stretched in long diagonal streaks, their grey fringes suspended over the church. A heavy shower fell intermittently, like someone turning taps on and off. The translucent droplets sprinkled the black trees along the avenue; a timid ray of light still peered through the damp air. Nature had once more imposed the rule that all funerals must be accompanied by precipitation.

I had arrived a little before a quarter to three. The possibility of being present at the funeral mass had seemed increasingly unlikely as the morning wore on. It isn't just that Papist buildings always give me a sense of collaboration with the forces of Evil; their dampness always made the joints in my neck ache.

The village was a marvel of low-key baroque, with its radiating avenues and centrifugal public spaces. A measured art of promise and imminence, a systematic deployment of potential reined in by a spirit of modesty. Would a stay in a place such as this help an American or an Eskimo achieve an understanding of France? I tried to imagine what kind of knowledge might arise from aimless days and insignificant nights spent walking those streets.

Suddenly I felt so tired that I reclined my car seat to rest for a quarter of an hour, just until the ceremony was over. I couldn't close my eyes. My attention was constantly being drawn by the tiny sounds that drummed against my cerebral cortex. I let my eye wander across the raindrop-scattered glass. From my reclining position, the row of houses opposite the church looked strange and immaterial. The rough facades, glistening after a succession of showers, the imposing mass of the building and the crenellations of the chimneys topped with spidery aerials seemed to be sliding along beneath the sky. It was not the dappled clouds in the background that were moving, rather the houses that were drifting by, like a stream of crème caramel.

A tolling bell dragged me from my dozing state. I sat up in my seat with the painful sensation of having been asleep for several hours. The church door had just opened up to reveal the first two pallbearers. Carrying the coffin on their shoulders, they made their way slowly towards the cemetery, a few hundred metres down from the church.

As my car was parked opposite the entrance, I wasn't able to see the rest of the cortege. I slid towards the passenger seat and opened the door parallel to the pavement. Squatting on my heels, I tried to move along the parked cars like a crab to achieve a more complete panorama of the situation. I also wanted to find an appropriate spot from which I could join the moving cortege without drawing attention to myself.

'You look as though you're here incognito . . . are you an acquaintance of the dead man's?'

I twisted my head three-quarters of the way round to see where the voice was coming from. A woman who looked like a former television star after a course of aerobics was watching me, chewing gum, her right shoulder leaning against the frame of the door of an establishment that looked like a hairdressing salon.

'Not really, no.'

'Are you a journalist?'

'No, I'm carrying out my own inquiries.'

'Ok, Sherlock. Come in, you'll get more clues inside.'

I got up with some difficulty, resting my hand on a car door-handle. A heavy-duty brassiere held the woman's breasts out like a pair of threatening V2s, forcing me to sink into the opposite side of the door frame to enter a room that smelled of ammonia and turpentine. My hostess was about forty, dressed with the taste typical of former beauty queens on the slide who haven't entirely abandoned the seductress's role. The deep hollows at the base of her neck suggested a drastic diet. A hazelnut-cream-coloured neck was topped by a face whose complexion was concealed beneath a thick layer of caramelised coating. Her heavy eyelids were purple, her false eyelashes sticky with mascara, her lips a shade of lilac, and a rhizome-shaped beauty spot formed a trigonometric point on the wide surface of her cheeks. She closed the door without taking her eyes off me. It was the first time I had been inside a ladies' hairdresser's, and the fact that it was empty only served to accentuate my unease. I felt as though I had been pushed into a sex shop.

'They're all at church. Bad business, isn't it?'

'What is?'

'What the hell do you think? . . . The Capadis boy and his fake suicide, obviously!'

The unhealthy, predatory curiosity that glinted in her eye seemed to contradict her languid voice and her accent, which dragged at the end of each syllable. Her pseudo-proletarian syntax was supposed to bear witness to her consummate honesty. She slumped in one of the rotating chairs. When she leaned forwards slightly to face me, I had a view of the freckled valley of her cleavage, as well as the hem of her bra, which peeped from her lurex tee-shirt.

'So he didn't kill himself?'

'Listen, I was the one who popped his cherry.' (Pause.) 'No point spinning me a line . . . I was quite well acquainted with him, if you catch my drift! The only people whose hair I did apart from the ladies were the little boys . . . that was how I met him, he would have been just fourteen when he first came here, and he kept on coming here until he went to university . . .'

'And you didn't see him again after that?'

'No, he never came back. When you see this hole, you can't really blame him, can you?'

'How did you learn of his death?'

'From the papers. About how he'd chucked himself out the window before the kids came back to the classroom.

Utter balls! . . . If you're naive enough to believe that, I'll give you some advice, and have the wit to follow it: join a sect or sign up for a political party, you're the ideal customer, the guy who doesn't go asking too many questions, who'll swallow more or less anything, and the worst thing is that you'll go on thinking you're a real cleverclogs.'

I tried as best I could to adapt to this new image of Capadis as a young virgin losing it to the village hairdresser. Another unlikely couple, I thought, the everfluctuating and incomprehensible aspect of nature's perpetual disorder. She waited for me to react, crossing and uncrossing her legs and tapping the side of the armrests with her resinous nails.

The snaking line of the cortege was beginning to wilt. The children followed immediately behind the pallbearers, and after them came all the teachers. I hadn't seen any members of the dead man's family, and wondered whether Capadis's parents had gone to the church. So far they were nowhere to be seen among the last members of the procession.

'I've got to go,' I said, heading off without looking towards the exit.

She rose abruptly to her feet and came and held the door open for me. Her face was a few centimetres away from mine. Like people from the Far East, I had never been able to bear people standing less than a metre from me. I had adopted this preventative measure since a vague acquaintance from school, whom I had bumped into near the toilets at a New Year's Eve party, had taken advantage of the fact to press me against the wall and stick her tongue down my throat as though rodding a drain.

'I close at half past seven. You could drop by . . . let's talk.'

'I'll see after the ceremony.'

'I'm sure you'll come.'

'Why?'

'Because you're curious. You'll be interested in what I have to say.'

I left her on that hopeful note.

The priest was busy delivering an impassive address about the gates of paradise and eternal repose. His breath formed little white clouds. He had a hawk-like face, one of those harsh physiognomies in which the bones lie right underneath the skin. Looking at him, I recalled the funeral of a family friend, and the ceremony in a crematorium in the western suburbs of Paris, the coffin clattering along on its rollers, the remote-controlled curtains and my mother's hiccup of emotion when the teak doors opened briefly for one last time before finally closing.

There were about forty of us waiting for ecclesiastical permission to pass by the coffin and scatter our ritual fistful of earth, as though there might be a possibility of the dead man growing again. Heads were lowered, eyes avoided both the casket and the voracious grave that was about to swallow it up. Only Christine Cazin watched the box jerking its way down, delivered into the earth by the pallbearers' straps. Capadis's parents had stayed at home, repaying their son for his absence. The children, their hair damp with rain, formed a colourful double row to the right of the coffin – little ones at the front, big ones at the back – as though posing for a class photograph. The black-clad adults looked stiff with their hands gripping the

handles of their umbrellas. The gravediggers were prop-
ping themselves up on their spades some distance away,
smoking cigarettes. Their caps were perched on the back
of their heads, the brims pointing towards a whitening
sky.

Standing between Poncin and Butel, I was able to take
advantage of their umbrellas and watch my pupils on the
sly. Their eyes were focused on the hole. They seemed
transfixed with cold, but they didn't move more than a
centimetre. There was something vaguely menacing about
their stillness. When the priest finished his address, they
raised their eyes towards us with a bored look, as though
there were a good and a bad way of considering the situation. Poncin chose that dangling moment to take from
his pocket a piece of paper, folded in four, unfolding it
only when he was standing by the grave. Before doing so,
he collapsed his umbrella with a crisp and jerky motion.

He delivered his oration in a devastated, almost confi-
dential voice, as though he had been carrying on a conversation with Capadis that had been suddenly interrupted
the previous day. I listened distractedly to his address, with
my eyes fixed on the chalk-tinted uppers of my black
moccasins. I didn't raise my eyes until he began to intone
that he was sorry that the deceased had chosen this way
out, because life, he added, slightly raising the tone of his
voice on that word, had the great power to bring the most
desperate among us to the togetherness of humanity. He
finished, addressing everyone in our name, and seeking,
with significant looks, the mute approval of our scattered
ranks.

The cemetery was as quiet as a sanatorium. All the
mourners hunched their shoulders as far as they could, to

avoid catching anyone's eye. The rain had stopped, and white clouds were bathed in cold neon light. The cries of children at play revealed the presence of a nearby playground. I caught a smile of contentment among the pupils as they heard the warm hubbub, which contrasted with the expiatory mood of the graveyard. The priest held the holy water sprinkler out to Poncin, who made the sign of the cross in the direction of the casket before passing it on to the next teacher so abruptly that it looked as though he wanted to get rid of it as quickly as possible. Everyone took part in the ritual in an insultingly casual manner. Their coldness seemed to indicate that the dead man hadn't had the time to carve a niche for himself at the college. He hadn't left the slightest trace of sympathy in anyone's mind; no meaningful handshake, no slap on the back, no colluding laugh. The tenor of the relationships that had brought the living together with the dead man was so functionally expressed that I almost felt disappointed on behalf of the man in the coffin.

Politely, the children looked straight ahead at the filtered light brilliantly reflected in the brand-new coffin. They looked drained, with a hint of that ecstatic zest that you only encounter among people coming back from a period of solitude in the mountains. When the priest approached them and held out the aspergil, one of the boys, a wiry pre-adolescent dressed with slightly scruffy distinction, shook his head and, pointing at the ground, indicated to the priest that the group would prefer to throw a handful of earth on the coffin. The priest appeared so startled by this plan that he leaned his head on one side, put the device back in his cassock and turned on his heels. One by one, the children followed each other to the graveside.

Beneath the inquiring eyes of the gravediggers, who had drawn nearer, holding their spades under their arms like baguettes, each of the children crouched down and threw a little earth, thick and rain-drenched, upon the coffin.

And that was that.

Passing through the centre of town again, I was tempted to stop off at the hairdressing salon. But a curious and apparently insignificant event diverted me from the prospect of an evening in an empty pizzeria with a strange woman whose chest measurements and emotional life were a little too oppressive for my romantic nature. Furthermore, I suspected that the reduction of our evening to a banal exchange of information on Capadis – and information that was broadly predictable – would produce an effect of psychological feedback a few days later, and could only prejudice the course of my February holidays, for which I had as yet made no plans.

As I was about to get back into my car at the way out of the cemetery, Clara Sorman, one of the brightest pupils in 9F, intercepted me with a degree of authority that surprised me. I had already noticed her during the ceremony. She had dark glasses on, and was constantly chewing at her thumbnail. She had taken the liberty of breaking away from the group to come and talk to me on my own. The bus, to judge by the wisps of exhaust escaping from the rear, was waiting only for Clara before setting off. The pupils watched her irritably from behind the misted glass. In the distance, I saw them shaking their heads suspiciously and murmuring words I couldn't make out.

Clara Sorman's story was disconcerting, and known to all the Clerval staff. In her second year as a pupil there, she had had an illicit relationship with a thirty-year-old school supervisor, who had since been struck from the lists of the education service. The story had been hushed up by the school board under pressure from the parents themselves. A psychologist diagnosed compulsive sexuality which could see no correlation between the idea of the act and its realisation in daily life. Rumour had it that Clara had lost her virginity at the age of nine to a fifty-year-old family friend, and that she regularly had sexual relations with her eighteen-year-old cousin. Photographs had even been found of her at 'special evenings'. Of the people around Sorman, those adults who were convinced of the innocence of children remained offended until Clara confided in them that she had organised the orgies herself when her parents were away. Since then she had been under special supervision. Poncin had told me about these stories at the end of the previous year, and when Clara asked me if I could spare her a moment I thought that perhaps she was at a loose end during the holidays as well, and that my lonely expression revealed me to be so obviously available that a nymphomaniac pre-adolescent might have been tempted to project upon it a vague hope of an affair. But that wasn't it. She stood there in front of me, her face tense, the muscles in her jaw working away.

'I've got to talk to you. It's important. Act as though you're not looking at me. The others are watching us.'

'I'm listening to you.'

'Don't take the class again after the holidays.'

'I don't know what you're talking about.'

'They'll destroy you.'

'When?'

'In a moment of trust, when tension and rivalry are at their lowest level.'

'I still don't understand.'

'I haven't much time.'

'I could almost think you were being serious.'

'I'm completely serious. I know them very well. We grew up together. Leave before it's too late. They'll get inside your loneliness the way they did with Monsieur Capadis.'

'I don't know what to say. Why should they, as you put it, get inside my loneliness?'

'Just leave!'

'I think you should try and calm down . . . we could talk about it some other time. After the holidays, for example.'

She shook her head without a word. Then she raised her chin, ran a finger along her temple to her hairline and glanced quickly towards the bus as though she had heard someone coming behind her. Her expression froze, two keen eyes assumed possession of her face, and all of a sudden its vague planes became sharper.

'After the holidays will be too late.'

'Why too late?'

'You just don't want to understand . . . have a good holiday.'

'And you.'

She turned around abruptly and ran towards the bus.

5

Ever since the start of my teaching career, the school holidays had often represented an opportunity to take stock of things, to appraise the objective conditions of my personal destiny. They were also a block of time beyond boredom, like an abandoned fragment of the spatio-temporal continuum.

I had spent the first week *entirely* at home, having my food delivered to me by young people wearing caps and fluorescent clothing, my finger hovering over the entry-phone. I got up late, wandering about half naked, holding a cup of coffee that I filled over and over again until my nerve-endings were in shards. I spent the rest of the day reading whatever came to hand. Magazines about firearms or aeroplanes, old movie magazines about forgotten starlets, or bestsellers from the eighties that I had bought by the kilo at Sunday boot sales.

From time to time I would open a biography telling the success story of some celebrity or other, hoping for a single paragraph, an isolated remark, that might turn up at the right moment to give me the strength to change my life, all those elegant phrases murmuring the word 'me'. I avoided television and any kind of nostalgic entertainment. I owed it to myself to innovate, to be less evasive, to rediscover a true sense of purpose.

My sister called me on Friday evening, just as I was starting to feel an insane craving to go away for a few days. Lying on a pseudo-Persian rug that I had bought from an unemployed welder just to get rid of him, I ticked off the least troublesome destinations (Liechtenstein, Andorra, Valenciennes) in a catalogue. It wasn't contempt for ordinary people that kept me away from sun and sand – although it's true that suntans do make people look a bit stupid – but the fear of finding myself even more alone than I was already, in a climate conducive to human relations.

(At this point in the story I should like to eliminate one misconception, and say that in my attitude towards solitude I had never flirted with the post-modern miserablism often associated with the term. In my eyes the condition did not represent a painful state, in so far as it had often made me less remote from the sufferings of other people. Certainly, I could have stayed in my bedroom until I died, but wherever possible I had always avoided this kind of negative thinking, which is based on failure, misadventure and loss. Sometimes I lost my nerve, imagining a lonely existence in old age, meals on a television tray in a dining room stinking of old socks, underpants stiff with dried semen. But I still wanted to talk to people.)

The previous day I had received a brochure from the Indre-et-Loire Association of Single Women inviting me to one of their soirees, at which I would be able to rediscover what they called 'the land of lost harmony and authentic values'. The accompanying letter explained that

I had been chosen according to very strict socio-cultural criteria, and because of my standards of morality. I wondered for a few minutes who might have supplied them with that information. My mother, perhaps.

The brochure was about twenty pages long, with photographs showing smiling, blooming women in their thirties, all thoroughly involved in their work and seemingly without a general grievance against life. Most of the women's profiles emphasised the jobs they did. They were teachers, consultants, highly trained computer technicians, product managers, software engineers, lawyers, some of them lowly secretaries.

Most of them were involved in communication in one way or another, and they were technically very rigorous, trained in the art of customer satisfaction and practising one of the most innovative professions in the key sectors of the economy. They were in search of an alter ego, a companion in arms to watch the first lights of day with, a shoulder to cry on, protection in the crowd, none of them things for which I considered myself particularly apt. The slightly blurred grain of the photographs unsettlingly resembled photographs of young women who have disappeared, which are usually displayed in service station windows. Just to be on the safe side, I had circled three advertisements that seemed to coincide with my own aspirations. I had not, of course, done anything about it.

My sister was at Nice airport. I heard the coins dropping bleakly into the phone. She explained that she had been staying in a two-star hotel overlooking the bay for a week, with the sole purpose of meeting a Nobel laureate in physics who had written, she said, a first novel of 'devastating honesty', a mixture of Lovecraft, Bellow and Andersen.

'And what about your work?' I asked.

'I can't do it any more. I need a new set of slogans. Being a teacher and not wanting children is completely immoral.'

'That's a good slogan. Have you thought of going into journalism? A lot of days spent at meetings, getting your pieces spiked, toeing the editorial line, keeping your records . . .'

'I value your support.'

'You'll have to cultivate a pleasant but vague appearance, a sophisticated kind of falsity in order to get hold of what you want.'

'Do you really think I'm heading in that direction?'

'The danger lies in getting used to vulgar forms of story-telling.'

'You know I've always loved that.'

'Your eyes are gleaming, I can feel it.'

'What are you up to right now?'

'I'm with friends.'

'I can't hear anything. Your friends are pretty quiet.'

'They're swimming.'

She laughed. An impassive, mirthless, almost specious laugh. I imagined her hand gradually easing its pressure on the black Bakelite, her eye passing over the oblong box, her finger stuffed in one ear so that she could hear with the other. I also imagined the smiles being bestowed on besuited men carrying attaché cases, as though to reward them for their patience, to promise them that she respected the rules which meant she would shortly be hanging up.

'Can you pick me up at Orly, gate 12, in two hours?'

'Can't your husband do that?'

'I've got to talk to you. I'll be wearing dark glasses, a pirate hat and a suitcase covered with stickers from cold countries. Can I crash at your place?'

'I'll put clean sheets on.'

'See you in a bit. Big kiss.'

Two hours later I was at the airport, sitting in the waiting room beside a former sports presenter who had disappeared from the screens when I was about fifteen. I hadn't thought about him for around twenty years. And now there he was, right next to me, like a ghost from the past. I was close enough to him to notice that his fair hair and fake tan couldn't mask a latent sense of failure, which a recent facelift had done nothing to disguise. Fat had built up on his cheekbones, and his angular jaw seemed to be ligatured by his facial muscles. With a melancholy smile, he glanced around him in case anyone remembered him. When his eyes returned to the arrivals gate with a painful fixity, his face seemed to die a little.

There was a ripple of movement in the crowd, a diffuse energy compressed by waiting. A voice with a foreign accent announced the arrival of the Nice–Paris flight, and the first passengers emerged from a double glass door to make their way to the carousel and collect their luggage. Léonore came out, wearing an elegant trenchcoat tied in at the waist by a large belt designed to emphasise her wasp waist. She actually was wearing sunglasses, her trademark chignon, which tilted like the casing of a chrysalis, and kid-skin gloves. Striding along like a pair of moving scissors, she suddenly stopped and looked around to see if she could spot me.

94

'Hi!'

She hadn't seen me coming around the circle of waiting people. As I saw her at the head of the line of passengers, I had decided on a whim that I wanted to startle her out of her familiar little script of sister–brother superiority. My hand closed over her right elbow, deliberately pinching the cubital nerve.

She gave a start.

'That hurt, bastard.'

She gave a little wave with her gloved hand to a slightly plump man of about thirty wearing a bland expression and a new suit, who darted furtive glances in our direction as he passed.

'An aerial encounter?' I asked.

'Exactly. The man in the seat next to me. An interesting guy, doing a doctorate at the management research centre of the École Polytechnique.'

'What on?'

'Air traffic control in Spain and France. He talked to me for the whole duration of the journey about the coming explosion in volume, the saturation of airspace and the limits of the system. I tried to let him know that I was a nervous flier, and that this wasn't really quite the moment, but he insisted on pursuing his topic. I think it's a hobby-horse of his.'

'And his obsession is?'

'That every year air traffic is rising by an average of seven per cent, we're about to hit an absolute limit, what he calls the wall of capacity. Nothing to get worked up about.'

'So?'

'Three possible scenarios, too long to expound in their

entirety. Which one do you want: death, chaos or putre-faction?'

'Death.'

'Thought so. You've always gone for extreme solutions. I'm very worried about you, Pierre. Have you had a fuck in living memory?'

'No.'

Her mouth stretched towards her cheekbones, mimicking boredom.

'I'll have to introduce you to Élizabeth. I think you know her . . . that party at Lambert's. Do you remember?'

'Tall girl with short red hair, pierced nose?'

'What a memory!'

'No way. Don't you know any normal girls?'

She smiled strangely. She still had that way of looking at you out of the corner of her eye that was supposed to tell you she'd seen right through you. Turning away, she pointed towards the carousel and I followed her long, elastic steps. After a minute's wait, during which neither of us uttered a word, she picked up an enormous garnet-coloured suitcase with straps so tight that I was almost surprised I couldn't hear the leather shrieking with pain.

The weight of her luggage nearly knocked her back-wards. She tottered for a moment or two, the suitcase pressed up against her, giving the comical impression that she was dancing with a slightly inebriated fat man. Finally I came to her aid. With each of us holding one handle of the suitcase, we made for the car park outside, where I had parked in a disabled space just out of curiosity. As we walked, she explained the death scenario with broad waves of her hand.

'Let's sum it up by saying that reaching the wall of

capacity is a terrifying prospect. According to the special-
ists, the increase in global aviation would create an avalanche
of accidents. The saturation would be such that the number
of collisions would finally put passengers off, and would
lead to the death of the air transport industry. The
controllers are talking of accidents so serious that they
would threaten the very existence of aviation. Do you see?'

'Did you get to meet your novelist in Nice?'

'No. Every time I called him to suggest we meet up,
it was his son who answered the phone. One day his father
had gone off to help an Australian film director who was
adapting his book, and the next he'd gone to a confer-
ence in Canada. Finally I dropped it.'

She suddenly stopped, exhausted, letting go of the suitcase. She took off her sunglasses and blew on the lenses,
her mouth an ellipse, then ran a cloth over the misty
surface and raised them towards a fluorescent light. Her
features were still as fine as they always had been, sharp
nose, angular chin and high cheekbones.

'Maybe it was really him, putting on a young person's
voice to screen his calls,' I suggested. 'He's already had
plenty of problems. Realism on the part of his women
readers, hysteria from the men. It's not unknown.'

She put her sunglasses in her bag, picked up the second
handle of her suitcase and darted me a reproachful glance.
We set off walking again.

'That's exactly the conclusion I came to.'

In the airport car park there was a smell of burnt excre-
ment that I hadn't noticed when I arrived. Doubtless a
nearby municipal tip. It was almost dark. The gloom
compactly enveloped us, discreetly protecting us from the
menacing silhouettes of the parked cars. Every thirty

seconds, the access barrier rose with a metallic drawbridge creak, letting out men whose foreheads were crumpled with the effort of concentration, who pinched their lower lips between thumb and index finger before they launched their cars towards more familiar surroundings, a universe of inner, domesticated pain.

My sister wanted to drive. I wouldn't let her. I hate anyone apart from me taking the wheel. Specially Léonore, who drives with her hands clutching the upper arc of the wheel, her fingers clenching and relaxing. It's far too emotional a way of driving, it demonstrates a lack of confidence. She avenged herself by not moving her lips once on the journey, knowing from experience that I would have to make a prodigious effort to fill the void created by her mute presence.

I sensed that she was tense. Her fingers tapped nervously on the face of her watch. She stared at the sky as though she might push it away with the pressure of her gaze. As a child she had been able to spend whole days without saying a word. She led a life independent of my parents, me, the dog, her sullen mouth in a dense and impregnable moue. I put a hand on her arm and felt her soften. She looked at me, surprised, her eyes bulging without her sunglasses, and reddened by the effort of staring at things.

'So you'll soon be thirty-six? In three weeks, I think?'

'In a month, steady on now, Pierre.'

'Sorry, that's unforgivable of me.'

'Are you going to give me some sort of escape route?'

'No. I was just going to give you a pair of slippers. I was wondering if you liked slippers. Tartan slippers with a lamb's-wool lining.'

She thought for a moment, then lit a cigarette which she immediately stubbed out in the ashtray with a grimace of disgust.

'Do you think that would get rid of my complexes?'

'Have you got complexes? I don't think you've got that many complexes. You're the least inhibited person I know.'

'It's other people who are inhibited with me.'

'You couldn't care less about other people. Is there anyone on this planet who cares less about other people than you do?'

She didn't reply.

A minute later she was asleep.

There was always a smell of damp when I switched the convectors off for two or three hours in winter. Léonore raised her glass of wine to me in thanks for rustling her up a quick meal. A moment previously, she had kicked off her shoes with adolescent abandon and folded her legs underneath her. Now she was facing me, curled up on the sofa, with her knees between her arms, sometimes bringing them right up to her chin. She was wearing an emerald green cashmere v-neck pullover, and had been chain-smoking for a quarter of an hour. Staying in the same position, she put down her glass and started smoothing out the cellophane on her cigarette packet. Smoke from the Chesterfield gripped between her teeth made her narrow her eyes. I wondered if she was wearing a bra.

All of a sudden she got to her feet and brushed some tendrils of hair from her face. I heard her filling her lungs, then exhaling slowly. She held her glass by its smooth round base; her lower lip had left a pink crescent of lipstick on it. Sudden curiosity made her grey-flecked irises shine.

'Are you writing at the moment?' she asked.

'No. Nothing for six months, apart from shopping lists . . .'

'Writer's block?'

'I don't know.'

'And what about your pupils? Things ok?'

'Does it matter? Yeah, fine.'

I was lying.

I didn't want to tell her the whole business about Capadis, the ins and outs of it all, I didn't want to go too deeply into the professional issues involved. After all, she was the one who had asked to make contact. Holding her head level, and with her mouth pinched in a mocking expression, she tried to find a way of framing a precise subject so as to give its features a line and a contour. The cigarette that she crushed on the side of her plate gave a little hiss as it came into contact with the vinaigrette.

I got up to go to the toilet, to breathe in a bit of intimacy and make up for the mess on the sitting-room table, which was overflowing with food, bottles and cooking utensils. The bathroom was smooth and casual, it had an identity of its own. Dried flowers on the cistern, little framed pictures of filmstars and a shower curtain decorated with little Smurfs. I slumped against the door, breathing in and out from the diaphragm. I was feverish. The latch suddenly jumped from its housing, pulling the catch from the spongy wood, and I found myself on the floor, arms and legs stretched towards the ceiling, like a little figure of a cyclist who has been taken off his plastic bicycle.

I couldn't get back on my feet. My sister came running

from the sitting room, and went into raptures when she saw my posture. She sat on her heels and looked me up and down with the rigid facial muscles that dictators have, and lion-tamers. The beginnings of a migraine were beginning to lacerate the back of my skull.

'Take my hand.'

She walked me to the sofa, her arm around my waist. I leaned against her with a sort of recklessness that I hadn't known since she had picked me up one evening from the town's main bar, where I was absorbing the after-effects of my first wretched love affair. I was eighteen. She was four years older.

As she put a cushion under my head, I caught another glimpse down the neck of her sweater. I was sure now that she wasn't wearing a bra. She sat next to me, lit her tenth cigarette of the evening, blew the smoke out through her nose to look like an elephant's tusks, and then stroked my hair with her free hand. I fleetingly noticed the flow of blood beneath the skin of her face like a pink veil, like a secret network of tiny guilt. She had a moment of panic, perceptible in the uncontrolled way in which her voice twisted at the corner of her mouth as it came out. A faint seductiveness, with a hint of fear.

'You're looking very Parisian.'

'That was my ambition from the start, you remember?' she replied with a pinched smile.

'How are our parents?'

'That's what I came to talk to you about.'

'I thought you'd come about me.'

'Not exactly. Mum's having an affair with a younger man. A guy at university, an intellectual. Tweed suits, a pipe, leather-bound books, cultural outings, that kind of thing.'

101

'Mum's always needed that.'

'She's been gone for a week,' she said after a minute, raising her eyes to the ceiling, the smoke rising from her nostrils, this time in swirls. 'It's hard to tell if it's a passing fancy or the real thing. You can never really tell with mum.'

'And dad?'

'Very negative. There's no talking to him. She's a slut, a trollop, an ingrate. He's pretty distraught. And very irritable as well.'

She stubbed out her cigarette with a sigh, and looked around for the bottle. She got to her feet. While she looked for it, the hollow that her body had left at the end of the sofa gradually disappeared. She finally found the bottle by the magazine rack.

'Glass of wine?'

'Please. What are we supposed to do in cases like that?'

'Nothing. I just wanted to talk to you about it, that's all.'

'Do you have a plan?'

'No.'

Lying on my back with my hands folded under the nape of my neck, I couldn't stop watching the ceiling spin. All the surfaces looked as though they were sinking out and swelling in front of my eyes, as though under the effect of an oceanic drag.

Léonore smiled nervously in an indeterminate direction, her jaw slack, her eyes clouded with exhaustion and the idea of a defeat that she alone appeared to understand. At such moments she was beautiful, a strange and taciturn beauty, like a painting by Modigliani. For a moment I had a sense that mist was rising from somewhere beyond her shoulders. Her lower lip trembled. I thought she was going to start crying.

102

'You remember,' she went on, 'when we were little, we had a notebook in which we recorded all the stupid things our parents said. We filled one every six months. Fine vellum, ninety-six pages, a moiré silk cover tied with a red ribbon. Our favourite day was Sunday. Dad would get so bored that he paced up and down the sitting room telling us anecdotes from his work, and giving us advice on how to live our lives. Mum was at church, her weekly outing. Dad had sixty hours of personnel management during the week, maintaining a Stalag-like discipline. He had to wait all week for his wife to leave him in charge of the place, so that he could arrange those mythical little father–child confrontations . . .'

'You're exaggerating now.'

'Not much, believe me. Do you want me to shut the door so that the neighbours don't hear?'

'Go on.'

'Remember him, the utter hell of the middle classes, a priest in his own church, every inch the altruist and with a total lack of self-interest, who acted out the tragedy of wisdom and generosity wrecked by human wickedness. How hypocritically we threw ourselves into the game, stifling our giggles, prepared to do anything for our pocket money. We were little bastards already.'

'Afterwards, we went up to our room, biro in hand, to record his *bons mots* in our notebook.'

'Mum came back from the village and found dad radiant, so happy that it was a joy to see. Sunday lunches were wonderful. I think I still miss that, thirty years on.'

I drew her to me. I slipped a hand behind her head, and closed my eyes, waiting for her lips to meet mine. I wanted to be swallowed up by her mouth, pressed against her heart.

My hand slipped under her jumper. Gently, she held it fast. I scrutinised her. Her eyes were hollow, her nostrils pinched, the whole effect like a dying flower shot in time-lapse.

'Steady now.'

Her voice was calm and soothing. My hand advanced once more, and its progress was immediately blocked. I tried to kiss her, but she kept me at a distance.

'No, that's not what you want.'

I put my head on her knees. She stroked my hair. Slowly, with infinite patience. I felt a hot tear fall on my forehead.

'We should try and find that notebook,' she said.

Léonore set off very early the following morning. I heard nothing from her for the next three days, and I didn't dare to call her, fearing that I might get her husband.

One evening at about eleven o'clock, just as I was about to bite into a soft caramel, he rang me. I recognised his voice immediately, although it sounded far away because of the crackling on the line. It still had the incredible strength that comes from a complete lack of interest in other people.

He told me that my sister had been suffering from depression for several months, that she was having random sex with men and drinking like a fish. She'd left her job as a teacher to work at home as a translator, and that gave her enough free time in the course of the day to devote herself to those abhorrent activities. Jean-Patrick Beaumont wanted to speak to me alone for the first time in five years ('man to man', he added, no doubt unaware that I loathed that expression, which smelled of sports clubs and macho drivers in Ford XR3s).

I remembered him as a young man with crow's-feet and a slightly greying mind, and wrinkled skin that looked as if it had endured all the gales of a life lived without any capacity for discernment. Being ten years older than me, he was part of that generation that had been the first to mock goodness and kindness, and whose hour of glory had come in the mid-eighties.

Essentially he wanted to have some psychological and biographical information about his wife, who he thought (wrongly!) was in my possession. I politely protested that I didn't know Léonore as well as he assumed.

'But you are her brother, all the same.'

'She's thirty-six. By the age of fourteen, she was never at home. At twenty she married you. Do the sums, you've shared more of her life than I have.'

'Aren't you going to help me?'

'Terrible question: in a word, no!'

'You're talking like someone with revenge on his mind.'

'I'm talking like someone caught off-guard.'

'I should have stayed in contact. It's a reproach.'

'No, I meant the phone call. It's late.'

'Sorry.'

'It doesn't matter. I hadn't gone to bed, anyway.'

In the background I could hear some metallic-sounding music hammering out with ferocious hatred, like a desire to smash hollow objects. I couldn't make my mind up: hardcore, maybe speed metal. Jean-Patrick sounded both focused and miserable. His voice had an inflection of dull feverishness. I wondered if he'd been drinking.

'I'm available whenever you want to see me,' I said. 'You have to show goodwill, that's all. You seem emotionally devastated by your wife's bad behaviour. Sooner or later in a marriage you notice that something's wrong, it's perfectly normal . . . and if you think I can help you here, you're barking up the wrong tree. Not being married myself, I haven't much experience of the subject. As to my sister, she's always had the charm of indirectness, it takes a lot of patience to tame a personality like that.'

'Astounding,' replied Jean-Patrick Beaumont, dragging the word out to try and make it sound shocked. 'So can't you help me?'

'Sorry, J.-P., can't do it.'

'Can I let you into a secret?'

'Who do you imagine I'm going to tell?'

'You have the wrong idea about me.'

'I'm sorry?'

'Sometimes I'd like to become altruistic again, I'd like to make sacrifices. But I don't know how to do it any more.'

'It's a lost art. There might still be a treatise or a manual on the subject.'

'But tell me something to help me get to sleep. I'm suffering from insomnia at the moment. I wake up and feel humiliated.'

'So do I, sometimes, I get scared when I wake up in the middle of the night. I have visions that make no sense whatsoever. A Librium and I go back to sleep. A Librium will sort you out, an hour before you go to bed.'

I suddenly felt exhausted, thinking only about stretching out on my bed and going to sleep. I imagined Jean-Patrick, his eyes lost in the darkness, nodding his head to the rhythm of my voice at the other end of the line. There was a brief silence, as though he were waiting for a consoling word before hanging up.

'Thanks for the advice, Pierre. I don't suppose there's anything else you can tell me about your sister. I love Léonore, you know that.'

'We both love her. I can tell that your attachment is sincere. Passionate concentration is a solid foundation in life. I almost envy you.'

'. . .'

'So when did she discover reality?'

'A year or two ago. It's got worse recently. What do you call reality?'

'A way of accepting things, letting your grievances invade your body, coming out of denial.'

'How does what you're saying have the slightest connection with Léonore?'

'Léonore's never been willing to negotiate, to learn the rules of the game. Any game. Just as she's always refused to shrink, to melt away, to become less colourful. She's been her own rival, more than most of us. She's hidden herself away behind rowdy behaviour. And now that the noise has abated, the game is beginning to crush her. No doubt about it, we're not children any more.'

I sighed. A broad ribbon of dust rose and fell slowly in the ray of light cast by the halogen lamp.

'You're talking like a teacher . . . I don't suppose you'd like to speak clearly for once in your life?'

'How do you want me to speak?'

'Normally.'

'Which is to say?'

'Use ordinary words.'

'Ok then. Sometimes there are black holes, moments of intense uncertainty. At such times, the only source of consolation lies in snow-covered abstract spaces, pictures of animal reserves in the autumn, ochre canyons or escarped fjords. You have to intervene and help these people find an environment of warmth, into which they can project themselves and shed anxious reservations.'

'How are we going to get her back on the straight and narrow?'

'If subjects don't become psychotic, which makes it easier for them to commit suicide when the time comes, they may take various alternative routes such as alcoholism or deviant sex, hurling themselves into their work, meals with friends, etc. What we in the education service call "a process of remediation". Are you still awake, Jean-Patrick?'

'I'm listening.'

'I saw Léonore a few days ago when she got back from Nice. She spent the evening here, at the flat . . .'

'. . . I know, Pierre, I know.'

'We talked about our parents. She isn't well, I noticed that, but Léonore has never been the perfect embodiment of the life-force. By the age of four she'd stopped believing in Father Christmas. We're very different. I would believe any kind of story, even the most unlikely ones, whereas the word "believe" has never been part of her vocabulary. You'll have to sort it out, Jean-Patrick, it's very serious. That's all I can tell you.'

'Thanks anyway. Come to dinner one evening. Léonore will be delighted to see you. And so will I.'

He hung up.

6

The week of holidays following my encounter with my sister passed without any anecdotes worth telling, apart from two strange events.

On Tuesday morning, a character with an impressive handlebar moustache, wearing a cap with a yellow insignia, rang at the door of my flat. He held out a parcel wrapped in green-and-orange-coloured paper. I was so unused to postmen turning up at my door that I thought it must be the Jehovah's Witnesses who had recently hit my part of town, and with whom I had spent hours at a stretch (I'm incapable of closing my door on people who have walked miles and miles in all weathers to tell innocent citizens of the coming apocalypse and the salvation of the righteous).

I signed the receipt and took the parcel to the sitting-room table. The name of the sender wasn't written on the back. The only clue was the place where the parcel had been posted, Brevigny, a village five kilometres from the school. I knew that many of the pupils lived there. I removed the paper to find a shoebox bearing the trade-mark of a make of boots for teenagers, somewhere between a space snowboot and a buskin. The box was padded with a significant layer of cotton wool, impregnated with a strong smell of urine. Clearly someone had thought it amusing to piss on it. But the cotton wool was immaculate; there was nothing suspicious to be seen, but for reasons of hygiene I preferred to lift the snowy layer with a pair of sugar-tongs.

Like a surgeon removing the bandage from a patient suffering serious burns, I delicately lifted the cotton wool and found an object wrapped in silver foil. Its configuration gave it the outline of a small-scale model, a wooden manikin, perhaps, its parts held together with wire, a miniature soft toy, a funny little figurine or a foetus from a Jivaro Indian ritual. I was spoilt for choice.

Kneeling over the low table with my shoulders bent towards the box, I must have looked like a mine-clearing expert on a Normandy beach. A few minutes passed like that. As I ran my eyes over the silver foil, I almost managed, with just the intensity of my gaze, to create a restricted space in which the rectangle of the box and the strip of cotton wool projected a sense of intimate confinement into the room itself. I folded my arms over my chest. Sweat trickled down my temple. My right hand trembled slightly. My brain pressed painfully against my frontal bone. My throat was tight, and I had a sensation of tissue swelling at the top of my thorax as though I needed to burp, retch or rip myself open from top to bottom just to feel a temporary relief.

A primitive cortical life seemed to flicker beneath the silvery carapace. My internal impulse relaxed as the seconds passed, and my attempts to act grew less frequent. Without knowing it, I was constructing a form of suspense, a wait that was becoming increasingly frustrating. I was mounting guard against an event which, in advance, I felt to be significant.

The object seemed to gain in strength with the passing minutes. Each time I went to pour myself a glass of water in the kitchen, or lit my first cigarette in six months, the box claimed a little more freedom. All of a sudden I felt weak and depressed. At the height of my confusion, I crossed my hands above my head and moved them back and forth, just for the immediate pleasure of a soothing sensation.

After a few minutes of this little game, without doing anything to anticipate my gesture, not even putting a hand to my mouth to repress the possibility of terror, I unfolded the silver paper. What I saw came as a great relief to me, although it was followed by a moment of disbelief. Even if I hadn't wanted to witness the unimaginable (and what I saw was far from that), I didn't usually have the stomach for anything beyond a certain level of well-defined meaning.

The mystery that the box yielded up was a recumbent little furry monkey, with a plastic dummy in its mouth and an air of anxious gaiety. It was a precise replica of a shaggy chimpanzee that my parents had given me for my sixth birthday, and which I had called Kikipinpon. That particular soft toy was to perish amidst the most appalling tortures after an attack of creative hysteria on the part of my sister, who had seen fit to paint a moustache and an eye-patch on the creature with black paint. Léonore was unaware of the corrosive properties of her paint on plastic, and poor Kiki's face melted like a human face under the effects of napalm.

I picked up Kiki No. 2 in the palm of my hand and decided to take a closer look. Soft fur covered the whole of its body apart from its paws and face. Around its belly, damp fur formed a regular square, like a tiny trap-door that could be lifted to reach inside. The line had not been drawn at random. It looked as though it had been cut with a Stanley knife. Bringing my nose close to the little monkey, I realised that the nauseating smell I had identified at first as urine more closely resembled silt or peat. An olfactory spectrum between decomposing vegetation and menstrual discharge. Although nothing was discernible to the eye, the stench revealed a subterranean life being played out behind the furry film that veiled the surface of Kiki's belly.

I put down the toy and, once again using the sugar-tongs, tried to lift the mysterious square of damp hair. As the artificial fur came away, a foamy liquid like the secretions of a slug threatened to flow over the brim of the suture. At the same time the room filled up with a harsh, almond-coloured light, and the pipes of the flat above started gurgling with a mixture of merciless realism and lyrical melancholy. The clear, pealing sound of a wineglass being set down on a glass table was followed by the dry click of a bolt, and then by the sound of footsteps leaving a bathroom. When I was sure that everything had finally fallen silent again, I gave it a clean tug. The square of brown hair came away and stayed stuck to the tongs.

A rod of ice flashed through my stomach. Paralysed with panic, I knelt open-mouthed, haggard-faced, over Kiki's corpse, which still held out to me its useless dummy. Where one might have expected kapok, little blood-worms wriggled within the fur, in a disgusting magma of sticky liquid whose resemblance to the whitish surface of a rice pudding caused me to jerk my head back. A few seconds later, I turned my eyes towards a light coming in from outside. A fly was climbing the glass of the balcony door: it slid halfway down, as though shaking off a small impediment, and then flew on. After spiralling around the room it landed on Kiki's head, near one of the long eyelids drawn on the rubber.

That must have been when I fainted.

Three days later, the phone rang at eleven o'clock in the morning just as I was having my breakfast. My immediate thought was that it must be a wrong number. I was ex-directory, and apart from my family and a few acquaintances with whom I had sporadic contact at best, no one knew what my number was.

I let the answering machine take the call, waiting for someone to put the phone down once the tape started running. For thirty seconds after the beep sounded there was silence punctuated by dry breathing. I leapt up and walked around the phone, tense to hear what would happen next. The breathing grew louder and louder, jerky and panting. It stopped, making way for something that sounded like parodic hiccups, followed by a mad chuckle that was supposed to be unsettling and sounded like a rather forced snort.

A moment's silence followed these catarrhal groans, a soft and pallid silence, of the kind which, in group conversations, usually precedes a personal attack. I froze expectantly, the heels of my feet coming slightly away from the rubber flip-flops that I was wearing. All of a sudden I caught my full-length reflection in a mirror on the wall.

I was wearing only a shapeless pair of cock-hugging Y-fronts, and couldn't help noticing my body, my sagging shoulders seeming to illustrate my odium at the sounds I was hearing. The tape was now recording a series of primitive chewing noises, the perfect imitation of a dozen adolescents stuffing themselves with the contents of half a box of popcorn.

In the gaps between the sequences of noise, I was growing increasingly curious as I tried to guess the nature of the object that was interrupting and then playing back the sounds. I couldn't make out a single word, not a voice, not even a vague murmur that might have personalised the message. There was no significant clue to indicate facial features, a form, an outline, any recognisable landmarks in this desert of white silence. The game went on for a good minute before coming to an abrupt halt. I felt damp shivers on my chest and my back. I resolved to analyse the silence, to subject it to systematic examination. I thought of the isolation in which I was living, the kind of solitude that could be startled awake by laughter in the night. Doubtless the person or persons making the phone call were well aware of that. It had been well thought through.

I was almost relieved when a contrived racket worthy of the Beatles' 'Revolution No. 9' set the receiver rattling like an ill-fitting ventilation grille. This time it was a tape-recording, there was no doubt about that. It was like the music of one of those early-eighties industrial bands who made tight, angst-ridden records, the Stations of the Cross set to music and extended to the point of nausea. When I put down the receiver the music stopped.

My telephonic bandleader had hung up. A general feeling of weakness invaded me, as though all parts of my body were suddenly gasping for air. A taste of acid metal and dry dust filled my mouth and throat. I dropped on to the sofa, exhorting myself to be calm, but the malevolence of what had happened still flickered in a corner. I got painfully to my feet and ventured as far as the kitchen. A blue light sliced across the grease-stained white formica. I opened the cupboards, the drawers, the larder in search of a jar of instant coffee. I finally found it in the fridge (in my flat it's always a great mystery where different foodstuffs might have been put), and made myself the equivalent of several cups in a hot-chocolate bowl.

As I waited for the water to boil, I cast an eye over a weekly magazine that I had subscribed to just in order to get some mail. After vaguely flicking through a long article on the finances of the various political parties, I fell upon the heading, 'Our times', an article headed by the picture of a teenager pointing a gun at the reader. The piece said that only a week after the murder of a teacher by one of her fifteen-year-old pupils, in class and in front of all his classmates, Germany had just avoided another such bloody episode at a school. As someone who thought of Germany – and I wasn't the only one among my colleagues who did so – as the country with the most civilised customs in Europe, and with an avant-garde educational system, I felt almost cleansed of the personal shame I had always felt about working in the education service.

Three fourteen-year-old pupils (a year older than mine, it occurred to me), who had been preparing a killing spree, had been stopped in the nick of time in Metten, a small town in Bavaria. They had been planning to kill a teacher who had been rather too critical of their behaviour in class. 'The pupils planned to shoot her in the legs to see her blood gradually drain away,' the state prosecutor in Daggendorf was quoted as saying. They also planned the murder of the headmistress of the school, who had arrived three months previously. The journalist had thought it proper to add that the children were fans of ultraviolent, pornographic videos, and collectors of swastikas and other trinkets designed to announce the guilt of society.

The trio had planned to follow up the murders by robbing a bank and, with their booty, buying grenades and mines. These teenagers had been terrorising their class-mates since the beginning of term. Some weeks previously, one of the three had fired a gun at a girl pupil without injuring her, but the teenager hadn't reported the incident to the police until after her attacker's arrest. She and a dozen of her classmates had known of the planned murder, but for fear of reprisals none of them had dared to say anything to their parents and teachers.

I thought again about another incident that had happened the week before, in a problem school in the suburbs of Rouen. A girl of fourteen, accompanied by one of her friends, had burst into the headmaster's office to ask him for a leaving certificate, because she wanted to leave her school which was in a socially disadvantaged area. When he had told her that he couldn't supply her with such a document before the end of the year, she had drawn a handgun from her bag and taken aim. The head-master had bowed to this threat, and allowed the girl to have her certificate.

Alerted by a teacher who must have been the first witness of the headmaster's terror, the police had appre-hended the girl, still carrying her gun. She had told the investigators that she always carried the weapon about her person, because she felt threatened at the college. She was charged with 'extortion of an official signature', and risked a sentence of up to thirty years in prison.

7

The light, the colour of white wine, heralded a cold, bright day. The previous night's frost still sparkled on the ground and in the hedges. There was no wind, and the trees, elms and beeches, stood solid and motionless on each side of the road. The deciduous forests passed by the car windows, rime illuminating their wintry geometry. But it was 14 March, and in a week it would be spring. The fields, covered with white ice, were punctuated here and there by sinister-looking copses, thickets sagging under the weight of winter, and vast, lumbering irrigation machines that looked like the vertebrae of some prehistoric creature.

Since leaving the flat I had found it difficult to concentrate on the road, as I did each time I returned from the school holidays. I felt exhausted, although I had done nothing but sleep for the previous two days. I had thought I might have contracted some kind of blood disease, a tropical illness or bacterial food poisoning, or perhaps some domestic pest had launched an attack on my nervous system.

The heating system, stretched to its limits in my attempts to demist the windscreen, puffed and whistled. In the dusk, my dashboard lights took me back to the film *Airport*, which I had seen on television the previous evening, with the hysterical cockpit scenes that I loved only because they reminded me of the early seventies, the end of a period of growth that was about to mark the return of unemployment and recession. I must have been about ten years old. I still remember the muffled excitement I felt at the very mention of the titles of disaster movies: *The Towering Inferno, Earthquake* (ah, Sensurround!) *The Poseidon Adventure, Soylent Green, Meteor.* What I couldn't have imagined at the time was the extent to which these apocalyptic fictions anticipated, with allegorical realism, the entry of the industrial societies into a new age of social anxiety.

I mechanically switched on the radio. The mere rotation of my thumb and index finger towards the left always gave me a sense of archaic satisfaction at owning one of those old car radios with knobs. A hostile and self-righteous voice emerged from the speakers, protesting against a legal project that it considered iniquitous, even accusing the individual who had promulgated it of irresponsibility. The vocal inflections had an artificial yapping quality, the usual short-term, selective indignation that you tend to hear on the morning news. I finally found a station broadcasting classical music.

My first class of the week was 9F, and strangely I didn't feel at all apprehensive about seeing them again. In spite of the anonymous phone calls that had punctuated the last two days, I felt as though a direct confrontation would sweep away a troubling veil created by the distance between us over the past fortnight. Perhaps their anonymity was an accurate reflection of the way they lived, a means of expression they had chosen deliberately, a kind of personal truth.

Most families used those February holidays to take their children skiing. I could already imagine their tans, their lungs gorged on alpine air, their gleaming eyes, vibrant with fresh vitality. From the first day of term, they would rediscover an acute awareness of the moment. Once more they would have to let school settle down, reconstitute itself and represent something that they would all finally acknowledge, like a return to rainy Wednesday afternoons spent on homework.

I turned up at the car park at the same time as Isabelle Gidoin, a colleague who taught French. Tall and haughty, she always wore an unfathomable expression that seemed to mask something hilarious going on beneath. I admired her greatly, and I think my esteem was reciprocated. We were about the same age, and we had a form of reticent respect for one another. She lived with an older woman who wrote novels for children and vegetarian recipe books. Élisa Berelowski, for that was her name, was also a militant member of a far-left organisation that supported certain armed struggles in the Third World. They were probably the sanest couple that I had ever met.

Isabelle always wore the same denim jacket, with the aerial of a mobile phone sticking out of a patch pocket to give a permanent sense of an intimate and boundless connection with the object of her affection. Her cropped, almost shaven hair, suggested a degree of scepticism about feminine accessories. She never wore make-up, and liked to display her chewed fingernails with the natural shamelessness of those too absorbed in fundamental tasks to be concerned about their outward appearance.

I switched off the radio, turned off the headlights and hurried over to her, an impulse that I tried to conceal by opening her car door with an exaggerated bow.

'Allow me, madam!'

'Why, sir, have we met? Pray introduce yourself! I am alarmed, sir – are you employed by this establishment?'

'My good lady, not at all. I roam the car park night and day and, in order to occupy myself, I sometimes open doors to ease the burden of poor mortal creatures. I became aware of your affliction the minute you passed through the gate. From it I deduced that classes had resumed; your face expressed the very essence of inexpressible melancholy.'

'Be not misled, kind stranger, what you took for affliction was merely a moment of regret for those fleeting desires that mourn for the things of the earth. But the enthusiastic heart is given up to hope of their renewal, rather than to tarnishing the present moment with miserable thoughts.'

She tried with difficulty to keep her features under control. I felt that she wanted to go on, knowing full well (and this lent piquancy to our past conventions) that the first one to laugh had lost the game. Isabelle loved to play out scenes from psychological novels with me, as they enabled her to yield to her nostalgia for the grand, dignified narratives, with their cascades of adjectives and their shielding, literary locutions.

It reinforced the vibrant memory of her identity of long ago, the character that had become detached from her with her acquisition of irony. Her taste for this type of verbal game had a function that was essentially one of confirmation.

'How were the holidays, then?' she asked, with that vague expression she usually wore when coming out with the ritual questions.

'I barricaded myself in with a rifle and a few hand grenades. Nothing special.'

'I was thinking you looked a little pale. You'd think you'd just spent a fortnight on a mushroom farm. Have you been eating, at least?'

'Jam, things in sachets, a few soups, vacuum-packed ready meals, bachelor food.'

'Why don't you get a flatmate? That's very fashionable at the moment. A girl with big breasts, amusing, warm, a student of sociology or perhaps a trainee teacher.'

'If I've understood you correctly, you want me to find my raison d'être in a pair of enormous knockers?'

She burst out laughing.

'Broadly speaking, yes.'

Isabelle, like some well-intentioned people of my acquaintance, could only imagine me with a person of an intellectual bent, in round glasses and mohair polo necks. My romantic ideal was in fact exactly the opposite of this, and was much more inclined towards secretaries, or what are nowadays called personal assistants. In my eyes that profession, which cultivates discretion to the point of secrecy, represented the most fruitful characteristics of male–female relations. It was the very image of devotion, the absolute icon of the eternal feminine disguised as a worker in the shadows, capable of adapting to any circumstances. Armed with word-processing packages and ultra-sophisticated telephones, they fascinated me with their legal and financial abilities. Right at the heart of the system, they were Mata Haris with college degrees, and they tended to play the role of the confidante in classical tragedy.

'And what about your holidays?'

'No comment.'

'You've aroused my curiosity all of a sudden.'

'Élisa likes the seaside out of season, particularly the beaches in northern France. It's her favourite perversion. We went to Merlimont. The local authorities have founded a clinic there, for people with physical disabilities. Élisa was unaware of that when she made her booking.'

'Certainly, from the tourist's point of view ... the disabled aren't necessarily much of a draw. I wonder why the municipal authorities insist on concentrating them in the nicest holiday resorts.'

'Apparently it's because they amuse the tourists with their uncoordinated little gestures.'

'Fine, but it's like a joke told too often, it ends up being boring.'

'I can't stand the disabled. They're always *moving* ... they're too small, they want to go to the seaside all the time. It's much too easy, you just have to be born disabled and they send you to the beach.'

'How's Élisa?'

'Knitting Tibetan hats for Amnesty International, and spending her nights on the internet trying to get in touch with Sub-Commander Marcos.'

'Any luck?'

'I've tried to explain to her that the number of personal computers in use throughout the world is about 180 million, in a global population of six billion, and that access to the internet is therefore limited to some three per cent of the planet's population. I have told her of my scepticism about the existence of web-surfers in Chiapas, one of the poorest regions in Mexico.'

'How has she reacted?'

'She tells me I'm being too negative. She says that kind of reductive pragmatism isn't much use in the struggle for the oppressed masses.'

Her voice had suddenly assumed a note of indignation, plaintive and prolonged. It suggested that it was very important for her to stress the fact that her concept of commitment differed from her partner's.

At the very same moment, Goliaguine, the art teacher, climbed out of his car with the embarrassed air of someone who has just overheard a conversation unintended for his ears. He was wearing a tight, grey, wing-collared chiné jacket, a Shetland pullover and a pair of square-tipped grey-green lace-ups so worn in appearance that he looked slightly sinister. He looked as though he had dressed up for a photograph. His trousers were shiny at the knees.

'I'm all stiff,' he said, extracting himself from his car with a smile full of innuendo.

'Backache is the occupational hazard of the professional seducer,' said Isabelle.

'It's not what you think. I've just spent the night in my car, in preparation for this morning.'

'I've got a pair of clean socks in my car if you like,' I suggested.

'What I need's some human warmth. Just think, a deserted car park, night-time, total silence in the car, the cold intensifying hour by hour.'

Since most of the teachers at the middle school were quite transparent, and worryingly conformist for people who were supposed be communicating the virtues of the critical mind, Goliaguine was greatly admired by those around him. He had understood that eccentricity was just as good a way of concealing one's feelings as respect for conventions. Isabelle walked towards him and threw her arms around him, before taking a few little dance steps.

'I feel better already.'

The ringing of the bell brought us back to reality. Goliaguine detached himself from Isabelle with a worried smile and looked at me tragically.

'The holidays really are over,' he said, struggling to comprehend the idea.

Isabelle interposed herself between us. She brought us to the playground, linking her arms with ours like Jeanne Moreau in *Jules et Jim*.

'I'd like to invite you both to dinner at eight o'clock on Saturday. You can leave it a little while before confirming, if you like.'

'We'll come,' said Goliaguine, without so much as glancing at me.

A little bit later, as I was climbing the flight of metal steps leading to the staffroom, I was already trying to come up with an excuse not to go.

They were sitting at their tables, and practically the whole class was there. Only Clara Sorman was absent. For five minutes now, her empty desk had been making me strangely uneasy. Holding my pencil suspended over the register, I waited for a few seconds as though trying to convince myself that she was going to appear at any minute. Twenty-three faces were gazing in my direction, backs straight, feet tightly together, as impatient as if they were waiting for me to start entertaining them with sexual anecdotes from my holidays.

The classroom was filled with a cold, sparkling light that made things whine. It was an ordinary school morning. The board-brush was dusty. It was the task of Marianne, a cleaning woman with dyed red hair held back behind her ears with bunches of black ribbon, to knock out the brushes every Friday evening. She always closed her eyes to keep the chalk-dust out. On the first day after the holidays there was always the same disaffection regarding simple, ordinary tasks. When the vacation began, the various members of staff made off as though they were never coming back, as though they were escaping a bushfire.

My presuppositions about their activities over the past fortnight seemed to be exactly right. Most of them had smoke-dried faces, almost auburn, with that slightly vulgar vitality that comes from holidays spent in large groups. Their anodyne provincial characters, borderline self-effacing, seemed to have acquired a little extra substance. It was manifested in the most ordinary actions, such as their way of unscrewing the lid of their fountain pen, or conscientiously folding the pages they'd already used in their homework notebooks, which consequently looked like a pile of origami.

Finally I wrote Clara Sorman's name down in the book of absentees. Sandrine Botella had crossed her pale hands in front of her as though they were a forgotten pair of gloves. She emanated a rather strange and terrifying intensity. Apart from Sandrine, each pupil had put in front of them a piece of paper bearing their name. They seemed to have done it on their own initiative, to make it easier for me to memorise their names. I stood up and began

126

to pace back and forth between my desk and the black-board. I hadn't yet taken off my poplin overcoat, and it rustled.

'Take out your geography exercise books and write the date, Monday, 3 March, the title of our first lesson: *Minorities in the United States: failure of the melting pot, or future of the salad bowl?*'

They leaned down to their schoolbags to take out their exercise books, which in fact turned out to be ring binders divided into three sections: history, geography and civics. No one corrected me. They all seemed to share a reasonable confidence in my observational capacities.

They were studying the United States this year. One of my teacherly caprices consisted of systematically constructing ideas that anticipated the usual course progressions by a year. Then, just after the final assessment, I informed them as I returned their essays that they had just taken a course that was actually a year higher than their current level. When they had received good marks, it inevitably boosted their self-esteem for the rest of the year. It wasn't a very orthodox method, perhaps, but it worked. I knew few people who favoured it apart from myself.

All classes on the United States inevitably involved a lesson on the population of America, in which the teacher evoked the classic notion of the melting pot, the crucible in which peoples of every origin merged together to give birth to *homo americanus*. The aim was to show, with a skilful dramatisation of the counter-argument, that this optimistic model of integration was increasingly contested within the United States itself, where the represent-atives of the various sexual or ethnic minorities were increasingly claiming the right to recognition of their specific qualities, so much so that the idea of a multicultural society was increasingly imposing itself.

Talking about her year tens, Christine Cazin had once explained to me in the staffroom that civics, history and demographics could be used together in such a way as to help pupils grasp an overall picture, and that it would all make perfect sense when assimilationist, Jacobin ideas were added to the recipe. I had taken her advice very seriously, working throughout the holidays on a number of educational magazines that had provided me with an impressive range of graphics and pictures.

I handed around a text by Jean de Crèvecoeur from 1785, his *Letters from an American Farmer*, in which he described the variety of forms of religious identification in Orange County, Nantucket, where he had lived. I walked down the aisles, handing out my photocopied sheets, leaning down to read each name. A smell of vanilla-scented Marseilles soap as well as a scent of cedar eau-de-toilette floated above the female heads. In the wake of the boys the perfume was a curious mixture of damp sawdust and burnt tyres.

Guillaume Durosoy, Richard Da Costa, Estelle Bodart, Franck Menessier, Kevin Durand, Sylvain Ginzburger, Mathieu Naudin, Cécile Montalembert (the row on the right as seen from my desk), Raphaël Leborgne, Pierre Lamérand, Julie Grancher, Apolline Brossard, Élodie Villovitch, Rislane Baroui, Dimitri Corto, Sébastien Amblard (the middle row), Maxime Horvenneau, Isabelle Marottin, Karim Chaïb, Laurence Guiblin, Brice Toutain, Mathilde Vandevoorde, Clara Sorman, Sandrine Botella (the row on the left).

Twenty-four pupils in all. Thirteen boys, eleven girls. Their places seemed to fluctuate from one class to another. This aleatoric geography didn't seem like a desire to confuse on their part. It seemed rather a kind of 'mixing' with no important significance. Generally speaking, the classes that binomially inverted themselves of their own accord throughout the year tended to get on pretty well. While I never took that kind of observation particularly seriously, I did find that it was often confirmed in the course of the year.

At the beginning of the left-hand row there were two names missing, those of Sandrine Botella – she must already have felt sufficiently well 'identified' to escape the obligation – and Clara Sorman, who still hadn't put in an appearance. The biology teacher had told me that they always sat side by side. She had nicknamed them 'The Inseparables', a classic of school nomenclature.

'I hope you had good holidays!'

They nodded in silence.

'You can reply with your hands if you like.'

I paused, staring at the ceiling, a bit of teacherly play-acting.

'And what about you?' asked Maxime Horvenneau.

'I just waited for you to come back.'

Élodie Villovitch wore a heavy metal bracelet on her right wrist, and its purplish reflections dazzled me at regular intervals. I asked her to read the text in the secret hope that she would straighten up her shapeless torso and cross her hands on her knees. A waste of time – she simply inserted the sheet between her forearms and started reading in a mournful voice. After the first paragraph, she asked me, with big lemur-like eyes, whether or not she should continue. Her face had that expression of sulky resignation that supermarket cashiers wear when they're forced to work on a Sunday.

I leaned against the corner of the room, one shoulder against each wall. I had rolled up the remaining photocopies like a telescope, which made me think all of a sudden of that slender North African nurse, walking off with her temperature chart. Nora's resemblance to Élodie's neighbour, Rislane Baroui, emphasised the analogy. I thought of a vague family resemblance. A younger sister? Perhaps a cousin? I reflected that 'Nora Baroui' had a ring to it, like an incontestable match between a person and her designation.

'Rislane, would you go on, please?'

Her eyebrows rose almost to her hairline as she checked that I was really addressing her, that there hadn't been some sort of mistake. Reassured by my nod and a discreet nudge from her neighbour, she began to read.

'"He believes in consubstantion . . ."'

'Consubstantiation, Rislane, again, please.'

'"He believes in consubstantiation; by so doing he scandalizes nobody; he also works in his fields, embellishes the earth, clears swamps, &c. What has the world to do with his Lutheran principles? He persecutes nobody, and nobody persecutes him . . ."'

I couldn't help smiling, not only because of this naive distinction between a Lutheran and his Catholic neighbours, but more particularly because of the sugary rhetoric being spoken in an angelic voice by a young Muslim girl in a tracksuit. As she was reading, I realised that Apolline Brossard was watching me curiously. There was something about her that had unsettled me since our first class, perhaps a frosty lubriciousness mingled with mischief, waiting only for an opportunity to manifest itself.

'Continue from there, Apolline.'

Once her initial surprise had passed, Apolline sardonically cleared her throat.

'You mean I really have to read?' she asked me in the familiar tone which she might have used to ask me if I fancied taking her to the cinema on Saturday night.

I looked at her insistently, to show her that I held her personally responsible for such an idiotic question. She sat there, immobile as a piece of granite, showing by her stillness that she was waiting for an answer that she saw as her due. Clearly, she was busy acting out a well-rehearsed scene from her repertoire of confrontations. The aggressive way in which Sandrine Botella was looking at her clearly indicated a feminine rivalry concerning the mastery of agit-prop techniques in class 9F.

'I don't know. But honestly . . .' I replied. Disconcerted by my answer, she blushed without taking her eyes off me.

'Is there something stopping you?'

'I don't like reading in public.'

'Are you shy?'

'Yes, that's it. I'm shy.'

'In that case . . . Who else wants to read?'

As the question flew around above their heads, I felt strangely detached and lonely. I became aware that my face was beginning to look complacent, an index of bad faith on my part.

'If no one can be bothered, then fine!' said Sandrine Botella, casting a contemptuous glance at her classmate. '"The Quakers are the only people who retain a fondness for their own mode of worship; for be they ever so

131

far separated from each other, they hold a sort of communion with the society, and seldom depart from its rules . . .'"

She declaimed the text in a brittle, bellicose way, detaching the syllables as though catapulting them out of her mouth with a view to injuring someone. Her voice fell away on the final words of the text, like the fade-out at the end of a piece of music. She lifted her eyes towards me, and for a few seconds she sought some signs in my face that might have assured her of a temporary sympathy, which she could then reject again at her leisure.

There was a knock at the door. Brice Toutain, who was nearest to it, got up to open it. I gestured to him to sit down. A veil of concern fell across the children's faces, and they all shrank nervously into their seats. Maxime Horvenneau glanced quizzically at Sylvain Ginzburger, who shrugged in reply. Cécile Montalembert fidgeted in her chair, while her neighbour displayed a grin that made her look almost idiotic. Her eyes were fixed on the branches of the chestnut tree, which cast shadows over her face.

I stood there with arms folded, trying to look impassive, careful to avoid any kind of risky impulse. All eyes converged on me. I leaned against a corner of the desk and took my watch off. A voice that seemed to come from my chest called, 'Come in!'

Clara Sorman appeared, or at the very least the image I had formed of Clara Sorman before the holidays, followed by Poncin, who was pushing her in front of him with his hand on her right shoulder.

8

'About ten gashes to the face with a Stanley knife. It's a stroke of luck that her eyesight wasn't damaged,' said Poncin. 'Did you notice that she was wearing a scarf?'

He was speaking in a low but firm voice. I studied his lips, which half opened when he spoke, before meeting again to form a soft line between each of his words. I also noticed the green irises in his eyes for the first time. They were spangled with a circle of tiny yellow patches against a rather waxy background. Cholesterol, probably.

'I don't remember,' I replied, breathing with difficulty. 'What struck me immediately was the bandages on her face. I hadn't expected that.'

'I see . . . she's wearing the scarf because of the finger-marks around her neck. They held her neck back . . . but it wasn't strangulation with intent to kill . . . that's what the police told me. Clara has been mute since the attack. She has been lying down at the police station. She won't give any names, she refuses to identify anyone and she doesn't remember anything. Apparently that's quite normal

with events of this kind. Particularly because of the drug
. . . a powerful narcotic.'

He started to fiddle with a thick yellow cardboard file
that he was holding in his hands and twisting nervously
about on his knees. Perspiration darkened the roots of his
hair and drenched the area around his shirt collar. Spring
sunlight filtered through the half-open shutters and illuminated a galaxy of particles of dust floating in the air.
He had called me in at mid-morning break to explain
what had happened to Clara on the Friday evening of the
first week of the school holidays. The police had phoned
him very early the next morning and kept him on the
premises until midday.

Clara had been walking back from a party held by a
childhood friend, at about eleven o'clock at night, when
she was attacked. Three individuals of similar build to
herself, and wearing carnival masks. She hadn't been able
to identify the sex or the clothing of her attackers. She
had been found two hours later, in a state of shock, by a
group of students on their way home from a club. They
had immediately taken her to the police station. She was
holding her carved-up face in her hands as though to
prevent a haemorrhage, and uttering muffled little cries of
pain. Because of the cold, the first clots of blood had
started forming between her fingers.

'Had she been drugged?'

'The report by the doctors who took charge of her
mention a quantity of GHB, a new drug that's been on
the market for some time, also called "the date-rape drug".
You might have heard of it.'

'My knowledge of drugs is very limited.'

Shouting and sounds of pursuit came from the stairs.

Poncin gave a knowing sigh. He looked at me as though I weren't living in the same universe as he was, as though I were the guardian of a piece of dusty knowledge utterly inappropriate to the cold requirements of this world, whose boundless complexity he himself had grasped.

'It's also called "liquid ecstasy". It's a substance used in anaesthetics. The scientific name is sodium gammahydroxybutyrate.'

He paused briefly and rested his left hand on top of a ream of photocopying paper, his thumb describing a straight line as though he wished to test the quality of the paper and discover a flaw in its smooth surface.

'I like to know the scientific names for things,' he added.

His features, which seemed to be directed towards the centre of his face by the effect of concentration, gave him a mocking and vaguely hostile appearance. A living nightmare of self-containment.

'The product exists in powder and granule form,' he went on, 'designed to be poured into a drink. It takes effect very quickly. It has the property of making the victim forget what she has been "chemically" forced to do at the instigation of her attackers. A bit like Rohypnol a few years ago. It seems that in some American bars there are posters warning drinkers always to keep hold of their glasses at all times. In Colombia it's a real national plague. The product can be injected into the bottom of a drinks can in such a way that it can still appear intact when the victim opens it. It's usually tourist women or couples who are drugged without their knowledge in order to obtain, with their apparent agreement, either money or sexual relations, you can imagine whatever you like.'

'A change to a will, for example.'

'You're getting there. In all likelihood Clara, after drinking a few glasses of something containing GHB, was taken to a place where certain people were waiting for her.'

'Have the police questioned the people who were present with her?'

'All of them, every single girl.'

'No boys?'

'Just girls.'

'Childhood friends? No . . . friends from school?'

'As a matter of fact there were. Three girls from 9F who didn't turn up, according to witnesses, until the end of the evening. One witness mentioned that they were slightly drunk, and speaking more or less incoherently.'

We said nothing for a few seconds. Poncin was waiting impatiently for *the* question, with a pose of exaggerated refinement, his finger held under his nose in the shape of a moustache, and his left arm perpendicular to the arm of his chair. I had to make a considerable effort to stay calm.

The phone rang. Poncin looked at it with an expression of headmasterly disdain, implying that people with real power don't lower themselves to the answering of telephones. He finally picked it up with a heavy heart, giving the impression that he was protecting it with his body. He spoke in monosyllables for thirty seconds or so, moving furiously around in his swivel chair. He set down the receiver and then put his fingers together in the shape of a pagoda.

'Voices keep reaching me through an increasingly awful crackling noise,' he said. 'It's very unpleasant. The region is reputed to harbour an excessive number of mobile phones.'

'Which three girls from 9F went to the party?'

He looked at me open-mouthed, as though he had suddenly become aware of my presence.

'Estelle Bodart, Apolline Brossard and Mathilde Vandevoorde.'

'Was there anyone with Clara when she left the party?'

'The four of them all set off together.'

The school wasn't the kind of place that encouraged relationships between teachers, but there was one colleague in particular with whom I had had a vague friendship during my time there. Jean-Paul Accetto had been a maths teacher at the school for thirty years and, with retirement five years away, he enjoyed the distinction of being the only one of the older teachers not to talk about the pupils in pejorative terms. A negative attitude towards children was one of the symptoms of the teacher mentality, in that age and routine took precedence over self-examination. But these men and women had acquired a perfect mastery of didacticism. They were balanced, level-headed and universally respected. Any traces of impulsiveness and insta-bility had gradually disappeared over the years. But the pupils remained a problem, those little bastards who had no respect for anything, least of all for the ageing people standing at the front of the classroom who were convinced that the older they got, the more the world fell into an irreversible process of decline.

When Jean-Paul Accetto spoke of a difficult case, he did so with the magnanimity of an abbot, although his authority was somewhat undercut by his scruffy appear-ance. It was not only that his clothes fitted him badly, but certain elements seemed to clash, or simply look not quite right. The bottom of a trouser leg would have been tucked into his sock, for example, or his shirt would have been buttoned wrongly from the top down, with button A in button-hole B and so on all the way down to his belt-buckle. Accetto compensated for chemotherapy thinness with a bushy beard that he never trimmed, along with a surprisingly youthful head of curly hair. But there was nothing in this socio-cultural leader's bonhomie to indicate any particular asceticism or ethical rectitude.

Jean-Paul spent his weekends studying political sociology, and had been the author about fifteen years previously of a book devoted to the history of genocides, which had caused something of a stir in university circles at the time. In particular he declared that the idea of genocide applied only to national, ethnic, racial and religious groups, and that it was difficult to employ the term for certain war crimes in which those qualities were not apparent. He had used the terms *politicide* to designate genocides based on politics, and *sociocide* for those with a social foundation, citing the example of the Chinese Communists and the Khmer Rouge. Having been accused of anti-Semitism by Holocaust groups, and of deviationism by Marxist history teachers, he had abstained from publishing anything ever again.

After my discussion with Poncin, I had five minutes before the end of break. I had a year-seven class who gave me no cause for concern, the kind that you go to without reservations. When I reached the staffroom, Jean-Paul was deep in conversation with Annick Spoerri, the deputy head. They were sitting at the central table facing one another, like patients waiting for a nurse to take their blood pressure, their attitude a mixture of abandonment and defiance.

Jean-Paul's hand rested on a large plastic ball with coloured stripes on it. He gave an impression of suffering from weakness, but from a willed form of weakness, like certain defensive illnesses. Annick Spoerri lifted her colourless face towards me with a forced smile. Her eyes behind the thick lenses of her glasses were tired. She held out a soft hand, which I pressed gently for fear of crushing it.

'It's terrible what happened to that poor Clara Sorman,' she said in a distraught voice. 'I was just talking to Monsieur Accetto, who had 9F last year.'

Jean-Paul stood up and nodded. He turned to me and looked at me with that air of profound weariness that clearly indicated that listening to him speak was going to be a trial: his phrases would be punctuated by interminable silences.

'How did they behave back then?' I asked.

'Just as they're doing now . . . I suppose.' (Silence.) 'They seemed quiet and submissive. No one ever knew what was going on in their heads . . .' (Silence.) 'No one ever tried to find out, either. It was really quite . . . how can I put it . . .' (he thought for a moment with one finger on his lower lip) '. . . enigmatic.'

'They're nice kids,' I said.

'That's true.'

'They have qualities that are immediately appealing. Punctuality, calm, order, attentiveness, vivacity. They don't have that unpleasant tendency to show off that you find in most pre-adolescents these days.'

'I can't argue with that.'

'They can also be weird and disconcerting. I have a sense that they're carrying lots of things inside them.'

139

'What do you mean? What things?' Annick Spoerri asked abruptly, trying to make her question sound casual.

It took me a moment or two to reply. I'd lost my thread. I tried to find a precise and incontestable meaning for her. Annick, like many people with an administrative mentality, didn't like anything resembling indeterminacy, vagueness, fog.

'I mean collective things that have nothing to do with the inner life of the individual. They give a sense of existing only as a whole, in a group. It's very disturbing.'

'As if the life of each was lit by the light of the others,' Jean-Paul went on with a complicit smile. 'It's a form of communitarian heliotropism.'

Annick Spoerri studied her nails, which were covered with a bright red varnish. They almost seemed to be telling her something. After a minute, she told me that the police had summoned the class one by one to the station to discover their whereabouts during the holidays.

'You'll be questioned as well, I'm sorry, I haven't got a date yet. They'll ask you some questions about their behaviour, their personalities, and so on. I hope you'll be a bit less . . . hermetic.'

'I have trouble talking about them any other way,' I said by way of apology, raising my right hand. 'After two classes with them I have nothing else to say about them. I sense rigid emotions, contradictory energies, but nothing I can really put my finger on.'

She stood up, stretching her legs out slowly, and then briskly crossed the room. Jean-Paul also rose to his feet, and took me by the arm to lead me aside. His smile was frozen.

'Those kids are weird, Pierre. No one's been able to

find out why, ever since their first year here. If you ask the teachers who have had anything to do with them, you'll see that they lower their heads, they start being evasive, they try and make you think that you're the one who's being strange. They're frightened! They're terrified! I was scared myself, I always had a sense that they were trying to warn me about something.'

'About what?'

'No idea! That's the disturbing thing as far as I'm concerned. It was the fact of not knowing, that constant air of menace, that feeling of always being at a disadvantage from the very first moment when I stood up to them, when I asked them to express a simple opinion.'

He stopped and glanced around to make sure that no one had been listening to us.

'The important thing is not to reveal anything,' he whispered very gently, leaning towards me.

He had slightly bad breath.

I was called into the station on Wednesday. The inspector who questioned me was very young, with the impassive face of a fanatic. His office was arranged so meticulously that it looked like a showroom in a shop selling cut-price furniture. Milkily phosphorescent light swept obliquely across the uneven floorboards. Metal files cast flat shadows into the corners.

The inspector drank an espresso every fifteen minutes, adding three spoons of sugar as he listened to me talk. Like everyone addicted to monologues, he seemed entirely devoid of curiosity about anyone else, except in a strictly professional sense. He was the kind of person who had a solid, well-organised life, not very happy, perhaps, but pleasant enough. I was sure he bought his books in second-hand shops. Aside from the energetic way in which he questioned me, I couldn't help feeling that he was emerging from a long period of depression.

For three-quarters of an hour he had been talking about my pupils with a worrying sort of enthusiasm. I felt as though he was trying to prove that he knew them better than I did. He hardly ever looked at me, as though he didn't have time. For two days he had been tallying up their timetables, calling their families in to confirm their statements and drawing up a precise organisation chart in which certain suspects were already appearing. Dozens of Post-it notes bearing familiar names were stuck to his desk.

'And what were you doing that Friday?'

'I went to pick up my sister from the airport. We spent the evening together and then she stayed over at my place. She left at eight in the morning.'

'She stayed the night at yours?'

'Yes, why do you ask?'

He suddenly pulled down the corners of his mouth in an imitation of fake consternation, and then took a sip of coffee.

'Could we possibly check that?'

'You can ring her up if you like.'

'What's her name?'

'Léonore Beaumont.'

'So she's not called Hoffman, like you?'

'Well, no, she got married at some point. Would you like me to write down her phone number?'

He handed me a notepad and a biro.

'I trust you. It's quite rare to find a bloke spending an

evening with his sister. Especially at your age, people have families, children.'

'Neither of us has children. And anyway, we're very close.'

His voice swapped its official neutrality for an inter-rogatory, almost sincere tone. I thought I spotted a trace of Belgian accent.

'Don't you miss it?'

'Miss what?'

'Having children?'

'It's quite an inspiration not having any offspring.'

He fell silent for the first time. He had that dazed expression characteristic of people who have just realised that there are possible lives beyond the healthy common sense with which they view their own. He seemed to be experiencing one of those moments of panic when you see the paths you have allowed your life to take without ever asking yourself a single question. I almost wanted to apologise. The fact of living alone sometimes gives you a perverse power, a kind of pagan joy in your relations with other people.

His eyes fell on the photograph of a young woman with curly fair hair, holding a Yorkshire terrier in her arms. He lowered his head in a gesture of deep satisfaction. Bubbles of saliva formed at the corners of his lips, then he coughed to clear his throat and stretched his asym-metrical torso, his ribs showing as knots beneath his shirt. An artery beat gently between the tendons of his neck.

'Let's run through the first pieces of the inquiry, if you don't mind.'

'Fine.'

'Most of the pupils went off to the slopes in the second

143

week of the holidays, apart from five whom we can already rule out: Pierre Lamérand, Maxime Horvenneau, Guillaume Durosoy, Raphaël Leborgne and Sandrine Botella . . .'

'Did you say Sandrine Botella?'

'Yes, why? Is there a problem?'

'No, not at all, carry on.'

I slumped on my seat, watching the inspector's thumb flick through a bundle of sheets of paper, his brown hair cut irregularly like that of a sixties guitarist, pale eyes set deep in a firm, narrow face.

'Twenty-three index cards in all. Minus five, so . . . eighteen suspects, from which we may subtract Richard Da Costa, Isabelle Marottin, Franck Menessier, Sylvain Ginzburger, Sébastien Amblard and Laurence Guiblin, who were all watching television with their families . . . Rislane Baroui went dancing at La Grange, and was formally identified by three eye-witnesses, Brice Toutain and Karim Chaïb were both in Paris staying with friends (confirmed by friends and parents). Nine people altogether. That leaves another nine, including Estelle Bodart, Apolline Brossard and Mathilde Vandevoorde, who walked with the victim and claimed to have left her five minutes later, near the war memorial . . . I called in their parents yesterday, and they all told me they'd heard their daughters come in at about half past eleven. The girls who had been at the party said that they left it with Clara at about ten to eleven. But . . . obviously between ten to eleven and half past you've got plenty of time to attack someone.'

'Obviously.'

'Do you have any objections?'

'None at all. Where do they live?'

'About half an hour on foot from the place where they spent the evening . . . if you walk slowly.'

'And the six other people?'

'Kevin Durand and Mathieu Naudin say they were at the Loch Ness, a games arcade, where they stayed until closing time, at one in the morning. The boss can't remember seeing them. It appears that on Friday evening the arcade's always full to bursting and you wouldn't necessarily remember any kids in particular.'

'And the four others?'

'The four others: Cécile Montalembert, Julie Grancher, Dimitri Corto and Élodie Villovitch.'

He took a bottle of lemon-flavoured mineral water that was standing on his desk, and slowly drained the contents. His Adam's apple moved nervously. I waited for him to explain. He gulped, with his fingers interlocking so tightly on the table that the joints were white.

'Cécile Montalembert spent the evening at Julie Grancher's,' he went on. 'Her parents had gone out for dinner with friends, and didn't get back until two in the morning. They told me that when they got back . . .' (pause) 'Cécile and Julie were asleep. Unfortunately there's no way of checking up on what they did that evening because they said they'd both stayed at home.'

He fell silent and sat there with his head bolt upright, his gaze lost somewhere over my right shoulder.

'Homosexuality isn't punishable by the law any more, is it?' I asked.

He stared at me as though I had lost my mind.

'Of course not, unless minors are involved. But that's not the problem . . . would you let your daughter sleep with another girl at your house . . . in her bed? Tell me, honestly.'

'Certainly not.'

'Well then.'

He received my reply with a smile that I couldn't interpret. I was behaving like anyone who's a little bit paranoid when they're asked a question that calls for a moral commitment. I tended to reply as the other person expected me to.

'There's one aspect to this business that we haven't yet looked at,' I said.

'Aha! And what's that?'

He got up and started pacing back and forth with his hands in his pockets and his eyes on the ground, then looked up to the ceiling as though mentally searching for the precise spot in the files that he had missed.

'Why should the perpetrator be someone in the class? Maybe Clara just happened upon a sadist. The region doesn't produce them in industrial quantities, but you can't rule out the hypothesis. You must be aware that Clara isn't exactly St Thérèse of Lisieux?'

'I'm aware of that. I've spoken to her parents.'

'And?'

His thin fingers started drumming exasperatingly on his desk-top. He sat back in his chair, took a deep breath and, suddenly plunging his hand into a desk drawer without looking, took out an envelope and held it out to me. I took it and opened it on my knees. It contained only a photograph, a class picture with that special grain they have. On the back of the picture a few lines had been scribbled in an elongated, hasty hand: Mme Recollet – CM2 – 15 September 19— (the last two numbers had been crossed out) – Maurice Nadeau Primary School – Jaillan-la Forêt – BODART ESTELLE (the name, written

146

in capitals, was emphatically underlined three times); then the signature: Françoise Recollet.

I turned the photograph around in my hands, twice, then looked up at the inspector who was looking at me in a falsely candid way, as though the picture had been taken in a sex club, and as though it showed me wearing some sort of exotic costume. I threw the envelope and the photograph on the desk. The inspector took the picture between his fingers, as you might hold out a hundred-franc note to a tramp. For a moment he said nothing, then he asked in a neutral voice:

'You know them, I suppose?'

'I expect there's a message.'

He sprang to his feet, and his chair toppled over behind him. Standing upright, leaning on the desk with his fingers parted, he smiled like a psychopath undergoing a personality conflict. He held out the photograph again with an insistent gesture.

'I've nearly had enough of you, Hoffman, acting all superior like the little provincial schoolteacher you are. Just look at the photograph and tell me what you see!'

Little folds of tension stood out around his mouth and his eyes, the pulse in his temples announced a battle of wills in which I wasn't entirely sure that I had the advantage. I took back the photograph.

'I'd say that this picture shows 9F almost in its entirety, before they came to the middle school. It was taken a year before I arrived in the region.'

'Exactly.'

'I suppose I should be surprised by the fact that they've all managed to stay together from primary school to their third year at middle school.'

'There's no explanation for it. The parents I met agreed that they considered it perfectly natural, that their children would be profoundly unbalanced if things were otherwise.'

'Which parents are you talking about?'

'Dimitri Corto's mother and Apolline Brossard's father.'

'I expect they must have put pressure on the headmaster to ensure that they stayed together.'

'That's what Monsieur Poncin told me when I asked him.'

'How did he react at that moment?'

'I thought he seemed uneasy.'

'Is that all?'

'That's all, yes . . . he added only that no one outside the school could imagine the dictatorial power exerted by parents within primary education. According to him it calmed down a bit once you reached the *lycée* – by that point the parents must have figured that their children were almost adult. So if they had set their sights on a single goal and were not satisfied with what they got, they went straight to the headmaster, who almost always went along with them. He gave me to understand that there was no point in resisting if parents wanted their children to be in the same class from primary school onwards. They would win the case anyway. A kind of banana republic, if you like, with codes and laws that don't tolerate any kind of interventionism . . . Do you see anything else?'

I'd obviously noticed the striking contrast between that photograph and the one taken at the beginning of term. In the first, confidence, credulity, quietude; in the second, anxiety, a failure to meet the eye, the vanishing of an enigmatic aura. In four years, they had become terribly *real*.

148

The inspector picked up his chair, drew it towards me and sat on to it like a cabaret singer in twenties Berlin. His sudden closeness threw an operating-theatre light on the picture. He scratched the back of his head. It was a gesture he had been making since the beginning of the interview, whenever he wanted to demonstrate his impatience. He suddenly exuded a quiet aptitude for mental torture. I sensed that he was very excited. It wasn't a banal homosexual impulse born of the proximity of his perspiration and mine; no, it was more the ordinary excitement of the guardian of law and order, which I associated with repression generated by countless sedative evenings spent *en famille*. I wasn't feeling especially calm.

'Why is there a white cross above the head of the teacher, and another one over the head of the child with the round glasses in the middle?' I asked by way of distraction.

'They're dead.'

'When did that happen?'

'The following year. The teacher threw herself under a train. No one has ever explained why she did it. No letter, no previous signs of mental imbalance; she had just got married and bought a house. As to the child, he disappeared, and for two months the theory prevailed that he had run away, until some holidaymakers found his body in a bunker on the Normandy coast. An inspector from the station in Arromanches has just sent me the report they made at the time. His mouth had been sealed with sticking-plaster. A handsaw had been placed near the body. According to the autopsy report, he took a long time to die.'

'That's horrible.'

'That's what I thought when I read it in detail. The guilty party was never apprehended. The case is classified as unsolved. But there are striking similarities between this double disappearance and the suicide of the class's history and geography teacher, followed by the attack on the Sorman girl . . . I'm sure it was a warning; if it hadn't been, she'd be dead already . . . But I can't prove anything. To answer your initial objection, I don't think we need seek the people who attacked Clara Sorman anywhere but in the history of this class.'

9

Leaving the station, I went to the nearby park to gather my thoughts. I had a terrible pain in my chest every time I breathed. There was a bench free. I tried to find a space free of birdshit so that I could think more clearly about the events of the past two days. At that time of the afternoon the temperature began to fall, and the sky was white and opaque with mist. The light was uniform, shadowless.

A young man with a pony tail and a goatee stopped to ask me the time. I told him, but not before pointing to the enormous clock on the wall of the town hall opposite. He asked me if I ever went to the Marino, a gay bar some way outside the town. I told him I didn't, that I went out very seldom, and when I did it wasn't to homosexual bars. He went on his way, raising his eyes heavenwards. I sank back, arms folded.

As I watched the children play, accompanied by their parents, in my mind I clearly saw the scene when Clara had appeared with her face bandaged, the hesitant way she walked. Poncin, pushing her in front of him with a little word of encouragement, had given me a nod whose meaning was still not entirely clear to me. I had a sense, although I wasn't certain, that by making her walk towards me, and by stepping backwards as she did so, he was trying to rid himself of a problem of conscience.

She was holding a note that she handed to me after apologising in a toneless voice. She went and sat down next to Sandrine Botella, whose pallor had made me concerned for a moment that she was going to faint. Her hands sat motionless on the table, her usual intensity had darkened into a look of sadness that briefly haloed her face. She sat rigidly, staring at a point in the wall above the blackboard.

The others waited for the rest of the lesson in a church-like silence. Apolline Brossard pulled on her chewing gum and rolled it round her index finger. I hadn't the strength to take it from her and throw it in the bin. I read in her eyes that she knew that, which made her provocation even more painful. Mathilde Vandevoorde, who was sitting just behind Clara, shivered a little too theatrically for a properly successful camouflage operation. Estelle Bodart's big dark eyes expressed a curious inner dimension, somehow contrite but at the same time without a trace of actual remorse. She had a hard face, with an extra-large mouth, broad and sensual, perhaps a bit vulgar in certain lights. She looked like one of those children who are constantly afraid of being punished.

Clara had got her belongings out without looking at me. When she raised her eyes towards me, her bandaged face bore an unbearably tragic expression. I glanced away towards my desk, took a photocopied sheet and handed it to her without a word.

'Where were we?' I asked everyone, without expecting a reply.

'I was just finishing reading the text,' replied Sandrine Botella, still staring straight ahead.

'I'd like you to take your rough-work books and choose from the text all the expressions illustrating the spirit of tolerance that the author values. I'll give you ten minutes. Then I'll ask one of you to go to the blackboard.'

They took out their notebooks with bad grace. I went and sat at the back of the class, near the window. During those ten minutes, I couldn't help looking at the bent backs of Clara and her neighbour. Sandrine Botella had moved closer to Clara, leaning on her left elbow, and was sulkily talking to her, glancing in my direction from time to time. I could hear a grumbling noise emerging from her throat, and her face showed not a hint of compassion. At that point I could barely have grasped that this kind of opacity in the general behaviour of the pupils was only the predictable extension of rituals to which I would never have access.

This time, I thought then as all the pupils bent over their notebooks, I was facing a real problem which came down to the level of moral engagement that my life was going to have to accommodate.

Placed by my indifference on the periphery of the national education system, of life in general, of everything, in fact, I had only ever been superficially affected by the little local perversions practised in the establishments in which I had taught since the start of my career. After ten years of adulthood, I no longer counted instances of passive paedophilia (masturbation under the desk during classes, the use of inappropriate language with the children), active paedophilia (various kinds of groping in dark corridors along with suggestive propositions) or sadism disguised as high-yield pedagogy: all such things were ratified in a staff room that was halfway between a dating agency and a wife-swapping club.

I had always behaved like one of those people the Nazis referred to as 'internal emigrants', the ones who worked within the system but weren't embarrassed about criticising it, with the complicity of some of its most servile collaborators. From now on I found myself at the epicentre of an affair that everyone had known about for years, everyone except me. I could go on pretending to take an interest in the teaching body, I could ignore the shadows, but I could no longer help wondering what Capadis, the primary school teacher and the child with the round glasses had done to deserve their fates.

Doctors had medical secrets, we had teacherly secrets, among the best guarded in France. Without those secrets, no one would have wanted to entrust their children to adults who – and this is a remarkable and rarely mentioned fact – were in general much more unbalanced than the members of most other professions. In comparison, the pre-adolescents I had before me seemed almost sane. But there was one very disturbing quality about them: most children tolerated the world that adults had built for them, and tried to adapt to it as best they could. Consequently, as a rule, they reproduced that world. Observing 9F, it was easy to guess that they had no intention of taking that route. They had chosen something much more catastrophic, which I could still not quite grasp. Something that had to do with secrecy, the territorial jealousy of childhood and the summary expulsion of any kind of otherness.

When the ten minutes had passed, I asked Dimitri Corto to go to the board. He slowly raised his thin, slumped form and picked up his notebook. As he brushed past Carla Sorman's desk, she raised her head towards him. Her face expressed a mixture of rancour and embarrassed constraint.

With his striped pullover, his extra-wide jeans, his little quiff and the casual ease of a Californian fashion model, the girls found Dimitri terribly attractive. His alpha-male status was not contested by anyone in the pack. He was the spokesman for the collective, the hero of the horde, carefully dissecting the mechanisms of anything that happened. His appearance upon the school scene always provoked a hushed delight in everyone present.

'Well, uh, in the text we read that the Catholic isn't shocked and if necessary the Quaker has the role of peacemaker . . . the term "enlightenment" is associated with the character of the Quaker . . .'

The bell interrupted the beginning of his disquisition. He gave an ironic bow, like a music-hall artiste, then returned to his seat with his eyes cast down. As everyone prepared to leave the classroom, I tried to catch up with Clara, who had left before everyone else. I ran almost as far as the disciplinary counsellors' office, in the wing opposite my building. As I stopped to get my breath back, I suddenly made her out among a little cluster of year sevens who were striding along in front of her. Her shoulders drooped, her head was bowed. I started running again. When I was almost level with her, she suddenly turned around. There were tears in her eyes.

'Stop following me,' she murmured. She stared into my eyes. 'Leave me alone. I should never have spoken to you.'

'I don't think you made a mistake.'

'*I* certainly think I did.'

'At the cemetery, you seemed absolutely certain that there was danger around. What did you mean?'

'You're the one who's put me in danger. It's part of your system, undermining people up until they come running to your aid. Go and find someone else!'

She raised her little fist to the level of her shoulder, her arm bent and her eyes suddenly wide. I took a step backwards. She dropped her arm again and lowered her head for a moment.

'I'm sorry, there's nothing I can say to you . . . I can't bear thinking about all that.'

'Who did it to you? Tell me . . . we'll protect you, the inspector promised me.' (I was lying.) 'You'll never get into the *lycée* if you stay here.'

'What's the point of us meeting like this? There isn't one. This conversation is stupid and . . . pointless,' she replied. 'Remember what I told you at the cemetery: leave, resign . . . you're in danger.'

She had moved away, instinctively shielding her face with her hands. I stood there rooted to the spot. I heard my heart beating, a deep staccato in my chest, like the sound of blood flowing through my aorta. I felt horribly guilty. For the first time in years, I wanted to cry. I repeated to myself that nothing could repair that life which would now be spent avoiding both mirrors and public appearances.

A woman sat down next to me. She wasn't carrying a toy, which would have suggested that she was the mother of one of the children. Her clothes were slovenly but not dirty. She had dark blond hair in curls that covered her eyes, hollow

156

cheeks and yellow teeth partly covered by her gums. Smiling with the beatitude of a mystic, she sat with her back bent, her forearms on her knees and the palms of her hands facing the ground. Her feet, strapped into beach shoes in spite of the damp weather, were spread wide.

I didn't know why, but the woman seemed to me to be extremely happy. She was sitting there like someone who didn't want to talk to anyone, but who was simply interested in the sight of children. Sometimes one of them would pull another's hair, throw sand in someone's eyes or yell as they ran around the flowerbed. Then the woman would smile at the mother very strangely, as though she weren't thinking about that woman in particular, or her child, but about some remote life that she had lived or wished she had.

After ten minutes of this business, she looked at me, still smiling. I got to my feet abruptly as though I had just emerged from a dream. I wanted to go home. It was going-home time for the office workers. More relaxed now, the people created a kind of relaxed topography, breaking up the harsh angles of the streets and shopfronts. As I crossed the streets, whatever the time of day, I always watched out for cars coming from behind, which seemed to be there only to show me that the town operated according to some principle of provocation.

It was a little cooler now. I was walking in a straight line, trying to forget my destination, when a group of boys and girls crossed the road twenty metres ahead of me. They were on their way to the park. The passers-by coming towards them gave them only the briefest of glances, as though they were nothing but a passing, familiar spectacle, serene young people who wouldn't steal their car radios or snatch their bags in an idle moment. I followed them for another hundred metres or so, without trying to catch up with them.

The traffic was gradually building up. There was a report from an exhaust pipe a little way away from their group. One of the boys and one of the girls turned around almost simultaneously. I stopped where I was, turning my head. I had just recognised Dimitri Corto and the gauze-whitened cheeks of Clara Sorman.

10

The group hadn't paid me the slightest attention. I was used to that. I hadn't met many people since my arrival in these parts. My anonymity outside the college had enabled me to establish a particular relationship with the region in spite of myself. A few exceptions aside, the pupils I had taught over the course of the previous few years pretended not to know me when we met by chance, as though they had only just realised that their teacher might exist in flesh and blood. For pupils in general it's hard to admit that a teacher might have a life of his own outside the classroom, hence the difficulty of living in the town where you teach.

I turned into a side-street, moving away from the group, aware that they couldn't be heading for anywhere else but the park. I emerged at the other end of the little street, at the spot where the barely moving cars, their headlights catching me in their saffron light, came to a standstill. I quickened my step for fear of losing the children. The fading light of day was growing increasingly stormy. For five hours, the sky had been as dense as slate. The birds were flying so low that you had to be careful not to bump into them.

I turned up my jacket collar and passed in front of a crowd of motionless people outside the municipal library. It was a bus stop with about fifty people standing in a more or less ordinary fashion, massed along the pavement almost on the steps of the building, ignoring the gusts of wind that were beginning to sweep the boulevard.

I didn't have a coat. I'd left it in my car. I huddled in my jacket and spotted my pupils passing by about fifty metres ahead of me. They were walking side by side now, like a squadron of planes approaching its target. They wore light clothing, jeans and hooded sweatshirts, but they didn't seem to feel the damp carried in the wind. They walked straight ahead, their arms swinging along their bodies with the regularity of a military exercise. They gave the impression that no one could have stopped them.

The park was now plunged into gloom. There was no one there apart from a pensioner who was letting his dog defecate in a flower bed. He called the dog to him when he noticed the teenagers heading in his direction. As they passed, he kept it firmly on its leash, and stared at them with a fearful movement of the head. His figure was caught for a moment in the bright halo of a streetlight, before he came towards me looking utterly astonished, as though the idea of an adult male following a group of adolescents in the dying light of a park was such a peculiar sight that surprise was the only possible reaction. He was a purple-faced old man, with little burst blood-vessels and a large nose. I couldn't help thinking of the sense of tragedy that I have always associated with people with large noses.

The pupils walked all the way down the central avenue. I bumped into two women who were walking along eating peaches, their heads tilted at an angle, their bodies strangely contorted to make sure that the juice didn't trickle where it wasn't wanted. They were speaking to one another with a liquid lisp, in short phrases that allowed them to remain as absorbed in their conversation as they were in their respective fruits. As they reached me, one of them began to inspect the fluff on her peach, as though she were contemplating returning to the supermarket. I heard them laughing and chattering long after I had passed them. I concentrated on my tailing task, to avoid reflecting that they might have been laughing and chattering about me. Turning around abruptly, I extended my fingers in the direction of their heads as though firing a revolver, and clicked my thumb. A gesture of pure frustration.

Eyes raised towards the foliage of the trees, I stayed there for a moment watching the birds flying around in the open patch of sky left amidst the branches. There was something unfinished and vertiginous in the pastoral image of a park at dusk. Silence fell as the sounds of the town subsided, and the footsteps of the two women faded away in the distance. I could almost hear the muffled scrape of my feet on the damp earth. The outlines of the trees looked as though they connected to a wider perspective which made self-consciousness grow to an overwhelming degree.

The wail of an ambulance siren reminded me of the existence of a world beyond this strip of green. About twenty metres to my right, I saw the back of a man relieving himself against a tree. As they struck the bark, the drops of urine emitted a faint splash, and gave off a cloud of steam that caught me in the back of the throat.

The man didn't even bother turning round as I approached, merely shaking his member with a comical rotating motion.

I was pulled from my embarrassment by the metallic clang of a gate being slammed shut. The pupils had passed through a gate into a garden of which I had until then been unaware. They were about to enter an unknown and mysterious zone that I hadn't anticipated. I made my way towards the gate.

The places where no ivy grew had assumed the colour of moss, and the whole fence seemed now to consist of plant matter. A rusted chain held the gate wide open. On one of the steel gateposts there was a sign covered with a piece of glass and lit by a neon tube. An inscription in marker pen was written on a piece of paper held in place by a rusty drawing pin: 'As this playground is unsupervised, the slide and swings are used at visitors' own risk.' Four small insects attracted by the neon crept among the letters.

Night had fallen without my noticing. It looked even darker beyond the gate than in the place where I was crouching. The damp wind started blowing even harder. Huddled in the semi-darkness behind the boundary formed by the illuminated gate, I felt the cold slowly enveloping my cheeks, hands and legs. Something invisible to the naked eye, like time, space or distances, started undergoing a strange distortion. I still couldn't hear any sound coming from the area sunk in darkness into which the pupils had disappeared.

I constructed the most baroque hypotheses. Perhaps they'd disappeared down a rabbit-hole, like Alice? Perhaps they'd noticed my presence and were hiding under the leaves waiting for me to pass through the gate so that they could ambush me? Or perhaps they had simply found the entrance to a grotto hidden from the eye, and reached another place that would allow them to shake off their pursuers via an underground tunnel?

The silence was becoming increasingly dense, like a pocket of emptiness in the darkness. During those moments of impotent tension, the imbalance of the world struck me in waves, along with the thought of my inability fully to occupy the centre ground.

I had always liked that sensation of being dragged in someone else's wake. Even when I was young I had sometimes tailed people randomly in the street. It gave me a feeling of escaping the force of serious events, of fear, of guilt. A wake as powerful as the one left by the children was a special state of consciousness, a world within the world, the revelation of an intimate obsession.

I allowed myself to wait for another five minutes; then I would make off as fast as my legs would carry me.

As I was getting up to retrace my steps, I was blinded by a geyser of light. I saw the sinusoid arc of a slide, along with a structure consisting of rings and lozenges. Just beside it, another more modest-sized structure supported two swings. The pupils were standing to the right of the perimeter of the playground. Dimitri Corto's hand rested on a rectangular console, set up on a steel tube. The lid that ensured its protection against damage dangled miserably from a single rusty chain. In the darkness of the park, the playground looked like an island of crystal in a sea of black water. Two halogen lamps projected cones of light, one aimed at the group, the other at the swings. The harsh light fell violently on the children's faces, which seemed even more pale and tense than usual.

I could now see the little group in profile. Each member appeared sculpted by the intense light. They were almost motionless, and standing a precise distance apart from one another. The whole scene seemed to correspond to an abstract calculation of perspective and tones, like dancers beneath a stroboscopic light. Beside Dimitri Corto stood Clara Sorman and Sandrine Botella. A little way back, Kevin Durand and Mathieu Naudin were keeping a close eye on the scene, their eyes narrowed, their hands held around their cheeks and forehead to shield them from the light.

The light made me invisible, and I stayed a few metres away from the children, as though I were watching them from another plane of existence. Slightly apart from the rest of the group, but facing me, Estelle Bodart, her arms crossed over her chest, gave a start at the slightest noise. At her feet was a canvas bag covered with sewn-on badges.

'How did you get hold of the key?' asked Kevin.

'Forget questions of that kind,' Dimitri replied coldly. 'Just enjoy the show. There's a waiting list.'

'What are we here for exactly?'

Mathieu Naudin had just asked the question in a voice so innocent that one wanted to spend the rest of the night giving him answers just to put his mind at rest.

'We're here to rediscover some sensations . . . and to do a swap.'

Estelle Bodart tapped the bag with a knowing grin. I liked the way her gums showed when she smiled. Despite the cold, she was wearing a man's white shirt knotted

164

together at the waist, and a pair of jeans cut off above the knees, with big socks and imitation Ranger boots. She looked at Mathieu, her eyes drained of expression, and nodded thoughtfully as though to suggest that his attack of stupidity was always liable to pass. She took off her shoes and threw them in front of her.

'Come over here,' she said to him after staring at him for a long while. 'People are worried about you.'

'Who, for instance?'

Mathieu came trustingly over to her. She stepped towards him, still staring him straight in the eyes, and standing on tiptoes. She came so close that her breath made his hair move. In front of everyone, Estelle undid Mathieu's belt. She didn't even lower her eyes, her fingers did the seeing for her.

'Me, for example.'

She ran a hand behind the nape of the boy's neck, drawing his face towards her. They rubbed noses like Eskimos, and then she tried to plant her lips on his. None of the others reacted. All of a sudden Mathieu broke away, and came and stood beside Kevin again. It was the first time that I had seen the slightest hint of sensuality among them.

'Piss off,' he spat at her between his teeth, readjusting the button of his trousers.

'Not like this – please!' she said imploringly.

Mathieu looked at her with the crushing expression that a gladiator reserves for his prey, and his posture revealed a desire not to succumb to the easy seduction represented by Estelle's capitulation, a kind of sober magnanimity. Estelle dropped to the ground and leaned her back against a tree, keeping the canvas bag between her legs, which

165

were parted in the V of a woman in childbirth. With her elbows resting on her knees and her fingers pointing downwards, her attitude expressed the anguish of someone who has been tortured all night. She snapped her chewing gum to show her defiance. In the silent darkness, her attitude of abandonment overwhelmed me: it was the ultimate expression of renunciation, like a fresh desire to speak from now on so as to be understood.

'What's in the bag?' asked Kevin suspiciously.

'A video tape.'

'Who for?'

'Some guys at another school . . . some guys like us.'

'That's not possible. There can't be anyone else like us. Are you quite sure about what you're claiming?'

'It's true,' Clara intervened dreamily, 'there isn't anyone else like us.'

Her words came out slowly, like the voice of a talking doll whose wire had been pulled too many times.

'Let them go on believing they're like us,' said Sandrine Botella, turning slightly towards the two boys.

She exchanged a look of approval with Dimitri. He suddenly looked very annoyed.

'So, where are we?' asked Mathieu.

'Who knows?' answered Clara.

'We're inside,' asserted Dimitri.

'That's obvious.'

'Quite reassuring to know that.'

'It's obvious because if we were outside,' Dimitri went on pompously, 'we would be powerless. It's the great technique of assimilation. Sooner or later the giant vacuum cleaner always sticks in its nozzle.'

As he spoke, he looked straight at the group, but with

no defiance in his eyes, no hint of tyrannical confrontation. I sensed that he had given those things up a long time ago, and that he now defined his position entirely through the concentration of the means with which he sought to achieve his goal. It was a tactical position that gave his audience an intoxicating sense of being neither tedious nor interchangeable. It was what some people call charisma, and others call manipulation, a method frequently employed by teachers.

The plot was beginning to thicken.

'I didn't know that, but I'm going to think about it.'

'By the time you've thought about it, it'll be too late.'

'And then?'

'Nothing. Evil will have arrived.'

'I'd just like to understand what's going on. I see myself as a guest, and guests are people who like to know what they're letting themselves in for,' added Mathieu, his face both servile and mocking.

For the first time I studied him carefully. He had the same big dark, bluish-grey eyes as Capadis, the same pointed ears, delicately rimmed at the tip. In profile, what struck me most was his nose, which was shaped like the shell of a snail. He was the kind of pupil who excelled at organising parties when people's parents were away, dealing with the music and telling dodgy jokes, slapping the boys on the back, and guiding his strange intensity into the hearts of the girls without ever externalising it. He seemed to be more disconcerted by Estelle's amorous display than by Dimitri's woolly speech.

After taking off his sweatshirt, and throwing it towards the part of the fence where I was standing, Dimitri dashed towards the slide uttering barbarian little cries. He climbed the ladder, then sat with his feet sticking out, as though about to slide down. He sat there with his arms raised, engulfing the others in the stylised gaze of a silent-film star. A gust of wind swirled up somnolent odours. The air smelled of children's vomit.

'Very impressive,' said Clara, clapping her hands.

'It's incredible,' said Sandrine.

'I love that,' said Estelle.

'I've done sliding competitions,' cried Dimitri, before making monkey noises and beating his chest. 'I can slide backwards, on the spot, standing up, lying down. I can climb the ladder faster than anyone. I've already managed to slide down and climb up ten times in thirty seconds. The supervisors in the Mickey Mouse club couldn't get over it, they thought it was completely incredible in a five-year-old. I don't know whether I could still do it!'

While speaking, he had wedged his right hand between his shirt collar and the back of his neck, his elbow level with his ear. I saw Clara staring at the sweat patch under his arm. She seemed to be holding her breath. It was one manifestation of the power that Dimitri had over the others. The sliding records at the Mickey Mouse club, thirty-second moped wheelies, five-minute kisses without suffocating. When he was eighteen he would humble the others by talking about Peruvian films that had been shown for a week in Paris, or Slovene Satanic thrash-metal bands. A kind of namedropping that placed deliberate stress on the unusual, a highly developed ritual of humiliation.

'Rumour has it', Mathieu called over to him with feudal obsequiousness, 'that your little brother had been tying fireworks to cats' backs. Three have died already. With their skin in rags, they go and die in gardens where there aren't any dogs. Or else they stay on the top of fences. One's even been found headless, hung up by its tail. It's really crap!'

'What else?'

'He blows up toads until they burst . . . he sticks his tongue out in a disgusting way at married women at the bus stop. He mocks disabled people and encourages tramps to masturbate into people's letterboxes.'

I stood up for a moment flexing my knees. My underpants had got stuck in the crack of my bottom, and threatened to pinch my perineum until they drew blood.

'Who told you that, Mat? I'm hearing a lot of bad things about myself at the moment. Too many, in fact . . . And I've decided to dye my hair yellow to make people think ill of me once and for all. I'll tell people, "Insult me and you'll see what happens!" And they'll have to take the threat very seriously . . . My big brother started doing that kind of thing years ago, shooting at cats in front of old people and pregnant women. My youngest brother must have been influenced . . .'

'You're paranoid, Dimitri,' said Sandrine.

'I'm trying to ease your anxieties. I'm taking all the blame. What are you complaining about, you ungrateful creeps?'

'Nothing. Where are we going? To do what? Those are the big questions. There's no getting around it. You can't be angry with us for asking!'

'I feel like a meerkat. They're little animals that look a bit like otters . . . they spend their time looking around the place to find things that are potentially harmful to the community. They die of stress in the end, but the community survives. That's the important thing . . .'

'Are you trying to tell us the world is a bad place?' said Kevin, astonished.

'There are various kinds of pressure, that much is certain. It's hard to evaluate at the moment. I can't prove anything. But what we've done in the past we were obliged to do. It's a good thing we're not here for very long.'

Clara turned an anguished face to the two boys who had stayed in the background.

'It hurts,' she said.

'What does?' asked Kevin.

'The feeling of being confined, of reaching the end.'

'What's she saying?' asked Dimitri, who was too far from Clara to hear.

'She says she's in pain,' Mathieu replied.

'Does she really have to say so?' asked Dimitri, addressing Mathieu as though Clara didn't exist. 'I know it's been getting worse for some time . . . but does she have to talk about it?'

'Certainly.'

'Fine.'

'I'm scared, too,' Mathieu went on. 'It's not a fear of being physically hurt, or disabled for life. It's the idea of what they really are that scares me.'

'I know what you mean,' said Dimitri, lowering his head. 'Does anyone want to dissolve the group?'

'No one. That would be even worse,' said Sandrine.

'And what about the others?'

'I haven't noticed anything.'

'I agree.'

'Let's get going.'

Dimitri clapped his hands.

'Fine, let's go!'

He slid soberly down the slide, his arms stretched out along his thighs, his head held straight. The others stood with their hands on their hips like footballers waiting for a decision from the referee.

'It looks as if your power is growing', said Clara to Dimitri as he passed in front of her to pick up his sweatshirt and walk over to the box.

'It isn't his power that's growing, it's our fear,' said Sandrine, not looking at her.

'He's busy banishing sadness,' added Kevin. 'That's his job. He does it quite well, don't you think?'

'I've got a birthday coming up,' said Dimitri, ignoring Kevin's question.

He was standing in front of the steel parallelogram, stroking its surface, concentrating like a synthesiser-player. Estelle came and stood next to him with her shoulderbag, and murmured something in his ear.

'How old does that make you?' asked Mathieu.

'Fourteen. In a month. I feel as though I'm about to enter a long period of anxiety. I'm trying not to panic. My parents are organising a do for my birthday, a little party. They've given me a budget and ordered up some invitations. I haven't sent any out yet.'

'Try not to think about it.'

'It's hard not to. What time is it?'

'Ten to seven.'

'We'd better get back. They'll be home soon. I'm going to cut the lights, switch off this thing and we'll go, ok!'

'What shall I do with the bag?' asked Estelle.

'Give it to me.'

She took it off her shoulder and held it out to him. He undid the straps and removed a black video cassette

171

with one hand, handing her the bag with the other. He was standing next to a knotty oak tree, with a wide crevice in the middle. He stood in front of the tree, hoisted himself up slightly on the tips of his toes and placed the box into the cavity. The dull clatter that the video made as it fell indicated that it would be deep enough to be totally invisible. Without warning the others, Dimitri switched off the light and then, in darkness, skilfully replaced the steel cover on the console. Shortly afterwards I heard the click of the padlock, like a final signal. The children left without a word, following Dimitri's shadow. He moved as easily as though he could see in the dark.

Once they had gone, I left my kneeling position and lay down in the damp grass. I don't know how long I stayed there, pressed against the earth, but I can still remember the sound of the gate clanking in the wind. Then I got up on one elbow and concentrated my field of vision upon it. Its indistinctness made it seem even more dense and present in the semi-darkness. I was seized by a panic that was like the return of an ancient childhood terror, and I fled.

It was only when I reached my car that I realised I had left the cassette behind.

I didn't know why, but I had the feeling that the car was zigzagging across the road.

On the way back, I struck the steering wheel hard, uttering brief two-syllable shouts that sounded a bit like foghorns, a bit like the cry of the Algonquin or the wail of a train screeching around a bend. The tape lay on the passenger seat. The last time I glanced at the box I had had a vague feeling of exhaustion, and had pressed myself into my seat, swearing to ignore it until I got home. To trick the enemy, I had switched on the radio, and changed stations every five seconds. After five minutes of zapping, a presenter with an accent from the province of Berry brought her programme to a close with the noise of a sizzling frying pan. A few seconds later, she was followed by another voice, the gentle voice of an arts programme, whose generous timbre seemed to be attempting to ease any possible disaffection that the listener might feel in response to the austerity of the programme's content.

When I reached my block of flats, two children were sitting on the steps of the building, playing jacks. The pale light from the lamp over the front door drew a circle around them, bounded by the shadow from a billboard that swayed in the north-westerly wind. Once I was out of my car, I made a clumsy attempt to hide the cassette under my jacket, holding my arm bent against my right side. The children remained silent as I passed. I tried to think of something amusing to say, but their attention was focused on the hand throwing the jack, while the other hung in the air for a fraction of a second. The game seemed to be wholly engrossing. It couldn't accommodate an exchange of points of view.

The bins were out. A bus passed in front of the building, tired faces pressed to the windows. I stopped on the threshold for a moment, powerless in the face of that form of déjà-vu, like matter madly returning to its original state. Just then the concierge of the building came out. His left hand was jumping about in the pocket of his overalls as if he thought he'd been caught *in flagrante*. Sweat run down his temples, tracing pale stripes on his alcohol-reddened skin.

173

I was sure he had been stealing the mail addressed to the women in the building again. He passed by me with a nod. I turned my head away, slowly raising my right hand to scratch myself under my itchy armpit. The video fell to my feet with a terrible crash. The concierge turned around and, with his eyes fastened on a spot between my feet, gave me a complicit smile. He brought his hands together to improve his posture.

'Nice evening ahead,' he said finally, in a lascivious voice, before going on his way.

I went back up towards my flat, this time with the cassette clearly visible in my hand. I was neither worried nor excited about the idea of discovering what it contained. The spectacle I had just witnessed, as well as the lack of clues on the box, were enough to reduce my expectations considerably. I did some tidying when I got home. I wanted to put each thing in its proper place. The phone rang. I picked it up in the secret hope of hearing Léonore's voice. At that moment I had a real need for her sardonic inflections, and her rather dry form of affection. But it was Goliaguine inviting me to a lunch with my colleagues on Sunday.

'Nothing fancy,' he added before I could say a word. Caught on the hop, I didn't feel in a state either to refuse or to lie. It would have taken too much preparation. I accepted, asking who else was going to be there. Goliaguine evaded the issue, on the pretext that I was one of the first people he had phoned. He claimed it was because of the way I lit up a room. I had a sense that he wanted me to talk about him, but I had no desire to launch into a frank and open conversation.

I gently put the phone down, then lay on the sofa for

an hour with my hands behind my neck and my eyes fixed on the ceiling. I'd left the front door light on as I had done when I was little and my mother left me alone in the sitting room in winter, late in the afternoon. The cassette, on the sitting-room table, now seemed to me to be the only fixed point in my life, the only area of stability. The black case sparkled with a fixed and frozen light. Its solidity absorbed all the attention in the place, draining the room of the level of solitude it attempted to achieve, and exaggerating the obviousness of its presence by remaining provocatively motionless.

I was tempted to throw it into the building's waste-disposal unit, to dispatch it far beyond the pain and shame that I was liable to feel once I knew what it contained. I knew that I should have to take these images *literally*, without casting them back into a symbolic background in which all threats to the social order normally dissolved. If I could remain alert and concentrate upon those images, if I could think clearly about them, if I could know with any certainty the range of the impact they would have upon my future relations with the children, only then could I begin to look at them while at the same time separating them from their grim sociological reality.

In the end I rose from the sofa to check that the windows were properly closed, the roller blinds lowered, and that no one, whether from a neighbouring tower block or an upper storey, could spy on (or hear!) what I was about to view. A burst of routine paranoia, very much part of the order of things associated with mass habitation. I brightened the halogen light lest I find myself in violent confrontation with the television screen. I brought my chair half a metre from the screen, not because I wanted to give myself the chance of putting the tape on 'pause' (something that I could do with the remote control while ensconcing myself on the sofa), but more that I wished to be able to turn off the television if the images became too disturbing.

I took the cassette from its box and checked that it was properly rewound, then inserted it between the jaws of the video recorder, which swallowed it up with a cash-register click, and switched on the television as I did so. I was so close to the screen that the electrostatic flash almost blinded me. The only noise I could hear now was the whirr of the tape passing through the video player. A snowy film appeared on the screen, then a light-blue back-ground trembling to some quick, cheerful music on a player-piano accompanied by a big bass drum striking out the beats, as in the film of *Pinocchio*.

A stretch of beach appeared on the screen, with the cries of children in the distance. They weren't the kind of cries that suggested a danger or a threat, but those of a noisy and disordered rabble of children, along with the sounds of arms splashing in water. The picture was crude and primitive, like holiday films shot on super-eight before being transferred to video. The cameraman was a long way away, and walked jerkily forward so that the screen showed, first of all, a patch of blue sky and an area of sandy beach. Some of the children were playing ball on the shore, now and again glancing curiously at the camera. The cameraman stopped as soon as he could capture the children on the beach and the ones in the water in a single shot. It now became apparent that they were splashing one another.

For several long minutes the shot remained fixed, with the camera a slight distance away from the scene. I pressed fast forward until I could make out some movement and grasp anything at all, the start of a story or an event that might justify the anxious apprehension which the cassette had provoked in me. But nothing happened. In the rapid sequence of images nothing moved, everything had a strange fixity, apart from the playful movements of the children.

All of a sudden, one child seemed to break away from the group on the beach, and I released my pressure on the button of the video machine. A little girl of about eight or nine came towards the camera, dragging her feet. When she was close to the lens, I was frozen in my chair with fear. She stuck out her tongue, grimacing horribly at the camera, and then waving at the cameraman to stop filming. The tape stopped abruptly, and I rewound the cassette. The film had lasted barely thirty minutes. As the tape rewound, I thought of the photograph that the inspector had shown me.

Later I would see the film again and identify all the protagonists of 9F one by one, but I would never forget the face of Mathilde Vandevoorde, authoritarian but facetious in the pale summer light, gesturing to the cameraman to stop filming herself and the others. Then I identified that refusal as the first in a long series, the inaugural gesture of a total war waged against the outside world, as though by that gesture Mathilde had wanted to tell the adult who was pointing the camera at her that they weren't yet ready to enter the world of death.

11

When Goliaguine laughed, I saw that his mouth was speckled with bits of cheddar cheese. Whenever he liked a remark, he stretched out with a smile, in a sort of ecstatic yawn, his hips and legs motionless, the top of his body arched backwards. Between two bursts of laughter, his face expressed a sceptical vigilance, followed by a fear of being caught unawares, a sort of sheepish perspicacity.

We had been sitting around the table for two hours, in a posture of hushed weariness, a conscious lethargy that we had all decided to adopt in unison. Everyone was already a little tipsy. Everything seemed to be in a state of dissolution. The sounds of conversations were beginning to melt in my inner ear like the sound of a bumblebee flying around a room. I mentally recomposed the diagnoses being sent out by the messengers of my natural hypochondria: symptoms of tinnitus? Tachycardia? I decided to arrange a meeting with my GP the following day.

As a musical background, the rhythm track from an old Prince song, 'Let's Go Crazy', did its best to drag the guests out of their post-prandial torpor. Goliaguine reminded us that the album *Purple Rain* was recorded as early as 1984, a time when the Minneapolis midget was already able to beat Michael Jackson on his own territory.

'Back then,' he went on almost to himself, gazing vaguely into the distance, 'nearly anything was still possible . . . I was working on my visual arts degree, I was in there for six hours a day . . . from dawn . . . a coffee, and off we would go! I could recite you Panofsky's main theories by heart and talk Greenberg to you for hours on end, I fiddled around with autobiographical triptychs in charcoal, and in distemper on crinkled paper, like Schiele.' (There was a framed reproduction of the *Portrait of Hugo Koller* next to his bookshelves.) 'I was just back from Addis Ababa, and we hadn't had Christophe yet.'

He gestured cynically, as though chasing away a fly.

'I know . . . there are little local difficulties, nothing of any great import . . .'

His glazed eyes rested for a moment on his wife Maeva, as though he held her responsible for his personal collapse. In a sudden flash of lucidity, he tried to detach himself from the micro-disaster that his speech had produced, by bursting out laughing with his arms raised. All the guests lowered their eyes towards their drinks.

After the aperitif – Michel Goliaguine had given each of the guests a large glass of planter's punch – Jean-Paul Accetto's wife had made some unworthy remarks to Butel about his crotch, which was thought to be largely inactive. It was at that precise moment that the alcohol had started to take effect. Jean-Paul had been barely able to contain his giggles. He had always hated Butel, and had been careful not to intervene, dispatching his wife to the front line as you might send a henchman to get a contract signed. He had merely lowered his head and run two grimy-nailed fingers through the thin hair on his cranium.

The most troubling aspect of the Accetto personality was that way he had of holding out the apple and waiting, with a glance out of the corner of his eye, for someone to make off with it; I had recognised his talents for manipulation only after an inexplicable delay. That perversity, probably the product of innate cowardice, had always cracked the façade of the good maths teacher who was involved in educational problems as a *humanist*, when his sole concern was really his character as a pedagogical mediator, an impotent witness of the disaster that was his private life.

I was utterly mesmerised by this unstructured reproduction of the staffroom, with all that was unsettling and slightly hysterical about it. Christine Cazin had come with her husband, a tall, dark-haired man originally from south-west France, who worked for the council of Loir-et-Cher and ended all his sentences with the languid phrase: 'don't you think?' At the other end of the table, Isabelle and Élisa sat with their little fingers hooked, and by refusing to be complicit with the other people present, they expressed the mute image of resignation.

Goliaguine's wife, who was Anglo-Caucasian but nonetheless possessed of an oriental reticence, came and went from the kitchen to our table with the regularity of a restaurant chef. Whenever she spoke to someone, she talked in an exaggeratedly low and formal voice, almost without moving her lips, forcing the other person to lean forward to catch her words. From time to time, Michel

Goliaguine looked at her with a smile of satisfaction, his hands crossed over his canonical paunch, as though his wife were a reassuring extension of himself.

One of his guests was Ali, a shy young man with a childlike smile, a passionate enthusiast for painting and medieval scholasticism. To support his family and fund his studies at art school in Tours, he worked as a supervisor at the *lycée* in Amboise. He tried to start a conversation with Butel, who gave him his full attention, having successfully fended off the attacks of Catherine Accetto. Butel turned to his right and his left, accompanying his speech as usual with flaccid, jerky gestures.

'I'm a halfwit,' he said, shaking his head with a dazed expression. 'I am, and I know it. And I confess that it's true.'

His words were drowned by an explosion of laughter. Accetto slapped him on the shoulder, saying gently, 'And it's very honourable of you to say so, Butel! A fault confessed is a fault half pardoned.'

'I hope you won't tell anyone!'

'You may count on me, my friend! Your secret's safe with me.'

Butel was sitting next to Vincent Crochelet, the music teacher who liked to tell superannuated jokes involving stupid stereotypes, which we were supposed to enjoy even though we were utterly resistant to them. In these witticisms, Jews were always avaricious and self-serving, blacks had natural rhythm and enormous penises, and women were venal, submissive and motherly.

Crochelet's wife, a plump little blonde with broken veins in her cheeks, seemed so simple and open, her eyes so unambiguous, that in comparison the other guests would

181

have passed for unsavoury perverts the moment they opened their mouths to ask for the salt. She stretched herself from time to time, smiling with a sort of delighted yawn as though she had just woken from a marvellous dream that had taken her to far-off and unfamiliar lands. Then, leaning on the table, she took her head in her hands, apparently counting the pulses in her temples, which were forced into an indigo hair-band.

'I think I'm going to end up an alcoholic,' said Goliaguine, 'I give myself one or two years, perhaps, no more than that.'

'You've got a Russian background, there's no way out of it,' said Crochelet. 'They knock back ninety-degree spirits over there, you know. Life expectancy has dropped to fifty-five for men . . . I don't know about the women, but it can't be fantastic.'

'Same difference,' said Butel.

'Do you watch television in your bedroom?' Élisa abruptly asked Crochelet, whom she had just met for the first time, and who seemed to have been annoying her since the start.

'Yes, of course. It's the only way I've found to avoid going to sleep on the sofa.'

'You know,' Élisa went on, 'that five years of that and brain death's inevitable. How old are you?'

'Thirty-eight.'

'Ouch!'

There was a long silence during which everyone looked at Élisa, wondering where she was going to take this. During that long silence, you could almost hear Accetto's beard growing. Isabelle desperately tapped her spoon against her cup as she stirred in her sugar.

'Are you referring to people who've stopped going to the cinema, to the theatre, to parties?' Crochelet asked shyly. 'It's difficult when you've got three kids, specially when two of them are very little. But we've always been left-wing, you know! It'll come back, I'm absolutely sure of it.'

'It'll come back?' asked Élisa sceptically.

'If you're left-wing it always comes back sooner or later. You just have to forget your past failures . . . and recognise the state of things in good time, as well. It's a matter of circumstances and vibrations.'

'And a matter of the will, perhaps.'

'Yes, a matter of the will, you're right, but specially circumstances . . . You can forget about the vibrations.'

Crochelet glanced at me for approval. My face remained rigorously neutral as I scratched the brownish dregs of a congealed drop of punch with my index finger. Goliaguine started distractedly running the edge of a matchbook under his nails.

'You sound as though you're straying a bit from your theme . . .'

'Do you think so?' said Crochelet with a hint of irritation.

Élisa nodded.

'A Swiss linguist', she went on, 'has calculated that women use the conditional voice twice as much as men, and five times as many qualifying expressions such as "perhaps" or "a bit". Women ask three times as many questions, don't finish their sentences and apologise more often, and this seems to be confirmed by our little exchange. Men are so lacking in self-confidence that they consider women's speech to be hesitant, even unimportant.'

183

'Not me!' said Crochelet in his own defence, banging his fist on the table.

'Tell people you're writing a novel! It's a very good way of restoring your self-confidence and catching your audience's attention. For years I used to tell people I was writing a novel. All of a sudden my conversation became interesting. When people asked me about the book, I did the mustn't-give-the-game-away thing, "No, you understand, I can't talk about a current project, it would completely destroy the creative tension." Since then I've advised everyone who suffers, as you do, from a lack of identity or a lack of interest on the part of those around them to use the novel trick.'

Isabelle blushed slightly. She seemed disproportionately apologetic. Élisa's spontaneity always made her sour and intractable very quickly. Like all combative women, what she enjoyed wasn't parties as such, but the self-satisfaction with which she presented herself for other people's appreciation. She said little, and instead spent her time studying people's faces to gauge their reactions to the group's interaction. Her life was perfectly calculated. One extraordinary thing was that her view of the world had never been tainted by cynicism. It was just that she'd stopped believing in people a long time ago.

'If you like, we could leave the two of you alone,' Accetto announced in his deadpan I'm-here-to-ease-the-atmosphere sort of way.

All of a sudden I felt cold. A kind of stiffness rose along my spinal column and compressed my skull. I felt a burning sensation in my oesophagus, like heartburn. I recognised the symptoms of critical indecision. I wanted to intervene, to stay silent, but also to leave and get back to my flat, all at the same time.

Maeva Goliaguine poured everyone coffee again. She constantly gave the impression of devoting herself to a necessary task from which no threat could divert her.

'I fancy another glass of wine,' Crochelet said finally.

'Me too,' said Butel.

'Coming up,' said Goliaguine, nodding to his wife with his index finger raised.

Catherine Accetto was looking at her husband now. He had picked up his paper napkin, which was printed with motifs of fish and shells, and was making stripes down it with the tines of his fork. Bent over his task, he held his cigarette at eye level, and his face was animated with a faint smile or a frown, according to his progress. Jean-Paul seemed to be stimulating his fogged brain in preparation for the hour to come.

With her milky-white, bluish and transparent skin, Catherine Accetto, who was sitting just opposite me, emanated an almost abnormal pallor. She had large, mobile breasts, restrained by a plumb-coloured pullover with a crossover top, and seemed entirely unaware of the amount of cleavage that she was displaying.

Isabelle Gidoin had recently told me confidentially that Jean-Paul's wife was a French teacher in a big *lycée* in Tours, and that that had always made her husband sick with jealousy. The fact that he had been working in a rural middle school for years had done nothing to diminish his frustration. Furthermore, I imagined that the ostentatious nature of her décolletés – the kind of generous abundance that could excite a corduroy-suited father encountered by chance in a school car park after a PTA meeting – could

185

not have done much to assuage Jean-Paul's paranoia. But over time, it seemed, he had learned to respond in kind, despite his obvious physical disadvantage. He was often encountered pathetically trying to seduce the young students who worked for him as classroom assistants. Françoise Morin had even surprised him one day in the computer room, standing with his trousers round his ankles, and feeling up a Ghanaian cleaning woman who went on running her duster over the computer screens as though nothing was happening.

Ali, who was sitting next to Catherine, kept staring at her chest every now and again. This fact did not escape the inquisitorial eye of Jean-Paul, particularly since Catherine had been provoking the young man for ten minutes by thrusting her bust exaggeratedly forwards. In an attempt to maintain his composure, Ali was forcing himself to talk to me about literature. He had a big, narrow mouth full of brownish teeth all going in different directions. Contrary to what one might have expected, his breath didn't smell fetid, just a little sweet, as though he had rinsed his mouth with vanilla essence. He was talking about Flaubert and Kafka, and making grand gestures with his hands that contrasted with the reserved attitude he had shown up until now.

'To express life, you need not only to renounce many things, but to have the courage to keep quiet about that renunciation,' he said sententiously.

At the other end of the table, Élisa applauded.

'Where did you read that?' she asked, bold as usual.

'Give it a rest for a minute,' Isabelle said to her gently, pressing her cheek against her fingers.

'It's from Pavese,' Ali replied without looking at anybody.

'It's in his journal, *The Craft of Living*.'

'It's lovely,' said Isabelle with endless compassion. 'Don't be vexed, Ali, Élisa's always a bit harsh with people she doesn't know. Some women love to make men feel uncomfortable.'

'It doesn't matter,' Ali said softly.

'That's funny, that's what Éric always used to say,' said Goliaguine, tugging at his right earlobe and staring at his plate. '"It doesn't matter, it doesn't matter," he used to say it over and over again.'

Then he burst into hysterical laughter. A startled tension ran through the company.

'And how's your health?' said Élisa after a few seconds, pulling herself up on the arms of the club chair with sly delight.

'So you're interested in people's health all of a sudden?' replied Goliaguine in a brittle voice.

'Mostly yours, darling.'

She rubbed up against him, tapping his thigh beneath Maeva's horrified gaze. 'How are your erection problems?'

'You're a pain in the arse, Élisa,' said Isabelle, getting up to go towards the parrot, where the coats were hanging. I'm off, you're unbearable . . .'

Élisa was delighted, twisting her arms around on the table-top like a mental patient. No one dared say a word.

'I know I'm an awful bitch,' she said, pointing towards Isabelle. 'I'll be punished when we get home . . . Zaza is going to spank me. Bang! Bang! Bang! Bang!' she said, slapping the table with the flat of her hand.

I had to keep myself from bursting out laughing. Something was finally happening. Maeva Goliaguine was the embodiment of nervous collapse. Her little mouth, surrounded by soft fluff, formed a suggestive O, while her eyes were narrowing to slits. Her husband had a stupid smile on his face, and kept his eyes fixed on the ceiling.

'Don't worry, my dear colleagues,' said Isabelle finally, slipping into her sailor's jacket, 'it's a fairly common mental illness. It's sometimes curable. Infantile histrionic syndrome accentuated by apopathodia-phulatophobia.'

Ali raised his finger like a schoolboy.

'What's that?'

'Fear of constipation, she can't keep anything to herself. Childhood in Orléans, education with the Jesuits, late discovery of sexuality . . . it can be treated with a pinch of cognitive restructuring and a dash of behavioural therapy. While the mongolism is pretty irremediable.'

At the sound of these words Élisa contorted in her chair, her hands clutching the arms. She uttered little feeble-minded cries, even going so far as to slobber on Vincent Crochelet, who leapt up in alarm. Isabelle went over to her and unceremoniously lifted her to her feet.

'That's it, home time, you coming?'

She uttered the phrase with a certain familiar energy. Emboldened by her own voice, she continued: 'If you go on like this, I'm going to tell everyone you eat dogshit!'

Élisa laughed like a madwoman and fell into the arms of Isabelle, who dragged her to the sofa. She didn't fight, but deliberately made herself as heavy as possible to keep herself from being carried. Isabelle had to stop breathlessly every few centimetres. The sweat stood out in droplets on her forehead. Weariness slid over us, like a rancid taste. Catherine blew a thick cloud of smoke over my shoulder. I pushed an ice cube to the bottom of my glass, held it down with my finger and let it rise up again.

I heard the phrase 'mad cow' behind me, accompanied by a little whistle of contempt. I didn't turn round. Vincent Crochelet, who had stayed on his feet, leaning against the bookshelf, helped Isabelle by taking Élisa's jacket. He tried in vain to make her put her arms in the sleeves. I was feeling increasingly ill at ease. I sat stiffly in my chair, looking elsewhere. I had a sense of seeing the history of the life of a couple, Élisa and Isabelle, played out before me. A history of perfect accord at home, and absolute discord the moment it came to confronting the real world. No one made any effort to see who they were. People asked them questions that they treated as insults to their intelligence. It was as though Élisa was able to see an appalling network of connections, a potentially lethal deluge that lurked behind the phrases of incredible banality that people were daring to exchange, here, within her earshot.

Goliaguine's phoney charisma, hidden behind his bat-like brows; Accetto's obsessive victimhood, his wife's compulsive nymphomania as she entered early middle age; the coarseness of Crochelet, the non-existence of Rebecca Crochelet (née Saltzman, married against the wishes of her family to a goy for whom she had dyed her hair blond to look less 'Jewish'); the submissiveness of Maeva Goliaguine, living in a state of mute separation from all the things she could have done in the outside world; Ali and his rambling conversations about literature that barely concealed his frustrated will to power . . .

She could see all that.

Like all temperaments more generous than tactical, her confrontations with the world always made her feel guilty, even if she felt she was innocent. She would go home and lie down in the dark, legs folded against her chest. Then

189

she felt small and lost. She resolved to stop trying to attract people's attention.

Then the next day she started all over again.

The Accettos were now wrapped round each other, waggling their heads as they watched Ali doing a demonstration of break-dancing to a rap remix of 'No Woman, No Cry', a record that seemed likely to belong to Goliaguine junior.

The first raindrops had begun to fall after most of the guests had gone, leaving filaments of liquid refraction on the glass to be blown about by the wind. The rain was now lashing the windows, drumming against the kitchen window. At the other end of the table, with my chin resting in my palm, my left arm bent, I studied the complex motifs formed by the contortions that Ali was making, having apparently forgotten that we were even there.

Maeva cleared up the torn paper napkins, the sauce-stained cardboard plates and the corpses of empty bottles which her husband studied dubiously with the melancholy air that befits the end of a banquet.

'You were speaking about Capadis a moment ago,' I said to Goliaguine with the same impassive tone of a clerk of court recapitulating some facts.

'I certainly did,' he replied, glancing fearfully towards the Accettos. 'Would you like to know why, young man?'

'Why was he always saying "It doesn't matter, it doesn't matter"? What was he talking about?'

Goliaguine lit his cigarette, holding it the wrong way round. He inhaled a great lungful of filter, which immediately made him sneeze. Jean-Paul got up to slap him on the back.

'You should stop, Michel,' said Maeva, coming back into the room with a bottle of carpet cleaner.

'You should certainly stop smoking,' added Accetto, 'especially filters! Filters aren't good for you.'

Catherine smiled. She was smiling not at her husband's joke, however, but at the bulge in the fly of Ali's jeans, which he tried in vain to hide by turning his back on our table. All of a sudden he stopped dancing and put on an old Steely Dan instead of the Fugees. He came and sat down at the table so hastily that Catherine burst into wild laughter that she could only contain by getting up to go to the toilet.

'You know,' Goliaguine went on, 'they gave him a hard time from the very first day. I've never understood why. He was young and enthusiastic, he wasn't there just to be a cog in a machine . . . He had never worked as a classroom assistant, it was his first concrete experience of teaching. The kids must have sensed that.'

'Why would he have been given that particular class?'

He hesitated for a moment before replying. A black cat appeared in the sitting room. It slid along the chairs like liquid fur. Jean-Paul raised his eyes towards the chandelier, clearing his throat.

'Because no one else wanted anything to do with them when classes were being assigned at the end of the year,' replied Goliaguine, detaching each syllable with an apologetic inflection.

'Why were they afraid?'

Goliaguine evaded the question by returning to the first thing I had asked him.

'He regularly confided in me . . . I was the only one he talked to, at any rate, I've never known why. Since I live next to the college, he often came to the house to tell me what was going on . . .'

'And?'

He looked at me as though wondering whether he could seriously imagine trusting me with a rather personal confidence.

'Well . . . things didn't really go as he would have wished. He came to ask my advice. He found Cazin incompetent. He spent whole afternoons here. Maeva can confirm that.'

She raised her head slowly.

'I *really* want to know what was wrong with that class.'

Goliaguine turned towards Accetto, who had by now risen to his feet and was watching us, standing in the door frame. He nodded to Goliaguine to continue.

'He started getting anonymous phone calls every day. Either no one spoke at the end of the line, or there was music or the sounds of a television. Like all optimists, he collapsed under the first blow. At first he was convinced it was the other teachers. He was a bit paranoid and thought his colleagues were angry with him because of his remote attitude. Poor thing, if he'd had any idea how little they cared. One day, he had naively gone to the cops to ask them if they could identify the guilty parties. He was hardly sleeping at all by now. The police referred him to France Telecom and it was there that he learned that you could find out the number of the person who had just rung by dialling a particular code. Since he rarely received any calls – he was very solitary, very closed in on himself, a rather schizoid personality, in my view – he had no difficulty in locating the number of his anonymous persecutor. And then, using Minitel, he was able to put a name to the number.'

He stopped and stared at a point above his wife's shoulder. I had a sense that the gleam in his eye was fading along with his story.

'I need the name.'

'I don't think that's of any interest. It's all in the past. Éric is dead now.'

'I'd be grateful if you'd allow me to judge what's interesting to me and what isn't.'

Ali had slumped heavily forward, slowly waggling his head, his elbows hovering above his knees, palms together and fingers pointing downwards. He seemed to be taking a great interest in our conversation.

'Clara Sorman. Then Éric worked out that they met at her place and phoned him up from there.'

'How did he know they met at hers?'

'She told him. He managed to take her aside and tell her that he knew.'

There was a silence. Goliaguine felt uneasy. He was constantly brushing imaginary dandruff from his head, and from time to time he would stick a finger in his ear and agitate it vigorously. Catherine listened with her hands clasped in front of her, observing Goliaguine with an intimidating fixity, as though she were frozen in her chair, incapable of moving. She had completely forgotten about Ali's presence.

'It's like that film *Les Disparus de Saint-Agil,*' I went on, 'a secret society in the midst of a school class.'

'No, Pierre. This time it's the whole class that's involved. Sometimes the pupils gang up against a teacher. It's a pure reflex of tribal cohesion aimed at a single individual. A sociologist might explain it better than I could.'

'It's your version I'm interested in. The bare facts related by an experienced teacher. Go on.'

'I don't like this kind of conversation.'

'Do you want to change the subject?'

'That's not up to me any more.'

At a nod from Accetto, Goliaguine went on:

'The calls resumed a bit later, but this time they were coming from a kiosk in a village on the edge of town. One evening he called me. He'd received a parcel. Inside it he had found the head of a cat, holding in its mouth a mouse in a state of advanced decomposition. There was no message. He was so shocked he could barely speak. He had spent all afternoon hidden under his duvet, weeping. From that point onwards he thought the children were following him all the time. He was constantly freaking out. I can't imagine what his classes must have been like.'

'Did he talk to Poncin about it?'

'That's what I told him to do. He wasn't much taken with the idea at first, but in the end he requested a meeting. He revealed the problem without mentioning the parcel – a mistake, in my view – and even gave the name of Clara Sorman. You'll never guess what Poncin did.'

'He called her in?'

'Not at all. He covered up for the girl and the whole class, explaining that they were a band of jokers, that they liked playing japes on new teachers. Then Éric got up and left. That was the end of the discussion. The end of every-thing, in fact.'

'And then he killed himself.'

'Sadly.'

194

The angle at which Jean-Paul was leaning seemed to give him a rare glimpse of his own height. He appeared absorbed in a tear in the knee of his jeans, rolling each bit of fluff between his fingers in turn. Then he lit a match and, cupping it in his hands against some imaginary wind, he looked towards Goliaguine once again, and made a vague gesture of supplication.

'There are a couple of things Michel's forgotten . . .'

The phone rang in an adjacent room. Maeva hurried to answer it.

'At this time of night it's bound to be either the mistress or the lover,' Catherine whispered witchily in my ear.

'Capadis was a depressive,' he went on, 'he had already made several suicide attempts. He was very introverted. Clearly other people's bodies made him ill at ease. I never saw him shaking anyone's hand, for example. He was very turned in on himself, he avoided all contact with anyone apart from Michel, whom he must have seen as a kind of ideal father.'

I remembered Father Capadis and his rough peasant features, his displaced sadness, his hair, with its slight widow's peak, thrown back in a smooth and brilliant parabola to reveal his wide forehead. Quite the opposite of Michel Goliaguine, who, to Capadis, must have represented the very archetype of the aesthete cultivating self-control. With Goliaguine, I imagined that he might have drifted beyond the margins of the things allowed by his education.

'It's a fairly crude hypothesis,' Goliaguine cut in, 'but it's acceptable.

'Worrying obsessions . . . you mentioned worrying obsessions.'

'I've said all I can say. After that, it's a matter of personal interpretation, you've got to be careful. He must have blamed them for his neurosis. I think they noticed. And they don't forgive that kind of thing.'

12

Whenever the opportunity presented itself, I always closely examined my sister's face in photographs, looking for features similar to mine. Was there something similar in the way our lower lips jutted out? A correspondence in the pronounced arch of our eyebrows? Might somebody think, seeing us side by side, that we were brother and sister . . .?

As far as I was concerned, there was no possible resemblance apart from our identical way of laughing. Since a number of people had pointed it out to me, I had made an effort to stop laughing like that. Léonore had the laugh of a child, an explosion of uncontrollable gaiety. I didn't laugh often, but when I couldn't help it I surprised myself by exploding just as she did. I sometimes told myself that I had worked on my appearance with the sole aim of looking as much unlike my sister as I possibly could. My tobacco-coloured eyes evoked a distant distress. My feeble expression, which I had deliberately stripped of all intensity, tirelessly constructed a space that none of my colleagues were able to enter. My face, without distinguishing features, deliberately apathetic in its movements, was designed to make me seem inaccessible.

As I yielded myself up to these reflections, looking for a few seconds at the photograph of Léonore taken during a New Year's party, for a moment I lost any notion of time, and any interest I might have had in the staffroom. The faint pulverisation of the raindrops bouncing off the windowsill led me to pay attention to the sounds around me. Once again, I listened carefully and for a moment I heard nothing at all. I even started wondering if, for those few moments of distraction, the few teachers present had not slipped out of the staffroom without my noticing. It was only when I saw the union noticeboard that I became aware of the reason for their absence. Most of them were on strike.

Like the return of the seasons and the migration of white whales, strike days had a benign, predictable recurrence, perfectly integrated within the course of normal school life. Each year those repeated, floating moments confirmed our material existence, gathered around a rough nucleus of protest upon which no ministerial changes could have had the slightest impact. I took little interest in the battles waged in the school arena. This always made my colleagues touchy, and they saw my bourgeois individualism as a shame to the profession. They avenged themselves by not letting me know when strike action was being taken. Duly noted.

A fortnight had passed since that Sunday at Goliaguine's. Three days after that social interlude, Jean-Patrick had rung me up again. He sounded crazed, and was speaking in the midst of an undefined hubbub. This time it was serious, he had told me. My sister had tried to kill herself. She had slit her wrists in the bath, like a Roman senator. He had found her floating in a crimson tide, her eyes rolling back like those of a madwoman, a terrifying serenity emanating from her naked body. The cut-throat razor was lying on the bathroom carpet. It was the first thing that Jean-Patrick had noticed. He had immediately had the presence of mind to get her out of the water, which was still hot enough to encourage bleeding ('Fortunately I'd taken a First Aid course!' he kept repeating as he ran through the techniques he had used to bring my sister back to life). He had made a tourniquet with his shirt-sleeve. Her hands and feet had already turned blue.

Léonore remained under observation for a week at the Trousseau Hospital. The artery in her right wrist had been completely severed (she was left-handed), but the cut in her left wrist was not very deep, and the underside of the artery was almost intact. She had had twenty stitches in each wrist. I couldn't help thinking of Capadis, who had died the previous month in the same medical department. I took a week off to go and see her every day, and bring her books and dark chocolate with hazelnuts.

My father and mother came too, but separately. Each in turn, they introduced their new partners. The roles seemed to be reversed now: the parents bringing their intended for the appraisal of the children. For them it was a way of continuing the family romance, while making us accept the fact that at some point in the scenario, someone had obliged them to split their roles in two.

At the ages of thirty-two and thirty-six, my sister and I still had no descendants; we were still *their* children. As such, implicitly, we thought that our parents were answerable to us. I've sometimes wondered whether the sense that we were still 'the son of' or 'the daughter of' had not broadly influenced the fact that we had never felt the need to procreate. I think it was a simple and rather non-committal way for us to preserve the illusion that we would never age.

Each time my father or mother had come into the room with their new companion, Léonore had cast them a glance of virtuous contempt. The survivor, lying stretched out on a hospital bed, she was able to make them understand that she was taking a great deal of trouble not to feel sorry for them. It seemed to be a kind of revenge on her part. During the whole of the conversation, her eyes seemed to say, 'As usual, you've managed to sort yourselves out, *and I haven't!*' She had always acted according to the principle that her suffering would have to be redeemed. Her whole, superficially mysterious strategy, had lain in suggesting to them the possibility that in flagrant contempt of the rules of transparency which they had inculcated in us, their children, they themselves had been quite scandalously leading double lives for ages.

Our mother had cut her hair quite short and dyed it ash blond. With her mouse-grey suit and her mackintosh over her arm, she looked as though she had stepped out of one of those fifties films in which severe but attractive-looking men with broken noses wait for women in limousines. The man with her was in his forties, and starting to go bald. He wore casual clothes, the kind that might be associated with medical doctors who have decided late in life to take up oriental therapies. His eyes were troubled, and gave the impression that he couldn't really see the person talking to him. Although we hadn't asked him a

200

single question, he confided in us that he was a 'research engineer', but that he also worked with old manuscripts (I wondered about the meaning and the range of that 'but'). They were holding hands, but their knees were not close enough to suggest a natural relationship which might have lent their game a more credible melodramatic truth.

As to my father, he still seemed to be affected by my mother's departure and the brutal void that it had left. His hair had turned completely white and his cheeks, congested with alcohol, sagged over his jaws. He no longer finished his sentences. The closing words petered out in the ruins of aborted protest, of barely contained rancour. His life now seemed to be passing by like a segment of abstract time, in a kind of compact blur. He looked increasingly like a burned-down house, of which all that remains is the shell. Unlike my mother, he didn't try to fool himself that he could try and persuade us that nothing had happened. And for that, I think, my sister and I were grateful.

He was in the company of a woman in her thirties. She invariably stayed in a corner of the room, her shoulders fixed to the wall, her arms crossed over an aviator-style blouse, staring out of the window. Tall and haughty, like a long, peeled stalk, she bore the resigned expression of an old maid who had always been let down by men. Her name was Stéphanie. Léonore hated her on sight. She called her 'Connie'. When she talked about her, she showed her slow, calculated, viperish smile. I couldn't stand her when she was like that.

Stéphanie worked as a data processor in a pharmaceutical laboratory. Something about her suggested that she probably liked animal magazines and warm, half-toned lighting. She conveyed a thwarted desire for well-being, pale pine furniture and shelves decorated in a touching and childish way. My father had finally confessed to us that he had met her through the personal ads.

Léonore thought that was 'romantic', while at the same time pointing out how appalling she found her tight leather trousers.

I took advantage of my visit to the hospital to see Nora again.

'Hello, Monsieur Pierre Hoffman!' she had called to me as she bumped into me in the corridor of the A and E department. She had slowed down as I approached, so that she could speed up again immediately if she had made a mistake. She held out her hand with a broad smile, as though I were an old acquaintance. I remembered that I hadn't mentioned my name in her presence.

'Once seen, never forgotten! Fantastic!'

'I didn't expect to see you again so soon.'

She was wearing an unbleached shirt and jeans, and the fact that she wasn't wearing white overalls gave me the impression that she was there by chance. She wasn't wearing spectacles attached to a string. She must have finished her shift not long ago.

'It's quite a morbid time of year,' I said, leaning my head on one side to give myself an air of grief.

'Who is it this time?'

'My sister.'

She didn't know whether to believe me or not. She looked around for a moment, took in the animation of the ward, turned around as she heard a fragment of a sentence emerging from a burst of collective laughter, and then decided to consider the possibility of what I had just told her.

'She slit her wrists,' I added, in response to her silence.

We went out together that evening. She told me she hated going to restaurants and the cinema. Especially going there with men who inevitably took advantage of the fact to suggest a bit of hanky-panky at the end of the evening. I pleaded my case, my hands held out in front of my chest like a volleyball player preparing to return the ball. It was decided wordlessly and without pressure of any kind: Nora and I would never sleep together.

She wanted me to let her choose the theme of the evening. I was to pick her up outside her flat at ten; then she would explain what happened next. As she said that, her voice assumed a theatrical intonation, a conspiratorial amplitude.

She lived in Blois, in an area that was supposedly 'difficult'. This municipal adjective was supposed to conceal a strategy of cramming together problem families. I admitted that I had always found it difficult not to take a pejorative view of those morbid concrete blocks, which seemed conceived solely to develop a negative self-image in the people who lived there. But Nora didn't seem to think that was of the slightest importance. She explained to me that she usually slept in a room at the hospital so as not to have to make the journey from Tours to Blois. At least she had television.

'The first time I went into the flat,' she had told me, 'the fitted kitchen and the electric convector heaters weren't working, there was shit from my upstairs neighbour floating in my toilet, everything was stale. I even found swastikas and inscriptions written in marker pen in the bathroom: "Fuck off nignogs", "Blacks to Auschwitz". I almost found myself thinking they were singling out the North Africans for preferential treatment. I must have spent weeks sleeping with all the windows open just to air the place, and got through litres of air freshener. I used to wake up in tears in the middle of the night, so often that I went and stayed with my parents for a week to recover. When I was passed on to the housing office, the people there treated me like crap. One person there said obsequiously that at least the Albanian refugees didn't complain. I could have kicked him in the bollocks. I left, spitting on the secretary's computer. Pathetic, I know, but I'd had it up to there.'

At ten o'clock I was standing outside a cluster of ochre buildings with purple lozenges on the facade. They looked like Social Security offices. As I parked in front of Nora's block, I had a sense of contemplating an infinite space, decorated with geometrical patterns. To my right and left, identical eight-storey buildings were lined up in rows of six. On either side of the axis formed by the road, the estate stretched like two wings, wider than they were long. The buildings were arranged in a zigzag, and probably because of the darkness, the eye seemed to encounter nothing but parallelograms supporting the dark arch of the sky.

Nora was waiting for me under the porch of block number 9, playing with the buttons of the entryphone. When she opened the door, I heard the sound of dogs throwing themselves against grilles.

Since she liked dancing, she took me to a club near Amboise. For fear of reprisals against a 'foreign plate', we left Nora's car and took mine, which had the local registration number, 37. Throughout the whole journey, Nora had been eating Ferrero Rochers. The pinchbeck-coloured wrappers lined up on the dashboard sparkled in the moonlight. I slyly watched her, facing the road and squinting at her in the rearview mirror, demonstrating a reticence about women that was closely connected with my upbringing. Her fingernails were painted black and her eyes were lined with kohl. Her mouth was bare. A ring encircled the thumb of her left hand, a coin set in a metal mount.

The Sunshine wasn't a proper club, more a kind of chalet planted in some fake sand between some large pine trees at the end of a valley. By the time we showed up at half past ten, there weren't many people there, about a dozen cars at the most. Some synthetic, monotonously rhythmic music reached our car.

Nora was wearing a grey hooded jacket and a short skirt with a pattern of trees. The metallic reflection of her boots, with their crimped seams and wedge heels, made it look as if she was making tiny sparks along the ground. Dressed like that, she looked like a curious mixture of Barbarella and Neneh Cherry. With her tight black curls, she made me want to fetch her some biscuits and a glass of cold milk. I followed her, unsuccessfully attempting to affect a casual gait.

An iron grille slid to one side, letting through a vinegary light. The scrutinising eye of the Cerberus on duty settled on Nora's low-cut tee-shirt. After a pause that lasted a few moments, the door opened with a sound like a sink-plunger. I should have suspected something as we went in, when the bouncer gave me a glance of manly complicity.

Nora left her hooded jacket at the cloakroom, and I left my bomber jacket. Now she revealed that she was wearing a tee-shirt with cartoon motifs and a dog-collar around her neck, with little roses looking like paste pearls. A long corridor lined with seventies cinema posters led towards the battle zone. As we walked in, a few couples were moving about on the floor to the rhythm of a gloomy techno track. The walls were painted a phosphorescent yellow that was almost painful to the eye.

The DJ was a girl, wearing a cap that bore the slogan 'Cool as Fuck'. Nora yelled in my ear, doubtless to put me at my ease, that the girl was a childhood friend. They had been at middle school together at Bégon College in the urban development zone. Between two pieces of music, her childhood friend called into the mic, 'Woowoo, it's hot, it's so hot in the Sunshine tonight!' Each time a new track came up, I felt my features tightening and my heart leaping in my chest. Nora's head rocked gently back and forth as she studied the people dancing.

She took my arm and led me towards the big purple armchairs surrounding the dancefloor. They smelled of damp and stale tobacco. Nora pulled a disgusted face as she sank into hers. 'At the end of the evening,' she said to relax me, 'apparently the rats come up from the basement and chat to the last customers.' She smiled that inner smile that was her trademark, and it slowly deepened, perhaps amused at having touched upon a truth. I didn't say much. Nora sat opposite me, twitchily smoking a cigarette. I was mesmerised by the strobes and the flashes that illuminated the dancers. A giant television screen showed music videos interrupted by advertisements for cocktail biscuits and mobile phones.

We danced for the next two hours. Nora was tireless. Every time I was out of range of her eye I slipped off, exhausted, towards the armchairs, but she always ended up catching me and beckoning me back on to the floor. On the perimeter of the floor a young man with an improbable mass of curly hair was performing some very curious choreography. Like Travolta in *Saturday Night Fever* (which I had seen seventeen times as a teenager), he was pointing his finger in the air in a very strange way: folding his thumb and middle fingers into the palm of his hand, he aimed his index and ring fingers towards his own testicles while his left hand extended towards the ceiling, his finger raised in perfect synchronisation. He disappeared as soon as I tried to point him out to Nora.

At about half past midnight, the few people who had been moving about on the floor with us for the last two hours disappeared. When Nora noticed that we were alone, she abruptly stopped dancing and asked me what I wanted to drink. I opted for a gin fizz, an elementary cocktail known to all the barmen in the world. She went and ordered at the bar, which was completely empty apart from a very young girl who seemed to be alone. I would have said she was fourteen at the most, and I was astonished that she was here because you had to be eighteen to get in. She must have been the daughter of the boss or of one of his employees. She was trying to communicate with the barman, a greasy-looking man with a moustache who was dancing on his own behind the bar as he wiped the beer glasses. He had a completely blank face and shoulders built for carrying heavy furniture up winding staircases. The girl was drinking Heineken through a straw, and as she spoke she watched her own reflection in the mirror opposite. The barman clearly wasn't listening to her. When Nora approached the bar, he almost threw himself at her to take her order.

She returned with an excited expression on her face, as though she felt she was living inside some wild computer game. She came and sat down next to me. The distance between our thighs suggested that she intended to be scrupulous in her respect for our original protocol.

'It's weird that everyone's left,' she said, 'Normally this is when most people would be turning up.'

'Do you come here often?' I asked, using the *vous* form.

'You can call me *tu* if you like.'

'I'd rather not.'

'Why not?'

'No particular reason. I was saving it for a bit later, not right now . . . I'm trying not to be too familiar.'

She started laughing, but it was a rather forced laugh that seemed to express a mild form of disappointment. The barman with the moustache arrived with his tray and our two gin fizzes with all the trappings. He put the glasses down in front of us with papal unction, then waited to be paid, holding the circular tray in front of his genitals, wearing a vaguely mocking expression. Nora took out a twenty-franc note, and as the barman started rummaging in his jeans to give her the change, she dismissed him without a glance.

Nora and I chatted for about half an hour as we sipped our drinks. She touched upon disturbing subjects like her job as a nurse and the unexpected nature of incurable illnesses. She went on to talk about her passion for the Accident and Emergency service, its unique character, linked as it was to a central and eternal vision of human nature. I broke in to ask her some indifferent questions about her work, and alluded to the delicate context in which our conversation was taking place.

'Sorry,' she said with a blush. 'Your sister . . . I promise I'll go and see her every opportunity I get.'

After a moment's silence, she asked me if I wrote books. She said my face suggested an inner life, the elaboration of a project on the edge of a normal idea of life. I disabused her by explaining that my greatest dream had always been to go to film school and learn to make documentaries.

'Reality!' I cried, almost elated. 'Reality! That's the whole purpose of my life!' I immediately turned around to see whether anyone had heard me.

The lights dimmed gradually, until they became a cotton-wool brown that enveloped things in transparent menace. Other people were arriving now, and mingling on the dancefloor without the usual preliminaries. Half-naked women, corseted and with accessories that suggested medieval cruelties, tore at the men's chests with their nails. Nora's eyes avoided mine. At the decks, a young transvestite had taken the place of Nora's childhood friend with the platinum hair, and was putting on pieces of seventies Italian disco with sinister panting, halfway between soft porn dubbing and the sounds of a fitness centre. It seemed clear that we were witnessing a kind of 'soiree' that Nora hadn't predicted. I felt the kind of refined unease you feel at the start of a film that doesn't match the title on the ticket.

The whole mechanism of this kind of party seemed to be organised according to a flow of sexual energy that rose and fell with the intensity of an equinox tide. When the young transvestite spoke into the microphone

– lowering the volume of the music as he did so – his voice was deliberately brusque, and he stressed every syllable as people do when yelling at strangers in the street.

A metal cage slowly descended, containing a girl in thigh-boots miming a wild beast that was about to leap at the members of the audience. They, in response, stretched their fingers towards her in a tigerish manner. Nora considered the spectacle of simulated clawing. All that remained of the vague interest she had shown initially was a seemly disgust. She expressed her scepticism by throwing her head back to cast long, oblique glances towards the dancefloor.

The advertising screens had made way for extremely violent pornographic films, exercises in humiliation filmed in super-eight, with a grainy texture that made their amateurism even more sordid than it was already. Harsh words were barked in military tones by men and women dressed like torturers. Different phases of a single sequence appeared on different screens, and the eye leapt from one screen to another, transforming the space of the club into a kind of visual chessboard.

Nora looked straight ahead, trembling slightly. I led her away from the couples who were starting to invade the armchairs. She clung to my arm as though she no longer had the strength to leave the club. I went to the cloakroom to collect our things.

The girl I had noticed at the bar a moment before was responsible for the cloakroom. She was now talking to the porter, still sitting on the stool on which she had been perched when talking to the barman. She must have carried it all the way there. He didn't seem terribly interested in whatever it was that she was saying. There was something prefabricated about her way of speaking, a weary volubility despite her youth. What she said didn't seem to mean much to her, she spoke as though she were somehow outside herself. All that mattered was the cadences, the highs and lows of her almost martial voice, the modulations, the arpeggios. Her eyes avoided the man as though she were addressing some invisible presence.

She was talking about soundproofing problems, about the problem of traffic in towns, of the regularity with which rubbish was cleared away, and so on. The man nodded gently with an automatic movement. For a moment I imagined him transformed into a huge ear, from helix to lobe, his broad, drooping shoulders forming a kind of desolate auricle.

I tapped on the counter. The girl turned three-quarters of the way towards me, almost surprised. I held out our tickets without a word. She nodded, then slipped off her stool and took them with a taciturn and fatalistic gesture.

'So, my little sweety-pies, off already?' the porter called to me. I took our jackets in silence and went to join Nora. She was sitting in a wing chair, her eyes closed. She coughed two or three times when she saw me. She apologised and then coughed several times in a row. The cough seemed to get deeper and deeper in her chest. She bent double and leaned towards the floor, breathing with difficulty.

'Are you ok?'

I went over and put my hand on her shoulder. Each time she coughed, my palm shook with the vibrations.

'I think we'd better go,' I said, holding out her jacket.

She shook her head with a smile, as though she expected that kind of meaningless observation from me. Once we were outside, she started walking very quickly towards the car, jacket over her shoulder.

'Thanks for everything.' Nora repeated when I came round to open the passenger door.

Then she burst into tears.

Léonore came out of hospital three days later. Before going back to work, I had spent most of my days with her, extended moments of utter calm. Together, we had reacquired a little weight, a degree of influence over ourselves as though we had returned to a time when events had a plausible dimension and direction. We reacquired our enthusiasm for talking about seventies television series about people leading rich, full lives, in which people sat in oak dining rooms and talked about trivia. We were happy in a way, as you can be happy to learn that your reasons for being what you have become are not so complex after all.

My sister absolutely adored Nora, whom she had met on a number of occasions during her stay in hospital. By the end they were spending a lot of time together. Their friendship seemed to be based on a direct and familiar language, which had enabled them to shrink the distances of their solitude from the first moment of contact. Léonore had always had an instinctive mistrust of female friendships, which she felt to be filled with intrigue, meanness and constant conflict. In Nora, she had found someone practical and entirely free of any uterine arrogance at her expense.

I finally discovered that Nora's surname was Curati and

not Baroui as I had imagined in my patronymic reveries. In my eyes, that confirmed Otto Rank's old idea that people were eventually fated to live out the meaning of their surnames.

13

Class 9F's progress meeting got off to a slightly late start, partly because the computer system was down. For the past two years, the school had been completely computerised, and at the end of each term all teachers had to input their notes into the database. The secretary's office then turned these notes into pie charts, statistics with different variables, typologies and highly polished factorial analyses. That allowed the headmaster, an indefatigable leader of staff meetings, to present complicated flow charts, irrefutable proofs of positive sanctions, rewards and gratifications to come.

The parents were dumbfounded.

Poncin was also delighted to distribute these documents. They gave him the chance to show his mastery of sociological terminology, which everyone present pretended to understand, nodding their heads sagely. It was always a pleasure to see him standing with his hands on his hips, his jacket parted over the beginnings of a paunch, considering the throng with a beaming smile every time he spoke of emerging effects, functional necessities, indexicality and margins of incompleteness.

Dimitri Corto's mother was the other reason why the meeting was late. For some unknown reason she hadn't been able to come the previous day. She cancelled without giving a reason three days in advance, which confirmed my suspicions about how independent the headmaster's office really was from the pupils' parents. The meeting was finally held on 22 March, a week after all the other year-nine classes.

Four teachers, Poncin, the two pupils' delegates and the two representatives of the pupils' parents were present, which gave the meeting the appearance of a tourist restaurant out of season.

First of all there was Annie Jurieu, 9F's class head, an emeritus Germanist just short of retirement, whose charm dwelt in a perpetual smile that exuded a weary and sentimental goodness. Patrick Borain was also present. He was a PE teacher of unparalleled stupidity who only took part in meetings to justify the additional allowance he received for educational support and orientation. Finally, sitting opposite Poncin and Annie Jurieu, Maryse Beauval – a teacher with so pronounced a Parisian accent that her colleagues nicknamed her Arletty – had pushed her way in between Borain and myself.

In the course of the afternoon, the teachers who were now absent had justified themselves in the staffroom like revolutionary tribunes, with the argument that we were not flunkeys of the pupils' parents, a protest delivered with a raised chin and in a dry tone of voice, with no opportunity for cooperation or reply.

Along the sides, facing one another, were the pupils' spokespeople and the parents' representatives. Isabelle Marottin and Dimitri Corto were writing conscientiously in a notebook what I supposed must be a list of claims that they would present us with at the end of the session. Isabelle had always had that evanescent air that made you think she hadn't yet acquired her definitive form. I remembered the offhand manner with which she had let Sandrine Botella call her a little cow, as though she had severed all the threads connecting the meaning of the word to the foul vocabulary that she heard at school. Dimitri was less at his ease in this context than he was among his classmates. He seemed almost out of place. He was much less charismatic than usual, and when he wasn't writing he stayed silent and motionless, resting his chin on the palm of his hand, sometimes merely staring at his mother with a strange smile.

She was sitting opposite her son, next to Apolline Brossard's father, a rustic type in his forties who looked at everyone with the desperate expression of a man condemned to empty a pond with a sponge. He had the kind of face typical of peasants around Tours, which hadn't changed since the novels of Balzac. He had that strictly abdominal paunch produced by an excess of alcohol. Over the years, the ancient ugliness of his face had been aggravated by swellings, jowls, wrinkles and broken veins, set off against a background slightly less intense in colour.

It was the first time that I had had the opportunity to make any sort of contact with Mme Corto. She was early, and had been hopping up and down on the spot outside the door when I arrived. As soon as she saw me, she held out a wolf-trap masquerading as a hand. She spoke very much from the front of her mouth, suggesting an affluent and proper upbringing. I loathed her on sight. Her mustard-coloured suit, her chest, which rose and fell regularly beneath her white blouse to indicate her outrage at the length of time everything was taking, her way of sceptically raising her head or untwisting a paper-clip, her neutral auctioneer's tone, all suggested the kind of phallic, authoritarian woman who adorns every word she utters with a kind of moral excellence, and who is almost entirely impermeable to irony.

Poncin opened the meeting by lambasting the lack of assiduity *in general* of the teachers at class meetings, thus ingeniously avoiding any comment on their absence *in particular* today. He was constantly turning towards Dimitri's mother for support, which she sometimes consented to give him with insultingly complacent twitches of her eyelids. Poncin frequently interrupted himself to sigh, and his eyes rested on Béatrice Corto's long legs (Dimitri had told me her first name just before the meeting with a kind of studied familiarity, adding that his mother was a 'stunner'), which she kept crossing and uncrossing without moving the upper part of her body, a performance which I associated with regular exercise for the figure and Tai Chi Chuan for the control. I imagined a sports bag in permanent residence in the boot of a car that was at once sober and sporty.

He then passed the baton to Annie Jurieu, who summarised the attitude and work of 9F, which she pronounced 'very good', with a 'winning profile' (the phrase sent me into ecstasies) that was constantly improving. In the fading light of late afternoon, Monsieur Brossard seemed to want to ask a question or two, his head on one side, a thoughtful expression on his face, a way of affirming the seriousness of his position in the eyes of his neighbour, who had barely addressed a word to him from the outset.

217

'If you don't mind, let us proceed one case at a time. Sébastien Amblard . . .'

The tradition was that each teacher, in strict and immutable order, should deliver a verbal appraisal of the pupil in question. Finally it was time for the headmaster to speak, and commit to paper a synthesis of what had been said. The class delegates took notes to draw up a report for their classmates the following day.

As no one paid any attention to what Borain said, since everyone considered the position he occupied to be too low-ranking to be taken seriously, he quickly fell silent and became absorbed in the contemplation of the logo on the cover of his notebook. Then he took a propelling pencil and immersed himself in the typography of his initials, inscribing on a squared sheet of paper a capital P in gothic script, along with an uncial B. Progressively excluded from the circle of the discussion, he suddenly seemed to have acquired the strangeness that comes from being aware of an anomaly within a group of people engaged in serious tasks. I think that with his silence he was trying to show us that it isn't easy to spend your time among people who don't understand you, and who see you as a negligible quantity.

There wasn't much to say about the pupils. None of them, that term, had smoked in the toilets, talked back to a teacher or questioned a school rule. All the same, at the name of Sorman, a slight shiver ran through the group, but order was soon re-established. At Brossard's name, his father gave a start as though he had just been told off. At the name of Corto, mother and son stared at one another, solemnly and insistently, then looked at Poncin, who lowered his eyes. At the name of Marottin nothing happened. Isabelle was top of the class. She didn't even bother raising her head. She was used to being thought of in this way, a long tradition of excellence, silence and anonymity that must have gone back several generations. It took us twenty minutes to get through our twenty-four clients.

'Good, very good,' Poncin concluded, glancing around the room, 'that's all ship-shape, then.' (It was one of his favourite expressions.) 'Do the pupils have any complaints?'

Isabelle Marottin shook her head. Dimitri glanced in the direction of his mother once again, and launched into some business about canteen timetables which enabled him to give free rein to his talents as an orator. It was clearly his intention to monopolise the discussion, and found approval in this in the batting of his mother's eyelids as she encouraged him to go on, as though he were busy telling a kind of family saga.

Silence fell once again after Dimitri's intervention, and Poncin asked whether the parents had any particular questions they wished to ask. Monsieur Brossard (Auguste, perhaps?) moved his head slowly and regularly from right to left. Everyone looked at him expectantly. Béatrice Corto turned abruptly towards him, her eyes shining and her shoulders thrown back, her hand forming a visor above her eyelids as though the sun were troubling her. Finally he said no. Dimitri's mother's hand fell with relief, and squeezed itself between the knee of one leg and the hollow of the other.

'I'd like to talk about the planned bus trip to Étretat,' she went on immediately.

Annie Jurieu looked at our trio to see whether we were as astonished as she was at Béatrice Corto's sudden announcement. Borain raised his head half-heartedly, before going back to his drawing. Maryse Beauval turned around to blush, making me aware how hot and stuffy it was in the room. She was silent, and visibly shaken. All of a sudden she turned very pale.

'What trip to Étretat?' she asked Poncin.

She had adopted an imperious tone, and threatened him with her raised index finger. He shrugged apologetically by way of reply. She sat up very straight on her chair, giving the impression that she was going to get up all of a sudden and leave the room.

'Is there a problem?' Béatrice Corto asked.

'A problem! She's asking if there's a problem!' Maryse choked, calling everyone else as witnesses. 'Annie, did you know anything about a planned bus trip?'

Annie Jurieu blinked very quickly, as though transmitting a message in Morse code with her eyelids. Clearly she didn't.

'No.'

'What about you?' Maryse Beauval went on, looking at Poncin.

'I'll have to explain,' he mumbled, a slight tension around his mouth.

His face seemed to shrink beneath the neon lights. Then his eyes became conciliatory to the point of self-abandonment.

'I'd like to understand what's going on as well,' I said, making enormous efforts to shake off the discouragement often aroused in me by this kind of petty secrecy that didn't seem to bother anyone else.

The words almost took me by surprise as they left my

mouth. My voice seemed to have assumed an unpleasant inflection. I was even sorry not to have punctuated my query with a hysterical giggle.

It was a matter of public knowledge that school trips had to be registered before Hallowe'en, the end of November at the latest, and it was now 22 March. This special dispensation only represented another example of Poncin's scandalous alliance with the pupils' parents. He slowly lowered his eyes and then raised them towards me once again. Monsieur Brossard was following the discussion with a gloomy attentiveness, which meant that he said yes in advance to anything that would allow him to leave this room without a fuss.

'Mme Corto discussed the trip with me in the middle of February,' he said, almost in a whisper, 'and I didn't see any problem with it since 9F were the only pupils in this establishment who had no end-of-year trip planned. I just forgot to mention it to the main interested party. I'm a busy man, I forget things. But none of that is of any importance; what matters is the place the children are going to, and who they're going with.'

'I don't know if I've understood correctly,' sneered Maryse. 'Many people could be worried if they didn't get clear answers. You want to send the kids of 9F to Étretat in a bus at the end of the year. Is that it?'

Poncin agreed.

'And I assume you've selected the teachers who are going with them? To my knowledge, no one has been consulted, there's nothing in the pigeonholes . . . Because you can't count on me.'

'I have a feeling the answer is very simple,' Béatrice

221

Corto interrupted dryly. 'The pupils have chosen Monsieur Hoffman and Monsieur Accetto. You see, no one's asking you anything at all.'

'I'll have you know that I'm a very experienced teacher.'

'And who are you?' replied Béatrice Corto icily.

'The one who never lets go . . . the beginning of the end . . . Make your choice!'

'I always enjoy talking to lunatics.'

'Delightful,' said Patrick Borain appreciatively.

Throughout the whole of that brief exchange Annie Jurieu hadn't said a word. She was still smiling, but she had a worried expression. While everyone was talking at once to communicate only a representative sample of their personal rancour, I was still taken aback by Annie's failure to assume responsibility on the strict plane of rhetoric. She gave the impression that she didn't feel especially concerned, as though none of this had any weight or density for her. People died, at least ten people in the world had died in the course of the past five minutes. That was all that seemed to have any meaning for her, a kind of generalised empathy for the species, a vast and delicate overall plan.

'There's always an authority higher than you think,' Béatrice Corto said with composure. 'Please allow me to take my leave now.'

'Wait, my dear,' said Maryse Beauval.

'Mme Corto will do.'

'What's your role in all this?'

'I don't have a role.'

'There are people in this college who would have liked to have a budget for an educational outing at the end of the first term, and who were informed at the time that it was too late. Well, I'd like to know how you managed to get one three months later!'

Béatrice Corto slowly put her hands together in front of her, and stared at Maryse, her eyes bright.

'I'll tell you how I got that trip in such a hurry. My son asked me a month ago. I then went to see Monsieur Poncin, who allowed me to have it without further ado. Especially when he knew that it wasn't I who made the request, but my son. As it happens, your headmaster holds Dimitri in special esteem.'

14

The news spread very quickly. Over the course of the week that followed 9F's class meeting, rumour – the dark harbinger of things to come – had it that Françoise Morin had fallen out with Poncin, to such an extent that she refused to go to his office after class. If the death of Capadis hadn't greatly stirred collective emotions, the Corto affair mobilised energies, sending such a tremor throughout the hierarchy that Poncin stopped appearing in the staffroom for some time.

During that period, placid Annick Spoerri addressed herself to the formation of 'relationships' with unfamiliar zeal. It was almost as though Poncin's guilt had helped to transform Annick's habitual attitude of rigid discretion into something more pragmatic and reassuring for the teaching body, so much so that the head's absence passed relatively unnoticed. But beneath her reserved bonhomie, Annick Spoerri concealed the temperament of a Medici. Instinctively, her job had taught her that the best way to tighten the bonds of the community when events had slackened them was to push those events into the background by brandishing a new threat. To paraphrase a Spanish Jesuit who spent his life freeing people from their errors, Annick Spoerri knew the essence and the season of things, and never revealed them until they were completed.

The end of March, in fact, was when timetables were issued, and passed on by the central board of education to the local education committee to generate national or inter-academic change. The timetable for each discipline was calculated according to the number of pupils expected within the catchment area of the school at the start of the next academic year and the number of classes affected, which would in turn affect the creation of new jobs or the loss of old ones.

The headmaster always feared the moment when he had to divulge the results, which became a pretext for staff representatives to get worked up about issues involving human resources. It was one of those rare moments when administrative failures on the part of the board came to light. No one with a clear view of things could be overwhelmed by the fact that the cosmetic measures taken by successive ministries, these judicious sprinklings of dust, were designed to conceal the most glaring discrepancies. At that level, reforms acted only as the natural laxative of educational science. They were like those basic mantras that relax the body, to dissipate tensions and ease pains related to the sensation of heaviness.

Every year some disciplines (visual arts and German, for example) faced death because of certain random factors related to intellectual demands. The ministry only expected them to expire once and for all as the result of departures through retirement or discouragement. The tactic was simple: by giving each new arrival two half-jobs thirty kilometres apart, in the short term one might expect the teacher in question either to resign or to convert to more useful disciplines. This administrative Machiavellianism meant that more and more subjects were consigned to the pedagogical box-room. As a result, the public sector was increasingly coming to resemble the private sector in terms of the refinement of its processes of exclusion.

This drift on the part of the civil service was one hobby-horse of SNIFE, the most powerful teachers' union at Clerval, which neglected no opportunity to denounce the neo-liberal tack that the educational system was taking. The union representatives sometimes took Poncin to task, accusing him of supporting this right-wing strategy. The headmaster sensed those moments of friction coming, and was able to avoid them by disappearing for a few days. Poncin had only to transfer responsibility for public affairs to Annick Spoerri and everything immediately fell into place.

The forthcoming job losses came at precisely the right time to let Poncin prepare 9F's little trip without anyone noticing. It had been decided behind the backs of the interested parties that the job of Annie Jurieu, who was about to retire, would not be renewed, and neither would that of Goliaguine, who had asked to move to the Lycée Grandmont in Tours. Having obtained twenty years' worth of seniority at the College, he had serious chances of getting it.

In its various actions against job losses, the union encountered a major problem for which it had no plan of action: the demographics of the department of Indre-et-Loire had been in free-fall for the past two years, which explained the reduction in the number of classes. This drop in the school population forced the representatives of SNIFE to elaborate an oblique strategy. They now brandished their secret weapon: the division of classes and the old refrain about teaching quality, invoking the pretext of over-subscribed classes (twenty-four pupils on average!).

As a rule, union thinking was not ramified, but rather linear and inductive. To put it another way, certain conditions had to be met before it became possible to move on to the following stage. So, for the present example, SNIFE began by loudly denouncing disinformation, a domain in which the union had itself in fact become something of a specialist. It then counterattacked with the argument that heterogeneity in the classes was an absolute necessity, and could only be effected by splitting them up into two groups so that the teacher would be able to devote closer attention to the problems of the individual pupil. This kind of proposition was supposed to demonstrate that, contrary to what the ministry had announced, the number of jobs per discipline needed to be increased rather than decreased. Anyone wishing to reintroduce streaming as a way of regulating the problem would immediately be seen as a dangerous reactionary. Generally speaking, alas, that was the price to be paid for living in the world of teaching if one had a jot of common sense.

It might also be added, without the slightest intention of denigrating anyone, that for several years people like Accetto, Isabelle and I had been impotent witnesses of the progressive decline in critical intelligence and linguistic skills, a development which the experts in the 'educational sciences' had overseen over the course of the past twenty years.

How many of us adapted to this failure of responsibility?

Why did we remain part of a system of which we greatly disapproved once we had passed the age of thirty? We couldn't avoid asking those questions, but we lived with the answer: it was our own kind of cowardice. With age, perhaps, we had forgotten how to interest our colleagues in ideas that had previously seemed quite fundamental to us. And that had become the new basis of our lives: pretending not to know. It was what our adult life was now devoted to: absorbing the fact that from now on every question had an answer, and then moving on to something else. But to what?

'Why did you choose me?'

A week after the disconcerting news about the trip, I finally asked the question as I stood in front of the drowsing class. I watched Guillaume Durosoy staring at a road map of Europe that was coming away from the wall.

Patches of colour started to whirl around me, heads turned, glances were exchanged, but no inner desolation, no interrogation, no anxiety filtered through. On the contrary, they seemed almost happy for me to ask them the anodyne question. A faint smile played about their lips, like an unnatural shadow, a single note played on an organ.

'Have you reached an agreement with Monsieur Accetto?' asked Maxime Horvenneau.

'Not yet.'

'You'd better get a move on,' said Richard Da Costa.

'It's in three weeks,' said someone else.

'Why did you choose Étretat?' I asked again, immediately realising that I hadn't yet had an answer to my first question.

'There are cliffs,' said Sandrine Botella.

'And water below.'

'The air's different.'

'We want a break from routine.'

'What could be more important than that?'

'Than overcoming our resistance?'

'Than forgetting our fear of water and craggy slopes?'

'Clearly nothing could be more important,' I replied.

Dimitri had remained curiously silent during this exchange. He was engraving sinuous motifs on his left hand with a white corrector pen, a kind of invisible scarification that followed a secret ritual. For a moment I observed his swollen face, his hollow eyes, his long hand flat on his desk, the slight tremor of his head. He mustn't have slept for a few nights. When he noticed that I was looking at him, he raised his head, and immediately he was in charge of the room.

'I'm getting the funds together, don't worry!' he said with the air of someone who is keen to stick to the rules.

'What sort of funds?'

'Whatever I can find. Windscreens to be washed, lawns to mow, cakes sold at the Sunday market, little jobs here and there. The whole of 9F has been hard at work. People sometimes give us their attics to empty. They're always keen on helping children go on holiday. They only ever want to help children. That's unfair, don't you think?'

'Certainly, Dimitri, certainly. Why are you so keen on the idea of financing your trip yourself? I don't understand.'

'We don't want to owe anything to the socio-educational fund,' he replied with a smile, after which there was a brief pause.

The allusion to this fund (financed by all the pupils)

revealed the profound nature of the interest that the class was showing as the trip approached. Their attitude from the very first achieved a mysterious coherence in this anodyne observation: the pupils didn't want to owe anything to anybody. It was their form of moral transaction with reality, an exasperating relationship for an observer accustomed to the pretence of sharing and permanent credit. Feeling a collective guilt for having decided on this trip so late, and for having resorted to external pressure to get it, they seemed to think it was very important to remind people of their autonomy.

Dimitri still wore his smile, but it was lifeless now. The late-afternoon light was fading. The classroom, located on a side of the building that didn't catch the sun, was lit by day, as at all other times, by the same homogeneous artificial light, an opal gauze that fell across the walls and the ceiling, banishing shadows and coldly emphasising the contours of a certain unease, without background or source. Estelle Bodart was talking to Franck Menessier with her hand over her mouth and her head held straight, but her efforts at simulation were rendered useless by an inability to lower her raucous voice to a whisper. As I stared at her, she began to cough into her hand to make her offence look like a misunderstanding. I started my class ten minutes late.

When I had returned to the board to write up the title of the session, I cast a glance over my shoulder and surprised Élodie Villovitch pointing her finger at a classmate at the back of the class. I went on writing, glancing back at regular intervals without attracting the attention of the class. Muffled sniggers started to emerge.

'What's going on?'

'It's Brice Toutain, sir, he's gone to sleep on the table!' replied Julie Grancher.

I hadn't noticed him from where I was standing, hidden as he was by the imposing figure of Karim Chaïb. I went over, and what struck me first was not his head, which had half disappeared into his arms, but the air of panic on the face of Mathilde Vandervoorde, Brice's cousin, who looked as though she herself was being told off. All the pupils turned around as I passed.

'He has sleeping attacks, sir,' said Mathilde, 'this isn't the first time. Attacks of deep sleep.'

'What sort of attacks are we talking about?' I asked.

'Sleeping attacks, regular and uncontrollable,' said Apolline Brossard enigmatically.

Brice Toutain didn't move. His crumpled face looked as though his skull had folded in. I took his little shoulder in my hand and shook it gently. His eyes stayed closed, two peaceful slits. He was breathing regularly. There was a whitish strand of dried saliva on his cheek, mingling almost imperceptibly with the pallor of his face. All the pupils had turned around now, with looks of concern on their faces. Clara Sorman had turned around too, her eyebrows slightly raised, and was watching the others with a weary and disdainful hint of a smile.

I clapped my hands next to the boy's uncovered ear. Brice gave a start, opened his eyes for a moment, stared at a tourist poster of Morocco and then went back to sleep. Opening his eyes again, he woke up properly with a start and stared with all his might at the faces turned towards him.

'My ears hurt,' he groaned, holding his head in both hands.

'What happened?'

'My ears hurt,' he repeated, 'I've got a noise in my ears . . . in my head, it hurts!'

He tried to leave his chair, still holding his head, then fell in a faint on the floor.

Through the frosted glass door of the supervisors' office, I watched Léa Kaminsky, the senior disciplinary counsellor, walking around the little body of Brice Toutain with her hands on her hips. He was prostrate on a chair by the window. Brice had taken off the woollen shirt that he wore in class, and was only wearing a long-sleeved thermal tee-shirt which had, I noticed, small holes at the wrists. His face was mild and serene, almost blank, an oval surface with no distinctive features. He was chewing gum, a sign that seemed to me to indicate a return to health. Léa stopped in front of him and took his arm, which she immediately dropped again, inert. Brice hadn't moved. Everybody was breathing slowly, as though with difficulty.

Faced with a case such as this, Léa Kaminsky had a weapon in reserve. It lay in a power that she had to extend time, to prolong its duration until it became a torment. She never raised her voice, asking questions in a perfectly neutral tone without any particular modulations, as though the instinctive, savage self that one sensed behind the inexpressive veil of her gaze had remained hidden behind the stage set of her deeper character. She was the kind of person one suspected of having, beneath her professional permafrost, the subterranean stratum of the emotions that never thaws, a particularly dense emotional life.

She finally noticed me, beckoned to me and went on

232

talking, raising her long brows in my direction. One of the counsellors came into the room by another door and put coffee and water in the electric machine which sat in a corner on a stripped pine shelf. The counsellors' office had always struck me as a rather disagreeable place. I never set foot there. Perhaps it was because, for reasons of intellectual jealousy, they didn't much care for teachers there.

It should be borne in mind that the counsellors, often young and considered as the lumpenproletariat of the secondary education staff, were all studying (their studies were compulsory if they were to achieve counsellor status), and that they were only there temporarily. Some of them were recruited from 'youth jobs', post-adolescents who spent their time showering the pupils with the most ludicrous nonsense. In principle they were supposed to act as educational support or back-up, but their status was so nebulous that they always felt obliged to speak more loudly than the teachers in order to reassure themselves about their existence within the school framework. They never missed an opportunity to remind everyone that they felt *close* to the pupils, whom they referred to as 'young people'.

'Did you want to see me?'

Léa Kaminsky's Asiatic face appeared in the doorway, and it was turned to me. The intonation was the one that people use when they feel they're being stared at in a restaurant and ask you if you have a problem. Here, the walls clearly had ears (even if it was hard to identify who those ears belonged to). Clerval was like a palace that you could be guided through by locating echoes, identifying breaths, rustling noises, complaints and imprecations around the next corner. Léa had been at the

233

College for ten years. She knew all the tricks of invisible horror. Her professional life had been gradually reduced to a process of selection and refinement, something like complete withdrawal and silent but omnipotent presence, which exerted an abstract attraction on some of the teachers.

'I just wanted to know how Brice was.'

'Come in.'

She dressed very ascetically, with that hint of impenetrability that you often find in service industries. She often wore a black trouser suit with square-tipped shoes. Sometimes, too – and I had noticed that this was always connected with an approaching birthday – she would even allow her imagination to run riot and wear polo-necked sweaters and stretch jeans with piped pockets on the sides for stowing away her secret notebooks. Léa's body seemed constantly in search of a mute ideal of inaccessibility.

She dropped into a revolving armchair and removed the defunct cigarette that hung almost to her chin, held to the edge of her bottom lip by a little dried saliva. She was at home in her office, as though in an immutable inner environment sculpted by years of taming the texture of the space. Just as some fish never leave coastal waters, Léa couldn't bear to talk to people anywhere but in this office.

'Have you given up smoking?'

'No, I'm trying systematically to stop lighting the cigarettes that I put in my mouth.'

'Did it take you long?'

'Six months. I thought I was going to go mad.'

'Wonderful, Léa, that's wonderful.'

234

'Wrong, Pierre . . . it's pathetic, the fear of cancer in a forty-year-old woman.'

Two little speakers in the corners of the ceiling were playing jazz.

'Miles Davis, *Seven Steps to Heaven*, she said, intercepting my gaze, 'I force myself to listen to it two or three times a day. My husband has four thousand bebop records, it's our way of staying in touch with each other. We only see each other once a week, on Sunday. But I'm well aware that it's brainless music!'

'There's something disturbing about it, it must have something to do with repetition . . . you get the sense that it's never going to stop.'

'That's a really pertinent observation, Pierre. I've been trying to work that one out for months. I'll have to talk to Antoine about it . . . that's my husband's name.' (An amused silence.) 'Do you want me to pause it?'

'No, no, it's fine.'

Léa's husband was a wealthy industrialist who had made a fortune in metal mouldings, a fancy way of saying 'tins'. Work was Léa's particular luxury. She could have stayed at home and spent her days making jam or organising suppers, but she needed to feel that she was useful. She had no children, but she did have two magnificent German mastiffs that she sometimes brought into school on Saturday mornings.

Léa enjoyed a superiority over the rest of us that came from the fact that she had not always been in the education service. This made her conversation richer and more varied than the average. For ten years she had been a tour operator with a large travel company that had gone bankrupt after disastrous speculation on the stock exchange.

After retraining as a partner in a high-flying marriage, she had finally passed the examination to become a disciplinary counsellor.

The teachers were a bit suspicious about a woman who had travelled all over the world while they were still sitting on their university benches trying to prolong, for a while at least, their immersion in a world of scholarship that sheltered them from reality. It was quite awkward to argue, in her presence, about the reduction of school holidays or the fundamental purchasing power of the teachers, when she had been to countries where the children spent their holidays working in brothels, and the teachers barely had enough money for a pair of shoes to walk to school. Because of the discreet critical perspective that she had, a good half of the teachers never addressed a word to her.

'What about Brice?'

'Nothing serious.'

'Could we talk about this on a more personal level?'

'Of course. You remember last night?'

'Yes, it was very cold for the time of year. Below zero, I believe . . . I had to put my pyjamas on.'

'Brice took his off. Then he opened the window, went and stood on the sill and spent all night counting the stars. Just before his parents came to wake him up as they do every day at seven o'clock, to go to school, he put on a tee-shirt and went back to bed.'

'Now I understand why he fell asleep on the table. And what about the fainting?'

'Hypothermia, I suppose. It's very dangerous.'

'I thought you said it wasn't serious! Did he tell you all that himself?'

'He came right out with it.'

'Why?'

'I don't think he's that keen on going off with the others. Clearly Brice has never been very much at ease in the school. I don't know why that might be, but whatever it is it must be pretty powerful for a boy to want to spend the night naked in weather barely warmer than my deep-freeze. Furthermore, I've noticed haematomas at the base of his spine. They look like blows from a baseball bat or a broom-handle. You'd have to look to his parents. But if it wasn't them, I don't want to throw them into a panic. What do you think?'

I didn't say a word. I was dumbfounded. If even Léa Kaminsky suspected that something was up, the situation was becoming desperate. I sank into the chair, literally entrenched in it. I waited for a concluding sentence or a final question before leaving the room. But nothing of the kind happened. Léa shook my hand, saying that perhaps I was a little tense and feverish, and that the sea air would do me good.

15

As soon as the decision of the pupils to set off for Étretat had been ratified by the body of teachers, the whole business became considerably simpler.

There were still recriminations, a few sleepless nights, some concerted attempts to block the enterprise, but in the end the stubbornness displayed by the teachers only reinforced the sense of class unity and the aura of mystery surrounding the little excursion. After a certain period of time, the adults almost assumed the appearance of vengeful fanatics. They had to admit: children who were as motivated as that could only see their efforts crowned by success.

What seemed surprising to several observers was the determination that the pupils had displayed in obtaining and financing the outing, not to mention the extraordinary relationship that they had formed with one another to get the trip off the ground. The obstacles they had confronted (the last-minute reservation of a bus, the collecting of funds, choice of accommodation, postponement of certain classes, etc.) had dissolved into thin air without any major complications.

It was the end of March, an intermediate period that marked the beginning of the third term before the second was quite at an end. During that time, my relationship with the pupils was marked by a sympathy I had not known until then. It was as though they wanted to communicate their delight but weren't sure how to go about it. My esteem for their collective singularity soared. Although I wasn't fully aware of it, the fact that they had chosen me redefined our mutual mistrust, bringing us closer to the prospect of an authentic exchange.

I continued to bear in mind the danger that they represented, but something was developing, inviting me to abandon the hard core of my ego, the protection I drew from my scepticism about them. From now on I felt obliged to place a certain amount of trust in them.

Accetto didn't see things that way. Since he had learned the news, his forehead had acquired an extra wrinkle of suspicion. He wandered around the school looking anxious, hands crossed behind his back, taking only a secondary, distracted interest in the people he encountered. Isabelle Gidoin and Vincent Crochelet had noticed him several times in the main bar in Noizay, where he owned a house, sitting alone at a table and gazing absently at the sparse traffic outside. Isabelle had even added, with some embarrassment, that she had noticed his lips moving.

'He must be crying day and night. He's frightened. Some people get very worried about bus trips.'

'I'm not sure that's it.'

'He could always just refuse to go.'

'Not him. He turns it into something personal. He knows the kids from 9F, and yet at the same time he doesn't. It's weird. I don't know what this business about the trip means for him, being chosen along with you and everything.'

'He's giving every sign of still being alive, at any rate, and trying to keep his apprehensions in check. He must just be going through a phase of doubt about his ability to stand up to things.'

'What sort of things?'

'The kids and this very strange relationship that we've built up. He's afraid of being excluded from it ... He's never been able to bear not being at the centre of all the projects he's launched. And now he finds this isn't his project.'

After saying that I cleared my throat noisily, a masculine noise, full of dubious self-assurance. Isabelle had studied me with the pleasure felt by a critical mind when it sees a caricature that confirms its opinions about the fatuousness of men.

'You've got tomato ketchup on your nose,' she said, pointing at her own.

From time to time Poncin reappeared with Françoise Morin, who was more concerned than ever. Annick Spoerri asked to see me in her office. Calmly inspecting the tips of her pointed fingers, she told me that Françoise hadn't very long to go, six months at the most. She had just received the results of her tests, incurable lung cancer. She got up one morning and spat blood, the sad banality of the signs that herald the end. I had asked her if Françoise herself had given her power of attorney to announce her coming demise. She didn't think the question worth answering.

Françoise was too self-aware to seek help from her colleagues. Her instinct told her to die with a recrimination or an idiotic joke on her lips, rather than a call for help. Attitudes such as silence and discouraged withdrawal were not among her astrological attributes (she was Leo, and born in the first decan). The pleasure of giving and winning comfort and professional acknowledgement, the delicious tremor of the soul when it witnesses the failure of others, all those strong inclinations were the broad stage upon which Françoise Morin still acted out her part.

There was one secret element in her life that she had once confided in me when we were speaking on the telephone: since childhood she had been haunted by her own incompetence. It was when she returned to the education service that she once and for all became that whirling thing, that girl in perpetual motion who put a space between what she thought and what she sometimes said. Her sexual episodes (she flattered herself over having exhausted three husbands and several dozen men under the age of thirty) were only a libidinous version of her lack of confidence.

Annick had asked me to promise to keep her biggest secret. She wasn't supposed to talk about it to anyone. Because no one, she thought she should add, was aware of it apart from the headmaster and myself. I didn't know how to react. At first I was very demoralised, unable to imagine the start of the next school year without Françoise, her stubborn presence, her special quality of mocking humanity. It was like moving from cinema to television, the demise of an eminence visible to everyone, which gives the life of a collective its bearings and its sense of direction. For me, Françoise was the familiar element, a kind of geodesic point. Her business was our business. From now on there was no one to keep our hackneyed phrases in check, no one who could, with a few well-chosen words, make us feel wretched. Some of us had had a glimpse of something, and now we were going to lose it. Dark things would return, whole areas of discussion would vanish. The destructive aspect of the school would be reinforced.

Nonetheless, I made the mistake of mentioning it to Goliaguine and Accetto. I had hoped to shed some of the burden of this news, rather than just cram my face into my big silk pillow as I usually did. Announcing the forthcoming death of a woman in her fifties to two men in their fifties was a risky and, more particularly, a ridiculous operation. It was like announcing the bankruptcy of a schoolmate to someone in their thirties who has just been through a divorce, a grotesque violation of the rules of group life. Their reaction was the opposite of what I had imagined. They looked almost gratified, and stopped just short of running about the place uttering loud cries of triumph. They smiled like people who have just been dug out after an earthquake, or like condemned men granted a reprieve. Accetto was the first to compose himself. He went and sat on one of the chairs in the staffroom and lit one of the little cigars he carried about in his jacket pocket. He inhaled the smoke, then twisted around to ensconce himself further in his chair.

'You want to know something?' he asked.

'I would actually be curious to know the reason for your hilarity.'

'Frankly I'd sooner it was her than me.'

'The explosion in the nuclear power plant at Chernobyl on 26 April 1986 contaminated more than 6,500 people, forced 135,000 Ukrainians into effectively permanent exile, and created a radioactive cloud, traces of which were found as far away as Haute-Provence. On 25 June of the same year, 2,000 researchers meeting in Paris alerted public opinion about the risks that AIDS posed for the future of humanity: to the 100,000 people who were already sick we should add seven to ten million individuals infected by the virus and thus capable of transmitting it and, unless some exceptional discovery were made, threatened with death. All of a sudden an illness and an accident that had been inconceivable before the late seventies began to haunt everyone's minds. No one had identified any symptom specific to AIDS, or anything to presage the nuclear catastrophe; there seemed to be something almost magical about their being unleashed upon the world, since there was no overall explanation for them. That double mystery prompted countless anxieties: was the virus born in Africa and did that mean that Africa, the crucible of all diseases, would be condemned? Would all nuclear power stations have to be closed down? Would industrial pollution destroy the balance of the planet?'

Estelle Bodart's arms sank, along with her notes, as she waited for a response. For about ten minutes she had been wearily reciting her exposé, but apparent in her attitude there was still an exhausted enthusiasm which conveyed a kind of materialised insecurity in every word. She had decided to speak on the subject of AIDS and nuclear power, those bridgeheads of millenarian unease. Estelle was the only one in the class who hadn't had a mark for a dissertation in the first term, and she had asked me to set aside twenty minutes of class time in the second so that she could express herself on a subject of her choice.

As she lowered her head, I noticed a little hive at her hairline, swelling the skin. She had just dyed her hair blond, and her new hairdo (with a centre parting, her hair falling on her cheeks in a single wave, stressing the elongated oval of her face) made her look indecipherable. When she raised her head and looked me straight in the eye, I realised for the first time that although she didn't actually have a squint, there was nonetheless a slight dissymmetry about her pupils.

'There's one thing I don't understand,' I said softly.

'What don't you understand?' she almost shouted, surprised.

'You seem to consider AIDS and Chernobyl as two ideal metaphors of a society that's worried about its future.'

'That's exactly what I've just said.'

'I didn't hear you.'

'That's exactly what I said.'

'You know, there is certainly a kind of unity in what we refer to as an era, but it may be something that's perceived by posterity rather than claimed by contemporaries. Mightn't you be a bit young still?'

She put her notes down on the desk and then moved her chair and sat down with a sigh.

'Perhaps,' she said leaning over the desk and slowly interlocking the fingers of her hands.

'Young people never go beyond the belief that they maintain with their innermost self. It's always charming to hear them expressing generalisations about the way of the world.'

'Haven't you ever noticed that children are very selfish, like everyone who is programmed to survive?'

She stared at me as she said it. I saw her big grey eyes,

244

dark and impenetrable. The whole of her life seemed to have been invaded by a profound, mineral calm. She was quite still, but for her protruding lower lip that trembled slightly.

'Young people these days are born old,' she went on, 'they want to know things. When your life is threatened by something invisible, you're no longer content to live without reservations. We're not living in the fifties . . . and you should know that I regret that . . .' (a silence) 'That *we* regret it . . .'

'Who do you mean when you say *we*, are you talking about young people in general?'

She lowered her head towards her notes and then allowed her gaze to wander vaguely around the classroom as people do when they are having lunch on their own in cafeterias.

'No, the people here.'

A shiver of relief ran through the class, a wide vibration of assent.

'Fine.'

'We need to explain why it is that certain of us have died, regardless of age, sex and profession, over the past ten years. Take what I am saying as a personal war that we're waging. The deaths of those people seem like a scandal to us.'

'I understand.'

'And what do you think about it?'

'I don't know.'

'People like doing that too.'

'What?'

'Saying "I don't know". It gives you a kind of moral superiority.'

245

'Please, Estelle!' (In a conciliatory tone.)

'The meaning of an era isn't very important. What's more important is why we feel so impoverished, so isolated, so abandoned ... why, today, you can't stroke someone's head without expecting to get your hand bitten off ... as to myself, I have to go round mercilessly whacking the heads of the very smallest children in order to survive. AIDS and nuclear power haven't killed this world ... for some time the feeling has been growing in me that the world died a long time ago. Do you think that's a very adolescent way of talking?'

'No, I'm fascinated.'

'These things are nameless. And anyway no one warns you. People in general don't say anything, or at least they don't say everything: they know all too well how terrible things are.'

16

Brice Toutain closed his eyes and let his head fall back on to a cushion. We stayed more or less in silence in the building attached to the school that served as a sick bay. Three metal beds were lined up against the back wall, lending the place a feeling of pure impersonality.

Brice was lying on the middle bed, with Léa Kaminsky and myself on either side. The light from the lamp on his bedside table put his childish form in shadow, making it look larger than it was. The monogrammed sheet that covered Brice was thrown back over a blanket bearing the same monogram, a sign that seemed to have been sewn on to demonstrate the rather tepid goodwill that often presided over the decoration of state schools. His breathing was so calm that he seemed to be asleep, but after a moment he murmured without opening his eyes or moving his head:

'I feel better now.'

'So, now, tell us!' said Léa, sponging his forehead, which gleamed with sweat.

It was the second time in two days that Brice had

fainted. At break time, Guillaume Durosoy had found him in a corridor, lying across a pile of schoolbags. He had dashed down to Léa's office, and she had sent two counsellors to carry the child to the sick bay.

Without hesitation, he started to tell us his recent history, omitting (deliberately, we supposed) any references to the class.

The previous day, Wednesday, he had been walking in the countryside around his home, when his head had been clouded by a dazzling, incandescent white light. Not a light that came from any particular point in the place where he was walking, but a ray seemed to issue from within himself, something at once unbearable and friendly, and he had fallen face down on the ground.

When Léa had asked him for details about the moment just before the fall, Brice had demonstrated a topographic precision rare for a child of his age, as though he had registered his journey with a view to a later reconstruction. He had gone for a walk, he said, to escape the malicious insinuations that his brother was making about some money that had been stolen from his mother's purse, 300 francs in all. His brother, he said, was trying to put the blame on him. Brice revealed this with a sense of absolute injustice, as though it were his first encounter with evil.

Leaving his house, he had followed a wide grassy path that skirted the edge of a forest, describing an irregular oval on a round trip that lasted an hour. He liked this place, because at certain times of day you could see vast fields through the trees; in other places, the path, smaller now, plunged into the very depths of the forest, the light barely filtered into it, and the grass made way for a vine that seemed to unfold in a tentacular fashion.

Brice added mysteriously that he had always been careful not to learn the names of trees so that he could intensify the sense of profusion that he felt when he plunged into the undergrowth. There was something so perspicacious about his remark that it made me feel uneasy. Brice was only thirteen and he spoke, like many of the pupils in 9F, like a trainee semiotician. He went on with his story after a little pause as though he wanted to think about the implications of what he had just said.

Wherever the path was broken by a little stream, a rock, a log or the vestiges of a Roman oppidum, a miniature Amazonia flourished, a jungle of moss, of fluorescent lichen, of microscopic trees. In front of him floated a curtain of climbing plants, fat as hawsers, through which the light filtered. The ground was covered with leaves, bracken and grass bent by its own weight. For a moment he thought he had got lost in a private garden.

Then he crossed a little clearing, and felt almost intimidated, as though he suddenly felt he was being spied on. He had sought shelter among the trees, and left the clearing as quickly as possible. He reached a place where the path he was following forked off at right-angles towards the interior of the wood, taking a little track that ended in a dip. The intersecting branches above the path formed a sort of baldachin ('it was like those big drapes they had over beds in the old days,' he said, giving the phrase a magical resonance) through which the setting sun cast orange shapes on the darkening grass. Where the path levelled out, there was a dead oak tree; its trunk almost rotten.

Brice was about ten metres from that oak when, walking around its trunk, he noticed a black shape moving between the trees that marked the boundary between the wood and a maize field. He remained motionless for a while, uncertain about the degree of reality that he should assign to this vision. The vague hint of a voice issued from it, hollow, crackly, with rustling consonants and muffled vowels. It was at that moment that he first fainted.

The child suddenly stopped talking.

'Try and concentrate, Brice,' said Léa, rising abruptly from her chair. 'What sort of a shape was it?'

She started pacing up and down the room. She needed to establish a connection that might begin a process of enlightenment and ease the child's anxiety. I was carefully watching Brice's face. He was thinking deeply about the counsellor's question, intent on cooperating with her. A small wrinkle formed between his brown, regular brows.

Léa approached him and put her hand on his shoulder.

'Seriously, love, make an effort.'

Brice, with his chin now resting on his hand, looked up towards her with such an air of powerlessness that I nodded to Léa to leave him in peace for a moment. I got up, took his arm, and led him away.

'The child is tired. He should be allowed to rest. He has his own reasons for not wanting to remember.'

She agreed and then left him alone for a few seconds before observing, 'You mean he's pretending he can't remember?'

'He hasn't been in a normal state for some time.'

She shook her head emphatically.

'So what's been going on in this school, and for some time? I don't get it.'

'I was going to ask you the same question.'

Her large eyes blinked twice, then she hugged her arms against her chest as though to protect herself from the cold, and shrugged her shoulders, smiling at me, a series of gestures that I immediately interpreted as a tacit wish to communicate her own sense of impotence. For her benefit I displayed a stereotypical version of an oriental smile, a kind of patibulary anti-smile that I had learned from watching films about the mafia. Léa was standing up now, near the only window in the room, her arms arched over the frame as though she were one of the building's pillars.

'It was a kind of troll,' Brice said all of a sudden, displaying, along with this reply, an infantile pride at our adult astonishment.

'A kind of troll?' Léa insisted, turning around in disbelief.

'Yes, like those evil spirits that live in forests.'

I remembered that trolls had a human form in Scandinavian mythology. They embodied the negative forces of nature, and Brice was not mistaken. Their noses, in general, were exaggeratedly long, and they had several heads, like the hydra of Lerna. In size they varied from the giant with pine trees on his head to the sly dwarf.

'Who did he look like?' I asked him. 'Anyone we know?'

'Yes.'

Brice said nothing more, and pressed the blanket to his chest as though defending himself against an attack.

'So . . . who?'

'Monsieur Accetto.'

Léa listened very carefully to his reply, with the fervent submissiveness of a patient preparing to undergo a serious operation. When he had finished, she leaned towards him and stroked his forehead. As well as being charming, Léa Kaminsky radiated niceness. I thought of the number of times when I had met people who were nice but completely round the bend. For a moment I wondered if the two didn't go hand in hand.

'Monsieur Accetto looks like a faun, Brice, not a troll,' said Léa with a strange smile. 'He has a beard, his clothes look like goat-skin, and he holds his pipe like a horn of plenty.'

She turned towards me, hunched her shoulders with an air of acute malice, and said *sotto voce* so that Brice wouldn't hear, 'And, like Greek satyrs, he chases young virgins. The resemblance is striking, don't you think?'

'I'd prefer to stick with the troll.'

I didn't know where this kind of comparison was leading us to, but it allowed us to maintain the conversation at an almost playful level.

'Are you sure?' she asked, raising an eyebrow to make her question funnier.

'Absolutely.'

She adopted an air of forced admiration. Picking up a pencil from the bedside table, she tapped it against her lower lip. Then she darted an amused glance at Brice, and murmured in an aside to me, 'I've always admired the imagination and coherence of your choices, and the two aren't contradictory.'

'Excuse me?'

'You heard very well.'

'What were we talking about again?'

She brought her two hands to her mouth and started chuckling into her striped tulle scarf. Brice no longer seemed to understand anything about the scene. He was disturbed to see two adults – with whom he had become used to having serious contact strictly codified by an absence of intimacy – behaving in a childish manner, and he tried to conceal his unease by curling up in an attitude of embarrassed apathy.

Abruptly Léa's face grew serious again, her features crumpled as though the covering of her facial skin were made of wax and had begun to melt. She lowered her pencil on to the covers, spinning it around like a majorette's baton, and then took Brice's hand and shook it in quite a familiar way.

'Ok, enough nonsense, Brice, what did you see yesterday in your enchanted forest?'

'I told you, miss, something that looked like a troll.'

'And it wasn't Monsieur Accetto?'

'No, I said it looked like him, but I'm sure it wasn't him.'

'What you're telling me is absolutely bizarre, couldn't you tell me something sensible for a change?'

Léa and I exchanged an apologetic look. Seeing Brice's big, wide-open eyes, I reflected that Léa always used intensifying adverbs to weaken her statements. 'Absolutely bizarre' was less intriguing than 'bizarre'. A television film she'd seen with a social theme was 'quite simply extraordinary', while a masterpiece by Dreyer, reseen at the Cinémathèque, was 'simply extraordinary'.

She stared at the wall above Brice's head and asked gently, 'Then what happened?'

'I started running, I can't remember in what direction . . . and I didn't care what direction, I was frightened!'

'Frightened of the figure you had seen?'

253

Léa's voice was softer now. Her expression was intended to be professionally compassionate.

'Yes, I thought it was coming after me.'

17

Three days before the trip, Jean-Paul Accetto fell ill. No one seemed especially shaken by the news. Goliaguine kept a circumspect silence; Isabelle, exhausted for some weeks by the effort to control a difficult class of year eights of which she was class head, observed a clinical detachment. Annie Jurieu wasn't really surprised; as to Crochelet, it simply wasn't his problem.

I decided not to talk about it to the pupils, convinced that I would manage that very evening to persuade Jean-Paul to come with us, despite his week's absence. My decision wasn't motivated by the pleasure of setting off with him, it was rather that the prospect of spending three days with a teacher of technology or maths with an enthusiasm for the internet and chess problems was enough to plunge me into a state of depression.

I had twenty-four hours ahead of me.

Leaving school at four o'clock, I took my car and headed for the Accettos'. Arriving outside their house in Noizay, I rang three times, but no one came. Putting my ear to the flaking wood of the front door, I heard the typical sounds of a fifties western, with its edifyingly dubbed voices, gunfire whistling through the sierra and abattoir whinnies.

My first reaction was to feel like an intruder, even though I couldn't even think for so much as a second of going away again. I didn't know what attitude to adopt: whether to wait, go away and come back in a quarter of an hour, or break down the door. I glanced around the garden. The fence was made of vulgar-looking chicken-wire, barely fixed to the ground. The grass hadn't been cut for at least two years, and made the house look as though it had been on sale for some time. The door was in a state of advanced dilapidation, and although it was March it still bore Christmas decorations. A pergola, collapsing in several places, stood next to an empty niche that held discarded bits of potato croquette and a few chewed toys. Nothing could be seen of the windows, which were closed off by railway-yellow blinds in poor condition.

An attentive observer might have spoken of decline, but the word 'abandon' seemed more appropriate, since the dilapidation on display showed not the slightest sign of any attempt at upkeep. I had just understood why the Accettos never had anyone over.

I knocked again, this time with the flat of my hand, producing, in the middle of the surrounding calm, the effect of a Gestapo intrusion. The volume of the television had been switched off, and a sudden oppressive silence fell. It was interrupted after thirty seconds by the sound of a heavy object falling, and I heard a male voice yelling, 'Fucking cunting bloody fucking shit!'

I looked around to see if anyone else had heard what I had. At that moment the door opened. A gaunt, lost-looking little boy, aged about seven and wearing a dirty dressing-gown, stood in front of me. His face was half covered by a fringe of black hair, and his large dark eyes gave anyone capable of reading them a brief summary of his life so far.

'How can I help you?' he asked.

'I've come to see Jean-Paul.'

'Please come in.'

I entered a large, empty hall lit by a bodged system of twenty-watt bulbs that hung from a wire stretched across the ceiling. Familiar smells – Catherine's perfume, Jean-Paul's cigars, dried flowers, coffee, the bakery smell of freshly washed clothes – reminded me why I had come. Doors opened on to several rooms, but there was no sign of life. Somewhere upstairs someone could be heard putting pieces of glass into a bucket.

'Do you mind me saying that it would have been nicer if you'd asked me how things were when you turned up?' said the little boy, 'I'd have been more at ease . . .'

'I can do that. How are things?'

'Fine, thank you. But who are you? My name's Jean-Baptiste The Killer Chauveau.'

'Delighted to meet you. I'm Pierre Method Man Hoffman.'

'Likewise.'

'A great honour.'

'J.-B., what the hell are you doing down there?' a male voice called from the floor above. Are you going to let that bloody dog in again, he's already shat all over the kitchen this morning . . . do you hear me, J.-B.?'

'Yes, J.-P., full marks.'

The child finished his sentence by sweeping the air

257

with a casual little gesture. He took a piece of snot from his nose on the tip of his index finger, glanced at it and wiped it on his dressing gown. There were some confused noises, then Jean-Paul's voice thundered across the space again and asked, 'Is there anyone there?'

J.-B. closed his eyes for a moment, like someone horrified by a stupid question.

'I'm with Monsieur Pierre Method Man Hoffman.'

'Who?'

'Pierre Hoffman, a mate of yours!'

There was the sound of rapid footsteps on a parquet floor, and then Jean-Paul tore the door open and ran to the upstairs balustrade. He was wearing a shapeless pair of jogging trousers and a tee-shirt bearing the slogan 'I'm a piece of shit'. His hair looked like a packet of cress, and he was barefoot. He was holding by the neck, squeezed under an arm, a large cat of an indefinable colour which was struggling and swinging its claws around.

'Come up,' he said, throwing the cat down the stairs, where it landed with a thump and a terrible miaow. 'Sorry about the mess, but I didn't know you were coming.'

'I should have rung.'

'It doesn't matter.'

He immediately vanished into the room. I climbed a staircase, my shadow lengthening as I did so. I also became increasingly aware of a sulphurous stench not unlike that left by tear gas, a searing, dry smell. When I entered the room, a kind of office that might equally comfortably have served as a garden shed, he was sitting down with his feet splayed and his arms not only wide open, but slightly raised on the arms of the armchair, which was so deep that his feet couldn't touch the ground.

On the other side of the room, parallel to his own position, there was a mirror, and beneath the mirror a rococo shelf bearing a late-Victorian clock. The double face, supported by four gilded buttresses, sat on top of a jumble of gear-wheels imprisoned by a transparent globe made of Swedish lead glass. The pendulum didn't move back and forth, but was disc-shaped and parallel to the floor, and was activated by a pin which, at six o'clock, formed an extension of the vertical of the hands. It was almost magical to notice this antique among the screaming chaos of the room.

But the room was softened by dust and darkness. The faint light, bluish in places, made everything look like flat, two-dimensional objects. There was a jumble of different things all over the place, most of them simply junked together and left to get on with it, to develop a familiarity with one another, every angle, surface and colour recalling the cosy intimacy of a room where the robes of some baroque drama lay softly on the fleshless arms of two rocking-chairs. It was like walking into an old turn-of-the-century photograph showing a decadent actress surrounded by her relics.

A cardboard plate and a glass of orange juice indicated that Jean-Paul had been sitting here for several hours. All of a sudden I felt defenceless, and I was sorry that I had no excuse for leaving. The floor around Jean-Paul's armchair was covered with a sticky yellow substance, probably some orange juice that he had spilt while pouring it.

As he began to drag himself from his chair, I rested my hand on his arm and studied him carefully. Some small things seemed to be scrabbling about in his beard, red and purple rings hung in rows of two or three beneath his

eyes. His face expressed that feeling of poignant contradiction that tries to survive at the boundary between
modesty and final collapse.

'Nice of you to have bothered.'

'How are you?'

'Better.'

'Meaning?'

'I feel more in phase with my usual karma. I have only
to spend two miserable days away from that school to feel
that I'm rising from the dead.'

His right foot fidgeted irrepressibly, apparently uncon-
nected to the rest of his body. Tapping his foot like that,
Jean-Paul resembled a household robot passing through a
phase of temporary malfunction. What worried me was
the abnormal and hideously deforming excrescence of
bunions on his feet. The bare feet of people of a certain
age made me uneasy at the best of times.

'Who was the child who let me in?'

'He's the son of some neighbours. I look after him from
time to time when they go off for the weekend. It's a sort
of compensation, I suppose, for the fact that Catherine
and I never had any children. At any rate that's what they
must have said to themselves, because they've never paid
us a penny for looking after him.'

'He seems quite clued up for his age.'

'You could say that. I'm often bowled over by the stuff
he tells me. Seven years of age and he's already an amoral
little son of a bitch!'

'Good to see you're ok. I was very worried. I thought
I was going to find someone who couldn't construct a
sentence or eat all by himself.'

His smile cut short any further discussion of the state

of his health. He coughed into the sleeve of his tee-shirt and then raised his left arm in a gesture of unconditional surrender. In his right hand he held a glass of orange juice. He tilted the glass slightly, and the surface of the liquid assumed an elongated shape. Then I watched him twist the sides of the cardboard plate that he had left on the table. He was folding it repeatedly so that a different part of the circumference would touch a small ketchup stain situated just slightly off centre. He carefully studied the resulting folds.

'What do you do with your days?' I asked.

After giving me a long inquisitive look, edged with darkness, he dropped his hands in front of him. He was on the defensive, attentive to the tiniest fluctuations in his little game of self-espionage.

'Nothing . . . do you really want to know?'

'What do you mean?'

'Do you like lying in bed all day?'

'Of course.'

'I love growing weaker hour by hour, from morning until night, convincing myself that I'm imitating one of those great writers in a dressing gown like Proust or Léautaud. In that apathy I find a kind of disenchanted pity for the world, the compensation for my social failure.' (Here he emitted a thick and typically philosophical burp.) 'My life is quite simply delightful at the moment.'

He spoke with his eyes fixed on his hands, which were motionless on his knees in the rocking-chair. A sullen silence began to accumulate in the room. I didn't like the tension. It was like the air in a cave, aged, stratified, damp with bodily substances. I didn't want the silence to become even bigger than it was already.

'I know why you've come.'

He waited for a few seconds – the Accetto pause, designed for effect – and drew a large breath before exhaling the following sentence.

'And the answer's no.'

I started observing him attentively as I normally watched people waiting for their change. There was a certain confidence in his voice. I decided to adopt a more oblique strategy, concealing my original intention.

'I came to find out what you were up to. It was out of pure altruism, not contempt.'

'How long do you think you're going to stay?'

'Two or three hours, I'd have thought, I don't know.'

He looked at me in disbelief, then lowered his eyes to his hands again.

'What else should I ask you?'

'I've found someone to replace you. Very quickly. When they knew you were taking time off, they all started guessing. I had to tell them that you hadn't gone to Mars. They didn't care, they all raised their hands: "Me, me! Take me with you, sir!" It was so sweet. Really, at their age!'

'So who's going with you in the end?'

'Vincent.'

'Good luck!'

'Why "good luck"?'

I knew Jean-Paul hated Crochelet. That was part of the plan.

'He's an absolute twat.'

'Your seat was highly coveted. I had no trouble at all.'

'All the better. Give the names of some of the candidates.'

'Everyone, as I just told you, was jumping up and down to replace you, I had to make a short-list.'

Now I put the second part of the plan into action. Jean-Paul was clearly ill at ease.

'Are you getting any exercise?'

'How do you mean?'

'I don't know, it just came out like that.'

He took a little orange pill out of his pocket and put it on his tongue. Then he closed his eyes and jerked back his head in an abrupt convulsive movement, swallowing the pill and retching slightly.

'What's that?'

'I have to zap my neurones from time to time.'

'Is it a capsule?'

'You swallow it,' he said, 'that's all.'

He rubbed his crotch briefly, then crossed his legs without taking his hand away.

'Nothing escapes the final collapse,' he said, pointing an ironic index finger towards an indeterminate place in the room, like a Methodist perched on a soapbox. His voice had assumed a Mittel-European inflection. 'You remember that marvellous bit in *The Third Man*: "In Italy for thirty years under the Borgias they had warfare, terror, murder, bloodshed – they produced Michelangelo, Leonardo da Vinci and the Renaissance. In Switzerland they had brotherly love, five hundred years of democracy and peace, and what did they produce? The cuckoo clock!" QED.'

He smiled sadly. His hand had burrowed even further between his thighs, and he was now speaking very slowly, almost mechanically.

'You know what the region around Tours is known as?'

'French Switzerland.'

263

'Quite. When I arrived in Noizay with Catherine, we were very enthusiastic. I was the one who sorted out the house, and all of a sudden, we don't know what happened, we started succumbing to the most deadly boredom. It's like a nineteenth-century building, all faded grandeur, and the person who lives there finds himself stuck in that painless disorientation. Everything is arranged to get worse around here, haven't you ever noticed?'

'I have, but it's all still quite new to me.'

'Our whole history has started to crumble and fall, like a house built on a swamp.'

'Nice comparison.'

'You know very well what I mean. I grant you that people like me, pretty ectomorphic by nature, have a natural predisposition always to set our sights on the worst.'

'The apocryphal fragments of Jean-Paul Accetto, the darkest section of his oeuvre.'

'You're not going to tell me you like it here?'

'I didn't say that.'

'Then why don't you believe me?'

'Can you get inside things?'

'No.'

'You have to make an effort to get inside things.'

'With a view to?'

'You can live anywhere, afterwards . . . it stops mattering.'

'When I was young I was like that. I lived in Romorantin, a little place in the Sologne, ignored by the world. I was even at school with a famous singer.'

'Who?'

'Can't remember. Curly hair, unbuttoned white shirts, sings with his hands in his pockets.'

'Tom Jones?'

'What? No, a Frenchman . . . Tom Jones is Welsh and he doesn't sing with his hands in his pockets. Anyway. I was a complete autodidact, you know, I took maths classes by correspondence course, I went to the library, I practically lived there. I know loads of people who throw themselves heart and soul into their jobs, but only the autodidact knows true obsession. My father was like that too. At that time I was inside things, I could have lived in Vladivostok or in the Niger, I had nothing in my head but science. It's since I started teaching that the world has entered my obsession and destroyed it. Nothing has happened, but in a strange way everything has changed.'

'Come with me and the kids to Étretat.'

'You told me you'd found someone.'

'I was lying.'

There was a long silence. Jean-Paul started coughing and spitting into a paper handkerchief. What remaining strength he had was exhausted by my revelation. His cough progressively assumed a desolate intonation, became an almost tragic bark, so much so as to define the residue of his existence. He plunged back into his rocking-chair, as though attempting to consolidate his connection with it.

'What are your suspicions about the trip?' he asked, staring at me.

The metallic undertone of his voice, when he spoke again, seemed to have assumed an additional nuance, like a grumbling tremor.

'None. Or rather I have too many. Some things aren't easy to sum up. I've had threatening signs, too, like Capadis. I don't know what they're expecting from us, but they want something, I'm sure of it. I don't know what it could be. What are the underlying reasons for this trip, which was decided on at the last minute? I think about it every day, every evening before going to sleep.'

'And you want to drag me into this?'

'I don't understand the question.'

'I'm afraid to accept, just because I don't fancy leaving you alone with them.'

'We're all afraid. Who isn't afraid? But no one mentions it out loud. You can't refuse on the basis of such a pathetic excuse. It's the oldest trick in the world, and it still works!'

'I wonder if I have the emotional solidity to bear the trip, especially at the moment. I'm anxious and depressed about the whole business.'

'You'll get it. You don't have to decide straight away.'

'How much time are you giving me?'

'Five minutes.'

He shook his head sceptically and put his right hand into his pocket. Still standing up, I didn't move, careful not to break a delicate balance between Jean-Paul and his decision. I felt he was ready to give in, if only to have the satisfaction of seeing me leave. He seemed to be shrinking now, or perhaps he was trying to withdraw inside himself.

In the end he got up, shook his head and slapped me on the shoulder. That movement, which I saw as a gesture destined to become Jean-Paul's equivalent of Pilate's handwashing, was like a form of unrestricted agreement, a complete involvement of the body which seemed to flow into the hand that touched you.

'I'm depending on you completely,' I added.

18

Before we parted, we summed up what we would need to take on the trip. I wanted to make everything black and white for Jean-Paul from the material point of view, because he seemed utterly incapable of preparing his bag for the following day. If necessary, I was ready to assume responsibility. Jean-Paul was one of those distracted companions who constantly maintained a degree of disengagement between themselves and their responsibilities, which he passed off as an education in autonomy. This strategy, used by many educators, was very popular at the time, and its purpose was actually to criticise any kind of rigorous or authoritarian attitude on the grounds that they represented a lack of trust in the children. That kind of nonsense, the product of libertarian culture, was unquestionably successful both with depressive and severely codependent colleagues, but less so among the more clear-sighted among them, who unmasked the deception quickly enough not to have to succumb to it. But as a rule Jean-Paul avoided such people.

'The trip lasts four days,' he said, 'including two days

taken up with the journey there and back on the bus, not to mention breaks and meals. We won't need to take a complete wardrobe. All you need is some reading-matter, sea-sickness pills and some fags. The kids know what they've got to bring . . . What else do we need to know?'

'Nothing – it's their trip, don't forget!'

'I hope they've at least provided food for lunch!'

'The canteen has been alerted. They've already got everything ready, the kids worked with the cook on the contents of their packed lunches.'

'And what about the hotel? Where will we be sleeping? Who sorted it out? Because finding a hotel that can accommodate twenty-six people at a week's notice isn't necessarily going to be easy! And I'm not talking about a flophouse with a view of the town dump!'

'We're in a bed-and-breakfast near Étretat,' I replied wearily. 'The kids reserved it . . . three weeks ago now.'

I sensed that he was appalled by what I had just said. The more concrete the replies I gave to his demands for information, the more clearly his lack of investment in the project appeared to him. Throughout the course of the conversation, his voice had assumed a slightly polite undertone of cunning. Some of his words seemed to vibrate with an underlying connotation of irony.

'Are we going to museums? To see monuments? Visit the Normandy beaches? Pick apples? Gather around André Gide's tomb? Can you tell me who's in charge of activities? That's the bare minimum for an old man like me.'

'Dimitri and Sandrine.'

'I expected as much.'

'It's only common sense.'

Jean-Paul was lost for words. He sat there in silence, visibly wounded, hating the idea that anyone might have been able to anticipate some knowledge that he had kept secret for years. He looked around, his head twitching. Visibly very annoyed, he didn't stop folding and unfolding his arms back and forth, his fists clenched as though he were doing articulatory exercises to combat arthritis.

'How do you know?'

'Observation of their personality, their relationship with the group, a mixture of dependence and indifference. Intrepidity, guts. Even some sort of magic power.'

'You could be wrong.'

'You're right.'

'Listen,' he said with an aggressive pout, 'these pseudo-observations of yours, delivered so objectively, they're just awful. Remind me how long you've been in education again?'

Such a reaction, as surprising as it was rare, was enough to reveal that rancour was Jean-Paul's natural state of mind, and everything else was just a massive effort of will to conquer his frustration.

'Not as long as you, it's true. I apologise for lacking breadth and perspective in my appreciation of a class; it should have been more nuanced by my lack of seniority.'

'You could put it like that.'

Curving his middle finger into the shape of a duck's beak, he slipped it into his mouth and chewed on a piece of nail, detaching it completely. He used the irregular clipping to scrape the dirt from the nails of his other hands. It was all utterly filthy. Then he got up and started listing the things he needed to bring, articulating them with exaggerated clarity.

269

'Socks, shoes, warm trousers with a warm inner lining, light canvas trousers, belt, how many days did you say?'

'Four.'

'So that's four tee-shirts, two pullovers, two shirts, mostly cotton if possible – the sea breeze is freezing whatever the time of year – a watch so as not to miss the timetable of the tides, a scarf to counter the risk of throat infection, a woolly hat (or something to protect my head anyway), a rucksack, no suitcase, some water and snacks for the journey, not to mention sea-sickness tablets, a Smurf, a Bugs Bunny and some sort of plastic gimcrack for peace of mind.'

Then he returned to his rocking-chair, openly expressing his apprehension in a fixed smile that seemed to bring his inventory to a kind of conclusion. All of a sudden he was so depressed that I had a sense that if I didn't speak during those thirty seconds, he would remain sunk in his chair for an hour, without saying a word.

'It's extremely detailed. It's perfect. How did you do it?'

'Experience, my boy, experience.'

I was about to brush my teeth when the phone rang for the fourth time that evening. I jumped, sending a jet of toothpaste shooting into the basin, where it formed a line and a curve that looked like a number four drawn by a maniac. Since my return from the school at about seven o'clock, someone had been ringing me up every hour and putting the phone down as soon as he heard the sound of my voice. It was an intimidation calculated to the very last minute, almost authoritarian and so precise that I could have stood next to the phone and waited for it to ring. I paced the room until my carpet smelled of grilled textiles, and then went to my bedroom and stayed there expectantly. I still expected to see someone turning up, or a note slipped under the door, or a video cassette emerging from the kitchen. But everything was calm again, apart from a monotonous noise in the distance, which sounded as though it came from nocturnal building work, somewhere above the ventilation grille fixed in a corner of the bedroom walls.

This time it was Nora.

'I wanted to wish you a pleasant trip. Léonore's just leaving my place.'

'Thanks, that's nice. I feel almost grateful to hear your voice.'

'Why?'

'I've had three anonymous calls since seven o'clock, from a phone box, I've tried to check the number, but it isn't listed against a name. What should I do?'

'You've got to call the police.'

She answered in a high, forced voice. She was speaking quickly, clearly wanting to give the impression that she was both efficient and stimulating.

'How's Léonore?'

'She's living with me at the moment.'

'You're joking.'

'Absolutely not.'

'Has she left her husband?'

'That's right.'

She was speaking in a sing-song voice, as though we were telling each other riddles.

'I'll have to leave you. I've got to get my things ready. I'll try and call Léonore when I get back.'

'I wanted to organise something with you for her thirty-sixth.'

'That was a week ago.'

'That's no reason not to.'

'I don't think there's any particular legislation inviting people in their late thirties to celebrate their birthday every week. And anyway, there's nothing to force their relatives to join in.'

'Are you refusing to come?'

'Léonore hasn't changed, that's wonderful . . . she organises parties at the drop of a hat. She gave a party for all the little girls in the neighbourhood when she had her first period. When she lost her virginity, she gave one for all the boys she had only ever flirted with. It's in her nature to be ceremonious, as though she needed that to move on to the next stage. That kind of information might be of use to you later on, without wishing to seem like a spoilsport.'

'Listen, I'll get the last details sorted out . . . we'll call each other to confirm. I'd like you to be there, at least for a while. Do you think you'll come? Tell me immediately, it would be a great weight off my shoulders!'

'I don't think I'll be going.'

'You have the whole trip to think about it, there's no mad rush. But I'd be terribly disappointed if you didn't come. So would your sister, I should imagine.'

'That's blackmail.'

'Think what you like.'

Hanging up, I stretched out my fingers and pulled on the phalanges to relax them. The gluey torpor through which I vaguely remembered my conversation with Nora made way for a feeling of guilt about her. It was always the same sense of admonition that I felt for anyone who tried to come between my sister and myself. It was nothing

272

to do with Nora. I had never been able to bear Léonore paying for a party and inviting anyone but me. It would probably take me years to get used to it.

I was sitting on my bed in my pyjamas, with my little finger on my belly, scratching the residues of dirt out of my navel, and that gesture made me think of Léonore and myself when we were little. The two of us used to go to our parents' double bed when we were alone in the house. Fully dressed, we could spend whole afternoons assessing our physical differences.

I took her hand and placed it against mine, and jotted down in a notebook the development of our fingers in an invariable order: thumb-index-middle-ring-little. We would then compare the lines in our palms to anticipate our chances of staying alive for a very long time, both of us if possible. Then came a mutual exploration of the rest. Lying on our backs, side by side, we compared our feet. Léonore's toes were generally longer and thinner than mine. We did the same with our arms, our legs, our necks and our tongues, but nothing looked so much alike as our navels. In that fleshy spiral, squashed on one side, we found the same fine slit and the same folds in the hollows. The exploration continued until I plunged my fingers into Léonore's mouth to count her teeth. It was at that point that we would burst out laughing at our inventory.

As I got older, I realised that it was Léonore who was the more remote from our archaic memories. Each time I alluded to one of our games, she seemed to withdraw, as though she wished to shake off her responsibility for having involved me in such stupid actions. There had always been something strangely restful for me in remembering chunks of childhood, while maturity and experience had hurled her light years away from that period in our lives.

Turning out my bedside light, I reflected sadly that that particular emotion was pathetically diluted by time and distance. It had been replaced by a vague surprise, a re-action to the depth of regret that followed attempts at commemoration. At such moments, I felt free all of a sudden to break away, to leave, to set off in a new direc-tion. It was time, I said to myself almost with delight, to bury the fundamental moments of my life.

The end of those afternoons spent on my sofa remem-bering the moments when I had passed a bit of string through a hole drilled through the middle of a conker, when I had made clay animals with my box of plasticine, the cherry stones I had buried and the people in whom I had placed an absolute trust.

Goodbye to the times when I used to plunge my head in the bath and count to thirty, the mouthfuls of ice cream that I ate with little emblazoned spoons and the vast wardrobes in which I was able to hide among my father's suits. Now you could count on the fingers of one hand the places where I could hide, the endless nights waiting for daylight to come, the days when I ran out of the house like a madman, yelling with joy.

After that I tried to convince myself that both the most intimate tremors and the major gear changes in my life were a response to a plan, a hidden logic that would be clear to me in due course, and that the organised move-ment of things would assume an obvious meaning, unmasking everything that seemed strange, reducing ambi-guities and shadows. Invariably I always ended up assessing the extent to which all reflection on the subject was pointless and banal. That kind of conclusion, exasperating as it might appear, was – and I am really sorry to say this to balanced, adult people – reached with relative ease.

A moment before, I had thought that Jean-Paul Accetto had been trying to be sarcastic. In fact, I understood later, he wasn't at all. What he had been expressing with his soft, half-open mouth had in fact been a mixture of anxiety and concern, when he had told Annick Spoerri that Brice Toutain was probably decomposing now in some municipal dump, with his head separated from his body in an olive-green plastic bag. There were big dark patches under his eyes. He must have spent the night tossing and turning in his bed like a dishevelled porpoise.

That morning, the sun couldn't pierce the wall of clouds, and the light seemed to seep from the ground through a magma of spongy fog, while I took a stroll on the footpath in front of the College. The children had been assembling by the bus for about ten minutes, getting out of their parents' cars, rucksacks on, jackets in their hands, with tired-looking faces accentuated by dishevelled hair. They had all arrived at the same time, at about half past seven, which gave their orderly movement in a semi-circle – from the rim of parked cars towards the centre symbolised by the bus – the appearance of time-lapse bacterial reproduction.

Annick Spoerri was holding the list of pupils, and put a cross beside the names as their owners appeared in the line. That gave her an initial count which she would then repeat more carefully. For this kind of routine operation, Annick had no trust in Jean-Paul, who considered roll calls to be a fascist attack on his right to self-determination. That belonged to the solid post-1968 armour which was the most immovable part of his personality, however much he might have denied it.

As the last cars set off with a wave from the children's parents, it became clear that Brice Toutain was the only one who hadn't rejoined the group. A short time before, Annick had asked us if we had heard of any possible dissatisfaction on his family's part, and it was at that moment, in response to my upset silence, that Jean-Paul came out with his remark about the municipal dump. I had consulted Léa two days previously to find out whether Brice was going on the trip, and it turned out that since the fainting episode she hadn't seen Brice either in class or in the sick room. There had been no letter from his parents excusing him. So it was clear *a priori* that there was nothing to stop him going on the trip with the rest of his classmates.

'Let's wait another five minutes,' said Jean-Paul with relief, as though he had just found an excuse for putting things off a little longer.

The idea of waiting any longer depressed me. I would have to talk to the pupils without revealing any of my dark conjectures about Brice's absence. The last time we had had to wait for a pupil together, Clara Sorman had finally arrived with her face carved up. Jean-Paul's joke, despite its bad taste and deliberate opacity, was beginning to look thoroughly plausible. Leaning against a lamp post, scraping the ground with my right foot and with my head at a slight angle, I thought about the fact that every time the cohesion of the group seemed to relax, someone disappeared or there was a serious incident of some kind. It seemed to be assuming the form of a real biological rhythm.

'Brice won't be coming,' said Cécile Montalembert. 'Normally he's always on time. He must be sick.'

'One more minute,' I replied stoically.

'He's not coming, that's clear,' repeated Maxime Horvenneau, staring into the distance.

All the cars had vanished now, and the bus driver, whose outline I could see vaguely through the bus window, seemed to be showing signs of impatience. He got out shortly afterwards and sat down on the first step of the bus to wait and see what happened. His left leg was bent, his right stretched out, and he was punctuating his silent remarks with jerky movements, flattening a lock of brown hair over his forehead. From a distance, I could make out his black moustache, so perfect that it looked as though it was made of plastic.

A Peugeot 205 appeared at the end of the street, and came and parked on the pavement opposite the bus with a screech of tyres. A plump man in his forties catapulted out of the open door. His sudden presence appeared too unreal, too cinematic to be rooted in the ordinary land-scape of a group of children setting off for the seaside. He was wearing a worn linen suit a little early in the season, an open-necked shirt and very unusual shoes for his age – brothel-creepers with crepe soles at least three inches high. He looked as though he had just emerged from a long stay in a psychiatric clinic.

As I faced the group of pupils, he came straight towards me, ignoring Annick and Jean-Paul, who had been talking in a low voice behind the bus for five minutes. He held out a slack hand. I shook it politely and immediately gave it back.

'I'm Brice's uncle,' he said.

'Monsieur Hoffman, French-teacher, pleased to meet you.'

'Don't you teach history and geography?'

'As a matter of fact . . . yes,' I stammered, confused at having forgotten my recent attributions for a moment. 'I'm the replacement for Monsieur Capadis and . . . Did you want to talk to me about Brice?'

'He won't be able to join the others. He's sick, his parents called the emergency doctor. He stayed out in the cold all night.'

'So he's started again.'

'Yes,' he said simply, lowering his head.

19

We had passed Vendôme ten minutes previously, and the landscape of the Beauceron, as we progressed through its strange vacuity, had finally provoked the same anxiety in me as those deserted sub-prefectures that you drive through at full speed at night, propelled only by the fear of breaking down. After passing Danzé, the bus had taken the D157 towards Mondoubleau, the regional capital where I had nearly been sent, upon my arrival in the area three years ago, to teach at the Central Academy. The vista of the Perche, a peaceful relief of hills beneath a vast sky north of the Loire, was picturesque in a cheerfully inflexible way. But there was a price to be paid for its rigour: the haemorrhage of the region's inhabitants was increasing year by year, leaving in place only an ageing population stuck amidst hedged farmland which was beginning to fray at the edges, as land was consolidated and hedgerows were uprooted.

All of a sudden I heard Jean-Paul beginning the first cycle of snores that went with this particular phase of his sleep. He was stretched out on the big seat at the back of the bus, and his head rested on his bag. Before arriving in Vendôme, he had taken a little bottle from his bag, peacefully unscrewed the top in front of the pupils, taken out the protecting cotton wool and tipped two tablets into his hand. He had swallowed them without water, and lain down across the seat without consulting Mathilde Vandevoorde and Clara Sorman, who were also occupying the seat. He had fallen to sleep almost immediately. Now he was sleeping with his thumb in his mouth.

We had been driving for an hour and a half in an abstracted silence that seemed to be confined to the surface of things, and in a general atmosphere of adolescent languor. The general silence was so palpable that it almost had a visible dimension, a sparkle or a bright flash, and a thickness not unlike that of freshly applied paint. Without exception, the pupils were sitting two per seat, so close together that they might have been handcuffed to one another, all looking straight in front of them. Their lids were heavy after being woken so early, but they seemed to be fighting sleep, just to test their own tenacity, and the persistence of their resolution to confront the fixed and irreversible plan of the journey that they were under-taking.

I was sitting in the second row behind the driver, next to Sandrine Botella, who hadn't addressed so much as a word to me since we set off. Her only significant gesture had been to press her fingers against the slightly tinted glass, marking it with her fingerprints. The serenity that she had shown since setting off was unfamiliar to me. At that precise moment, she gave the impression that she lacked nothing, that she wanted for nothing, and that she could leave all the miseries of childhood behind her.

She looked so withdrawn that if she could have done so she would have folded her arms into her mouth and swallowed them to the shoulders, followed by her legs and her torso.

Dimitri Corto and Élodie Villovitch were sitting in front of us. Élodie held her boyfriend's pullover carefully folded over her knees. Dimitri's hands were locked over his head. He rocked them back and forth, and the top of his head moved in accompaniment. Every time he looked at Élodie, she gratified him with a strangely penetrating, strangely sweet smile, her delicate lips spreading to the two corners of her mouth. For some time, Dimitri had been fully absorbed in watching the driving of the bus. He followed the driver's every movement, every time he changed gear, every time he braked, with intense concentration.

Glancing to one side, I noticed how my neighbour was dressed. She was wearing a tunic pullover with a black and white jacquard print on the front (a geometrical fantasy evoking Vasarely) and a pair of satin-texture leggings. The discreet elegance of the ensemble had almost made me forget the arrogant girl I had had to endure on the occasion of my first encounter with the pupils. Now there was a sort of rigorous commitment to her presentability. Her face looked as though it lacked consistency, exposing a semi-transparent pallor that looked like the very pulp, pale and naked, of her being. The well-proportioned quasi-neutrality of her silhouette, of her appearance, even in a seated position, the fragile rectitude of it all, evoked in me an irreversible negation, flaws concealed beneath a deceptive classicism. All of her activity seemed to be concentrated in looking through the window, dreamily chewing on the skin of her index finger.

Since the episode in the park, I had had trouble seeing her except as an adolescent tormented by an inner vision inaccessible to everyone else, a kind of vague mysticism. Her theatrical sarcasm, the impression of wild independence projected by her entire attitude, the austere fidelity that she seemed to profess towards her inner reality reawakened the latent feeling of my own compromise with life. She seemed to be thinking about something else all the time, as though her whole life was constantly passing before her eyes and she was trying to select the most interesting moments from it. She was increasingly uncooperative, and each passing day seemed to be heightening her level of self-consciousness until she finally abdicated any relations with the outside world. Over the past few days, however, she had passed from the status of difficult adolescent to that of detached young girl, discovering the virtues of emotional abandon in a normal existence. To put it another way, she was no longer really there.

To the right of Dimitri and Élodie, Cécile Montalembert and Julie Grancher were openly holding hands. They were talking in a low voice and with such absolute calm that they looked like those impassive silent-film actors that the advent of talking pictures had condemned to eternal aphasia. Thoroughly self-contained, Cécile and Julie, it seemed, could only be perceived in isolation, without any precise reference to the context of which they were an almost accidental part. Julie sometimes kissed Cécile's hair as she might have done in a Pre-Raphaelite painting showing two beautiful sleeping women. Over time, that pair of girls pressed against one another began to appear as an important element in the restful atmosphere that I attributed to the present moment.

Dense sensations were reduced to points, lines, planes. The 'expression' of the inside of the bus seemed to have been conceived in very precise terms, as though the space were keen to show me that something dangerous might happen at a certain moment as yet undetermined. But it was a fear based on irrational foundations, an anxiety that nothing could for the time being confirm. I thought often of Jean-Paul's apprehension, the nervousness that had gripped him as the trip approached, his pseudo-depression and its as yet invisible consequences.

Cécile turned towards Dimitri and his girlfriend every now and again, staring at them in turn, sucking on a sweet, her cheeks hollow and her thin lips folded into a vinegary pout. Then she looked in our direction and nodded to Sandrine, who nodded back; after that she stared at me, but the expression in her eyes was still indecipherable.

A sign indicated a rest area two kilometres away. The driver had taken his microphone to ask if the children wanted the bus to stop so they could have a pee. He had a Slavic accent that made his elocution hesitant and spasmodic. The absence of definite articles dissolved the meaning of his words, giving them a general scope of significance on the edge of abstraction. He couldn't have been in France for very long. He must have known deprivation, loneliness, the threats concealed behind the shortage of indispensable goods, all those limitations that made his current exile endurable.

That impression had been confirmed by the austerity in his face. Thirty-five years of smiling and narrowing his eyes in the smoke had carved crows' feet that reached halfway to his ears. The furrow that led from his nostril

to the corner of his lips must have been dug by dis-
enchantment. Apart from his fake-looking moustache, his
skin was riddled with pock-marks. He had eyes like slits
in the bone of his skull, grey-green arrow-slits that seemed
to say, 'You can try and look beyond these, but don't waste
your time . . . there's nothing there.' He looked desperately weary, and this was confirmed by a vast range of
jerky hand gestures which compensated for a face drained
of any force that might have animated it, as though he
had been driving all the time for twenty years.

Since setting off, I had seen him laugh only once – a
curious, trumpeting explosion, when I had asked him, as
I climbed aboard, if he was happy about taking us to the
sea. It had seemed strange, because his laugh had stopped
abruptly, as though he hadn't wanted to encumber me
with tiresome details about its meaning. His body was now
slumped heavily forwards, his elbows resting on the curve
of the steering wheel, his palms clutching it as though it
were the joystick of a gaming console, and his fingers
pointing downwards.

Twenty-three heads turned slowly from side to side in
a gesture of negation. Some had begun to eat their picnic,
cheese spread, crisps and chocolate bars. We had just left
the hills of the Perche, and we were now halfway between
Mortagne and Bernay, which represented the border
between Lower and Upper Normandy. For the three hours
that we had been driving, the pupils had preserved the
uneasy passivity of tourists visiting dangerous countries,
where routine checks could end in mass arrest.

'You like listen radio?' asked the driver.

Silence.

'If you have cassette, radio also do cassette.'

284

Silence fell again, but not the same silence. This one was more hostile, disapproving, as though the moment had come for the pupils to point out to the driver that they were the ones who might *possibly* ask him for something. He made a cynical gesture in the air and called to me, yelling 'Excuse me, teacher!' over his right shoulder. My legs were stiff, and I was busy trying to find veins under my knees so that I could stimulate them. I hauled myself to my feet and came to stand next to him.

'Don't they talk, these children? Never? They have language, though . . . if they don't talk and don't say problems, they maybe vomit in bus or have pee. I don't want that, no dirt in my bus, you understand?'

His voice was so drowsy as to be almost incoherent. Too much vigilance, perhaps, excessive reflex actions.

'Don't worry, if they have a problem they'll say so. How long is it before we stop?'

'An hour and a half, nearly two. At about eleven I've got to rest for a bit, drink a coffee.'

'Whereabouts?'

'Bolbec. I've seen the map and Bolbec isn't far from Étretat. It's fine, we nearly there. Everyone happy, I think.'

'Why are you so cross with us?'

'Never transported boys and girls like these. They don't move, they like little wax models in Christmas shop window. If my children could be like that!'

His flushed face turned towards me for a moment, then he focused his attention back to the road. His features then assumed an expression of inquisitorial uncertainty. The bus speeded up, unambiguously indicating that he was in a hurry to get there. I noticed that his forehead was gleaming with little translucent drops of sweat.

285

'Your colleague is tired, he sleep since beginning. Why you not sleep a little?'

'I'm not tired.'

'You being annoyed, I think. No?'

'Bus journeys tire me.'

'The weather is changing.'

I shrugged my shoulders and merely shook my head, then looked away to study the vast space that made up most of the landscape. The idea that human beings might live in such gloomy places always chilled my blood. They must have had some atavistic motivation, the sense of some obscure debt, a moral obligation, something of the order of a custom or an expiatory discipline.

Why else would you choose to live so far away from the world, forty kilometres from the smallest agglomeration of ten thousand inhabitants? Why flee life in these harsh, miserable, terminal villages? Why wait there to go grey and fat, to drag your feet, slumped, stuck in fleece-lined slippers pierced through at the end by unclipped toenails? It would be hard to get to the secret of the peaceful horror of those villages on Sundays, the Eucharistic secret of those ancient feet returning from mass, without already belonging a little to the kingdom of the dead.

I heard some children talking behind me, but had trouble making out what they were saying. The density of time enveloped everything. To keep my balance, I clutched two metal tubes on either side of my body. My elbows stood out like the wings of a hang-glider. The whole conversation had seemed to take place in a dream, and I found it hard to believe that we were talking like this when the driver barely knew the children. The slight migraine from which I had been suffering since the start had metamorphosed into a buzzing in my head, like the one you sometimes get after an injection of Novocaine.

'What do you think is strange about the children?' I asked solemnly and insistently.

He turned his face towards me and made a little bump in his cheek with his tongue.

'Nothing, ignore me,' he replied with a smile. 'I'm just tired or mad, much driving this last time, much problems too.'

I held back just in time from asking him to expand on his problems. There was no point, he wore his life on his face. That, as well as his mouth, gave signs of a life lived without material comforts. His eyes showed no experience of any kind of gentleness. I had a disagreeable sense that he was the perfect propaganda for the enchanted West plonked bang next to servitude, resigned but intense in his desolation. Perhaps what finally embarrassed me was his way of rolling his eyes, with that factitious and cunning wink that media stars have when spotted in the real world, in the street, when they know they're being observed.

I moved my shoulders back and forth to try and relax the muscles. I needed a little fresh air. With his thumb and index finger, the driver picked a crumb of tobacco off the end of his tongue. He examined it for a moment, then his hand returned to the wheel. At that moment his face manifested that exhausted tension that dims the eye and extends the sincerest smile to the point of stupidity. He was silent for a moment, then shook his head and went on:

'What will happen once everyone arrive, who know? Me, I will be off anyway, but you, I hope you enjoy yourself a lot with children and snoring friend. Me, I haven't even time to talk. I go one place, then another and between the two, nothing, I want to concentrate on direction and safety. No life through all that . . . sad, sad, only driving people . . . and people often rude and silent . . . not talk to me as though with me being foreigner I not understand what they say. But my ears can hear very well that they are mock me very quietly.'

He was now talking to me in the rapid and unmodulated voice that you use with a long-standing friend. I couldn't determine the bond that suddenly drew him to me. That new intimacy made me feel almost virtuous, in harmony with the good and social being that I sometimes felt I held within. It occurred to me that most people who formed friendships with me had confronted a private tragedy, often family-related. It was as if they had met me at the moment when they wanted to release a particular tension, a conflict, almost making my presence accidental and superfluous.

After speaking for twenty minutes to my new friend, who listened to me with polite attention, I turned back towards the children. Most of them were sleeping in a posture of complete abandon. Something in their trust guided the scene in the direction of silence and blindness, one of those unreal spaces from which suffering was banished and disappearance was always likely. Some children still persisted in staying awake. Richard Da Costa and Kevin Durand were quietly playing cards, Pierre Lamérand was reading a magazine and listening to what sounded like hip-hop, Clara Sorman was concentrating on a gameboy, and Mathilde Vandevoorde, frowning, was trying to solve a crossword.

Jean-Paul was still asleep.

Clara noticed that I was watching her. She raised her head and studied me for a few seconds in her tempestuous way. I didn't know what to do, but I felt that I had to respond to her gaze. I didn't know why, but I had to do it, it was like an imperious need, an entreaty that we alone were capable of understanding. Finally I gave her a little wave.

She got up and came towards me without taking her eyes off mine. When she was almost level with me, she dropped on to the seat where I had been sitting, next to Sandrine, who barely noticed she was there. I wondered what one should say or do in that situation. 'Tough', her expression seemed to say, or perhaps she only wanted to tell me that she was returning to her real seat, next to her best friend.

At that point a car passed alongside us. It was trying to overtake us, and it seemed as though the bus driver were accelerating on purpose to prevent it from doing so. I heard him sniggering as the car disappeared once again towards the back of the bus. The driver was furiously flashing his lights at him, and giving loud honks on his horn. It was at that moment that I chose to turn towards him.

'You shouldn't play with the kids' safety.'

'Ok, ok, boss!' he merely replied.

'I'm not your boss.'

'I know . . . is manner of speaking, that's all. Not get annoyed, is just I enjoy myself a bit.'

I undid the button of my polo shirt, the one that was pressing on my Adam's apple, and rolled up my sleeve. To conceal his embarrassment, the driver was busy sniffing the nicotine on his fingers. He hadn't had a smoke for three hours, and the dark sepia colour that covered the upper part of his middle and index fingers was the sign of a compulsive smoker who was constrained by regulations. The mere act seemed to calm him down. In ten years' time, he would have the waxy complexion of the inveterate smoker, constantly hawking, with a disgusting noise, a yellowish phlegm that he would spit on the ground.

Clara's face appeared in the rearview mirror like a shaky image from a hesitant camera. For the first time since we had known one another, I paid attention to her physical appearance. She was pretty, quite small for her age, with a narrow face framed by short brown hair. A classical, but spectral beauty. But she was curiously proportioned, a little as though she were in conflict with her own figure. Her face and her fragile torso contrasted with her wide, strong hips and her thick legs. With her very wide-spaced hazel eyes and her fluting voice, she looked, above the waist, like an ethereal Lolita, and below it like a sixteenth-century Carmelite, barefoot in her sandals. There was something mythological about her figure, there was something in it of both the centaur and the siren. Her skin was so clear that you could see the blue veins of her temples. The scars that marbled her face almost melted into the milky tissue of her cheeks.

She had noticed that I was looking at her in the rearview mirror, and each time she did so she tried to point out my rudeness, by crossing her eyes and casting me a look full of suspicion and numb bitterness. It was as though she had developed an almost pathological and paranoid sensitivity to the nuances of my various ways of looking at her. I went on uneasily admiring her from a distance.

All of a sudden Sandrine got to her feet and, making simple apologetic gestures, put her right leg over Clara's knees, immediately followed by her left. Then she headed towards the back of the bus to sit in Clara's old place, adjacent to the vague form of Jean-Paul, who still seemed to be asleep. A smell of crisps and strawberry-flavoured chewing gum now floated in the air. I heard a voice asking with an expression of respectful fear, 'Do you really believe what they say?' There was no reply.

Hesitant and anxious though I was, I decided to go and sit down in the place vacated by Sandrine. I looked at the road and mentally counted to ten before facing all the pupils. Those peaceful faces had an expression of trust so complete, so absolute that I couldn't believe it was unfounded. Those sleeping children looked like the pictures I was always being given by the Jehovah's Witnesses. At that moment I think I would have given anything to know the force that seemed so strong and formidable that it justified that inner faith. They seemed to be attracting a powerful beam of light from outside.

It was my turn to climb over Clara's legs. A wave of incredulity and resignation was immediately apparent in their three faces. (Dimitri and Élodie turned around almost at the same time), but I decided to lay claim to the normality of my position.

Silence fell.

This time Clara stared at me with an air of truculent surprise. A faint smile began to play around her lips. Dimitri and his girlfriend seemed almost delighted that I had made the effort to come and talk to them. They never looked as though they wanted to suggest to me that my presence might be a threat to their happiness and their safety; I always had a sense, on the contrary, that they sought and encouraged it, but had not the slightest idea of how to behave to provoke it. Their attitude towards me revealed an indirect form of goodwill, a tacit invitation to enter their circle.

'Nice of you to visit,' said Clara.

'Will we be in Bolbec soon?' asked Dimitri, with a voice of calculated concern.

'I didn't know you knew the itinerary.'

'We asked the driver before you arrived this morning,' replied Élodie in a coldly matter-of-fact tone.

'Which hotel are we staying at?'

'The Normandy.'

'That's original.'

'That was the plan.'

'The weather's about to turn,' said Dimitri in a slightly plaintive voice.

There was a long silence.

Clara was busy staring into the void straight ahead of her. She seemed to be afraid that the slightest change in the texture of sounds, movements and expressions might obstruct the sequence of events. Dimitri stood with his forearms crossed over the top of the seat as though the conversation were a triangle of which he formed the apex, and Élodie and Clara each constituted a side. My own position did not impinge upon their balance of forces. I felt utterly alone, and could do nothing but wait to confront this atmosphere of satin-soft expectation which – I now felt with painful certainty – would engulf us sooner or later. Élodie's lips murmured the words of a pop song that was constantly on the radio at the time. She smiled shyly when she realised that I was looking at her.

'I know that in this world you've always got to show that you're strong and ruthless,' Clara went on with calculated slowness, continuing the conversation she had been having before I arrived. 'All our lessons show that, but I often feel exhausted forcing myself to be a match for that kind of ineptitude. I don't want to spend all my time fearing the acceleration of time, I want to go on enjoying those slow and inactive days, those completely empty afternoons, those evenings with nothing in prospect. Unfortunately, we're going to have to find out about the activities proposed . . . It's a difficult, full-time job, it's not something you can just take for granted. That's why I fear year ten. How did you cope at our age? Try and remember.'

She had turned to face me. The look she gave me contained a perfectly studied desire for destabilisation. I averted my eyes, fearing that she might notice my embarrassment.

'I was impatient to grow up so that I would have access to all kinds of things. My education was very strict. My sister and I were in a hurry to go to the *lycée*. As far as we were concerned that was the gateway to a more exciting world. After the *lycée*, I wanted to leave the provinces to go and study in Paris and meet highly developed, subtle-minded people. I think that . . .'

'At our age, Clara meant,' Élodie broke in.

'I honestly can't remember.'

'That's not possible. Everyone remembers.'

'Oh, it's perfectly possible. I've talked about it with people of my own age. No one remembers the years they spent at middle school. There's a great blank. You can believe me on that one. But it's quite normal for you to reject what I'm telling you. When I was your age, thirty-year-olds seemed terribly old and corrupt. And I was convinced that they were all lying.'

Silence fell once more. We waited to see if the conversation was over.

'I can't believe it,' said Clara.

Her voice itself had the tone of a nostalgic reverie expressed without any concern for the people listening. I noticed the respectful and restrained attitude of Élodie and Dimitri. Their faces expressed disappointment at receiving confirmation of something they suspected, but didn't dare formulate given the current state of their knowledge. I had a sense that they must feel imprisoned in more ways than one.

'The only chance you have of growing up well', I continued with a sigh, 'is constantly to remind yourself of that part of yourself that has stayed behind during your years at middle school. Always saying to yourself: What did I want? What did I feel? Keep a very hard line.'

'Is that what you did?' asked Dimitri.

'No.'

'So what's the difference between then and now?'

'Often the relationship between adulthood and childhood is pretty much one of picking off dead skin, or even of bumping off an embarrassing witness. Children are universal truth, and everyone knows that. That's why people are afraid of them. That's why they talk nicely to them. Parents have a phrase for that: "Out of the mouths of babes . . ." And no one really wonders what the phrase means, nobody cares! As you grow older, that truth tends to be diluted with new voices that come from outside yourself. We begin to doubt, and to forget fundamental things. When I was a kid, I lived in the narrow cage of time, and

294

I felt good. My plan was to be a train driver. I really believed in it.'

'What do you do to stop believing?' asked Clara.

'As soon as I left middle school, I started to grow apart from my former classmates. I never saw them again, or if I did it was by accident. I had completely abandoned the very idea of the gang that we had formed, four or five of us. I became the ideal target for advertising companies. I had turned into an adolescent who was integrated into mass culture. In order for that to happen, I developed a strategy isolating myself from the rest of the group by distinguishing myself. It was at that moment that loneliness arrived. Fortunately I had my sister. But she quickly forgot, too. I became inconsolable, completely turned in on myself. I don't know why I'm telling you about that, it's very private.'

'So you do remember,' said Dimitri.

'Maybe I'm tampering with my own childhood!'

'We feel all the things you're talking about,' said Élodie, smiling into the void.

'We're aware of the trap,' added Clara.

'It's not a question of the connection with adulthood. The issue is rather how to reinforce the sense you have of yourself,' Dimitri intervened.

'And what does that mean?' asked Élodie, ruffling his hair with a gesture that was at once ironic and tender.

'I'm still a child. We're still children. How can you explain the fact that there's nothing at all childish in our school? Nothing at all, it's very weird. Something is taking its course, but you never know what. We never know what's really happening. You'd think that Poncin and the others were *organising* us. That's why I appreciate the fact that you were trying to tell us the truth without treating us as simpletons.'

There was profound gratitude in her eyes.

'There's a story that I like to tell. It was Clara who told it to me. Can I?'

'Please do.'

'It's the story of a Jew in a city in western Europe who meets another Jew heading for the station, loaded down with suitcases, and asks him where he's going. "To South America," the other one says. "Ah," replies the first one, "you're going that far?" To which the second one, looking at him with surprise, replies, "Far from where?"'

'That's funny,' I said.

'I feel like that, and so do most of us. Do we have a reference point from which we could be near or far? We're rooted in ourselves, we're always located within our own boundaries. We're appallingly isolated and no one else can put themselves in our position. How can you imagine that we can have the same centres of interest as the other pupils? They say we have this peculiar way of talking and behaving. I don't think so. How are we going to swap ideas with people who are constantly accusing us of speaking a foreign language, when we feel as though we're at the very heart of things?'

'It's sad,' said Clara.

'That's why we all get together at the slightest excuse,' Dimitri went on with a melancholic smile. We all feel – that is, our group does – very, very alone at Clerval. Loneliness among adults is the saddest thing in the world. School work becomes the only vaguely imaginative aspect of your life. It's very depressing. For us, the only way of surviving was to subordinate our existence to that of the group, to live as close as possible to its warmth. Not many people understand that. To move away from the group, to break the circle, is to be condemned to die alone, with your face to the wall, and that seems so frightening to us! Our class is the only way we have of attaching ourselves to our own life, otherwise we feel totally lost.'

'Why? How do the other pupils cope? They have a life outside. They do sport, they have friends who aren't necessarily from the same school, they join in.'

'I get frightened when I see the other pupils, I even feel sorry for them. The important thing for us is to go unnoticed, not to fight to become adults, which is the idea that drives most children these days. That's why people at Clerval think we're strange. Even dangerous.'

'Did Monsieur Capadis understand you?'

'I don't think so.'

'He lost his life over it.'

'What do you mean?' asked Clara with a sardonic flash in her eye.

'Nothing.'

'First of all, what do you know about that guy?' Clara went on, her face, this time, deliberately drained of all expression.

Since my exchange with the children had become animated, the driver was looking at me with sustained attention in the rearview mirror. His expression didn't inspire confidence.

'He was under pressure, wasn't he?'

'We're all sorry about what happened to him, if that's what you want to know. He was fragile, he hadn't enough faith in life, he was at the mercy of all sorts of enticements. It was probably the strangeness and the atmosphere of the

297

place as well as his young age that made him feel so impotent and abandoned at the school. I don't think he went out much, he had no friends, no social life. At first we tried to boost his self-confidence, to make him feel as though he wasn't frightened, as though he was safe. To give you a precise example, I can talk to you about his desk. His predecessor had put it in the right-hand corner of his classroom, just below the window. We put it right in the middle of the room. Why do you think we did that?'

'I don't know. So that he could have you within his field of vision?'

'Not at all. It was so that he would be at the centre of our attention, so that he would feel bigger, stronger. Everything was fine until . . .'

She put a finger on her lower lip, assuming a refined air of concentration.

'Until the Christmas holidays, barely a term in,' said Dimitri, slowly shaking his head.

'Then what happened?'

'He must have spent the Christmas and New Year holidays on his own. The atmosphere was charged with aggression and recrimination. It was as though he was cross with us for enjoying ourselves, whereas throughout the whole of that time he had been left to his own devices. We had made him feel that we had abandoned him, and that was utterly false and unfair because we had been nice and considerate with him from the very beginning. He stayed at the back of the class, leaning against the wall, arms crossed, and with a sullen expression on his face. He closed his eyes and clenched his fists as he spoke. We all felt awful. We were all picking up the bad signals, his dark forebodings and his sadness. It was then that he entered a phase of depression and self-pity. It looked as though he was feeling his loneliness with a terrible intensity. One day, right in the middle of a class, he sat down at his desk and started to cry with his head between his hands. We looked at him in silence, almost hypnotised, and he said, "I want to die, I want to die and come back to live another life, I can't bear this one any more." It was from that moment that he withdrew from the world formed by us, to take the path that was to lead to his own death. It was clear that he wanted to die.'

'And of course you approved?'

'We can't reject that possibility,' replied Élodie with a sad smile.

While Clara had been speaking, no one had questioned her story, no one had tried to introduce their own personal testimony. It was rather as if someone had evoked a portion of life in which they had not been involved. They seemed interested in what Clara was saying, and even curious about it, but they also seemed detached from it. Their nodding heads indicated that they trusted her to transcribe their own experiences, their feelings.

'But that's monstrous.'

'He always made me think of a powerful car on chocks,' intervened Dimitri in a different tone, to tell me that my moral considerations were vain and the important thing lay elsewhere. 'He had many reasons for leaving, even quite advantageous reasons, but the moment he sat at the wheel, he stopped moving. He was afraid of the class from the very beginning. He expected an approval from us that we never gave him. I realise now that it might have helped. Some people have suggested that we were the ones who killed him.'

'Which people?'

'Doesn't matter. You don't think so, do you?'

'No,' I lied.

'We just wanted to help him. In a way.'

All of a sudden it started raining and the driver switched on the headlights. The light faded as the sky covered over with big black clouds. Normandy was keeping its promises. The oblique rain was like a curtain that dulled the light of the headlamps. The metallic crackle of the raindrops, an almost unreal and magical noise, had interrupted our conversation. Something in the children's attitude prevented me from pursuing our exchange along those lines, as though they had passed from one level of existence to another. Suddenly it occurred to me that I might have sounded as though I were suspicious, and that might have made them anxious.

Dimitri and Élodie had remained in the same position, but their eyes wandered vaguely over the rain-drenched countryside. Élodie clung firmly to her boyfriend's fingers as though to boost his confidence, or to prevent him from abandoning himself to the sad thoughts she could feel inside him. It seemed that Dimitri depended entirely, drop by drop, on his girlfriend's affection. It was an aspect of his personality that was new to me. There was such complicity between the two of them that Clara and I felt like undesirable outsiders, characters introduced artificially into a genre painting. I observed Clara, who was studying the insides of her arms, apparently appalled, before folding her chubby legs underneath her to turn and face the landscape.

We were now following a railway track the slopes of

which were covered with plastic cups that had been thrown from a train or perhaps blown there by the wind from a nearby dump. A disused factory appeared about fifty metres away from the road, with hundreds of broken windows and its outside light hanging from wires. The worrying noise of the engine sometimes made me jump. Jean-Paul still hadn't woken up. I was worried that the tranquilliser he had taken was too strong. A sign announced that Bolbec was thirty kilometres away.

We'd be there in a quarter of an hour.

20

Apart from ten or so lorries lined up haphazardly to the right of the petrol station, very few cars were filling up from the pumps. The car park in front of the octagonal building that housed the cash desk was nearly empty. The service station seemed almost forlorn there in the middle of that vast stretch of forest, that sylvan solitude. It had been built below the motorway, and we could see the cars passing by on a slightly higher level.

The service station was called 'The Flowery Glade'. Was that a way of counterbalancing the effects of the damp from the deluges of rain that must fall here? What kind of important event could happen to us in such a 'flowery glade'? Was such a peculiar name supposed to make us think that our visit had coincided with some kind of reconciliation with nature? Generally speaking, I felt a sense of relief when I found myself in places with pleasant names. That was half the battle.

Some locals were standing in the blazing light, by enormous windows, watching us with perplexity. The rain was falling more densely now, accompanied by quite strong winds coming from the west. The windscreen wipers described greasy arcs through which we could sometimes make out the sparkling pumps that stood beneath multi-coloured banners. The driver and I exchanged a quick, concerned glance. We hadn't expected the rain to be so heavy.

'Horrible weather for a break,' he said.

'We have no choice.'

Jean-Paul was woken by the screech of the brakes. Shortly beforehand he had been snoring with the placidity of a diesel engine. He sat up with some difficulty, then stayed where he was for a few seconds with his hands on either side of his body, leaning against the back of the seat, turning his head from side to side with an air of hazy disbelief. The flags clattered in the wind. The children were looking through the windows, and their hands were pressed against the panes like big pale spiders.

The bus came to a standstill. The driver pulled on the handbrake and stopped the engine. He clicked his fingers, briefly swung his right leg around, then raised his eyebrows towards me.

'I'm going to toilets, smoke cigarette, then come back to sleep a little, ok?'

'All right. How long have we got before setting off again?'

'Let's say twenty minutes. Ok?'

'Ok.'

During our exchange, I had noticed Dimitri going through Élodie's canvas bag, which was full of sandwiches and various kinds of other food. From it he had taken what looked like half a baguette wrapped in a tea-towel patterned with little red squares. I thought to myself with a shiver that it could equally easily have been a machine gun or a length of electric cable. Dimitri is a pre-adolescent, I thought, to reassure myself, who likes to titillate people by preserving an appearance of impassivity, to lead them up the garden path, play with their sense of reality, let's not exaggerate. A sensation of impotence took hold of me when he noticed that I was looking at him out of the corner of my eye. We exchanged a look that was fraught with innuendo.

Five or six rows behind him, Richard Da Costa was explaining something to Sébastien Amblard about how to play a particular sport. He was gesturing a lot, sometimes pointing to himself with his finger. As I got closer, I realised that he was talking about the funeral rites of a vanished civilisation. Then his little voice was lost in the hubbub that pupils make when there are large numbers of them in an enclosed space. Mathieu put a magazine in his bag and looked at the rest of his classmates with a harsh, resolute air.

The pupils crammed into the middle aisle when the bus doors opened. Four pupils at the back of the bus formed a semi-circle around Jean-Paul. From a distance I observed this circle of listeners, their arms crossed and their heads leaning slightly to one side. Two girls in particular were looking at him, blissful with admiration. I wondered what Jean-Paul could have been saying to them.

'Time to go,' said the driver.

'I'll go and get my colleague.'

Pushing past some of the pupils, I made for the back of the bus. When he saw me coming, Jean-Paul adopted a sly, secretive smile that revealed his tendency to believe that he had a particular empathy with the pupils, and that

that empathy put him in the special position of a renowned guru or a famous medium. It was part of that eternal rivalry between teachers, invisible to the naked eye, and designed to ensure the momentary inveiglement of young and willing minds.

I was clearly cramping his style.

I walked further towards him and waited for him to finish his sentence before speaking to him. The children burst out laughing, and their heads danced. It was a complicit, slightly forced laugh designed to demonstrate that their discussion with Jean-Paul had forged new bonds between them.

'Excuse me, but we've got to get off,' I murmured.

'I'm going to give instructions before we go,' replied Jean-Paul authoritatively.

He abandoned the group, parting them gently with his hand, and stepped towards the front of the bus amidst the general uproar that was beginning to rise around us. His initiative, although it was an extension of his earlier attitude, surprised me and almost increased my sensitivity to the tension and anxiety that reigned at that precise moment. The children at the back began to follow him. I found myself alone at the back of the bus, and noticed that none of the pupils had taken their bags.

The driver held a microphone out to him, and he blew on it to check that it was working. His voice rose suddenly, almost creating an unexpected atmosphere of lightness and gaiety. It was like the voice used by former television presenters who have been reduced to working in trade fairs, where they deliver faked-up formulas solely to attract you to the sausage department.

'We are not letting you out of here!' he declaimed in

305

a Bavarian accent. He paused for a few seconds. There was a burst of applause. Some of the pupils clapped their hands and acclaimed the orator . . . 'Thank you, thank you! We're taking twenty minutes. The driver's going to stay on the bus to open the door for you when you get back. Don't spend all your money, keep some for your stay in Étretat. You'll be able to make any calls you want, there are phoneboxes inside. You'll also be able to go to the toilet. No one's to leave the group, ok?'

I listened carefully, trying to work out what he was trying to say. The rain hammered on the vehicle with an almost biblical force. Clara was staring at me from the front of the bus with an affected and contemptuous expression on her face. A blank and reflective moment seemed to descend upon us. The pupils avoided looking each other in the eyes. As time passed, it seemed increasingly clear that Jean-Paul had decided to see nothing strange in our situation.

I was filled with a sense of weariness. I became aware of the gloomy atmosphere surrounding me. The colours and smells seemed stronger. The effluvia of sweets and chocolate bars, the dull hum of a ventilation system somewhere in the distance, the rustle of bags being taken down and put back on the racks, the sound of the children whispering among themselves, the regular rumble of cars passing a hundred metres away, and particularly that sliding of feet, muffled and melancholic, that is common to all the pupils in the world at the end of the school day.

Now that we had got off the bus and were getting ready to go into the shop with the children, I surprised myself by discovering in their most ordinary gestures a surprising intensity, and an unexpected series of connections. For the first time I noticed how closely they all resembled one another, despite the general diversity of their origins. They seemed eager to leave the shadow and confinement of the bus for just a few minutes. They hadn't taken their bags, their clothes had stayed inside despite the damp weather. Some of them were whispering behind me, and when I turned around they stopped short, their eyes pointing at the floor. Some of them walked forwards, leaning against one another, tottering like lovers on the beach or like people who have just escaped a terrorist attack.

Clara and Sandrine had joined each other, and were walking next to Franck Menessier and Estelle Bodart. The rain no longer seemed to reach them. Sandrine still had her death-mask pallor, and Élodie and Dimitri brought up the rear. None of them tried to shield their heads or walk any faster to escape the rain. They wandered in disparate groups of three or four, little archipelagos beneath the grey, seeming to blur beneath their own momentum into a landscape filled with weariness and neglect.

The driver's hair fell into his eyes, making his forehead look like coral washed up on a beach. Jean-Paul covered his head with a plastic bag which he kept in place by holding the handles under his chin. I had put my hands over my head like someone who is afraid that he is going to be hit. I deliberately walked like a duck to lessen the ridicule that such a posture might have provoked. The children were now looking cautiously at us from a distance, as though we were strangers to their lives who had suddenly revealed their indelible status as adults.

'They're good kids,' said Jean-Paul sullenly.

With their identical sandwiches, their hugely expensive

souvenirs and the inevitable porn magazines for the lorry drivers, the service stations next to rest areas didn't seem to me to have changed the way they had operated since the seventies, as though they represented the crystallisation of a wide social sensibility in accordance with the fixity of the regulations concerning lorry drivers' rest and daylight robbery for everyone else. Jean-Paul, once he was inside, suggested that the driver have a coffee, but he refused on the grounds that he was tired and wanted to get back to the bus to have a nap.

'I'm going to have to go once I've dropped you off,' he said, perfecting his gruff appearance with a roll of the shoulders.

'Straight away?'

'Yes, unfortunately I've got another job before coming back to get you in three days' time. Another employer, but thanks all the same . . . tell the children not to be late.'

He headed off furtively towards the toilets, outside which the pupils were already queuing in complete silence. A jingle advertising fitted kitchens rang out through the service station. Inside there was an uneasy, cramped darkness. It clearly had something to do with a determination not to put on all the lights as part of an economy drive. A light set somewhere in the floor spread across the half-empty shelves. We had almost felt embarrassed as we came in, as though we had to apologise for the chain's imminent bankruptcy. The girl at the cash desk had a round, resigned face, and looked so bored that you would have felt like issuing her with an impromptu invitation to the zoo. Her face bore an expression of complete injustice, like an older sister who had just been betrayed once again by her younger sibling.

'Basically,' said Jean-Paul eruditely as he looked at her with a suggestive smile, 'there's only really one big problem in life: at what point do you become a ghost?'

'You mean, at what point do you become the ghost of your own life?'

'You're absolutely right, Pierre.'

To mask his hesitancy, he ran his fingers through his hair, at the same time looking for a reflecting surface.

'Particularly when you see this girl lost in some shit-hole in the back-end of Normandy,' he went on, 'you ask that kind of question. Even if you don't think that people are affected by places in general.'

'You said exactly the opposite to me at your house, two days ago.'

'So I did! You're quite right.'

There was something insulting about his casual accept-ance of the contradictions that had just come to light. When you talked to Jean-Paul, you almost became nostalgic for the time when people could die for their ideas. He seemed to reserve the sincerity of his observa-tions for his written work. It was the only thing that counted, he liked to say; and that explained the fact, to Jean-Paul's satisfaction, that great writers were often complete bastards.

Our remarks became increasingly laconic, as in a father-and-son relationship, where the brevity of the exchanges allows you to relax without sinking into an embarrassing silence. We bumped into two deaf-mutes who were busy showing each other different blocks of nougat and assessing their respective merits in terms of their price–quality ratio, which they evoked by spreading their fingers more or less widely. This was followed by a monotonous list, increasingly unintelligible and pathetic, of articles that they showed each other one by one. Tiring of their mime, we set off again towards the coffee machines at the back of the shop, next to the toilets and the phone.

'How do you feel?' I asked Jean-Paul, taking some coins from my wallet.

'Well. Very well. What about you?'

'My eyes hurt. I think I should consult an optician. I'm a bit tired. What bloody awful weather! Sugar? Short? Long? Espresso? Tea? Tomato juice?'

'Espresso. I've got to wake up. I feel as though I've slept for a week.'

'You were asleep for four hours.'

I clicked on the espresso button and the cup fell immediately with a factory clunk. I heard Jean-Paul whispering behind me. I hadn't known until then that he talked to himself the moment he felt no one was looking at him. Léonore had told me one day that half of the human beings on the planet talked to themselves when they had only themselves for company. It was an identity reflex, a way of reinforcing our self-image, a method designed to capture within ourselves whatever it was that constantly escaped our private nucleus. I imagined a vast chorus of people moving their lips all over the globe. Thousands of imaginary conversations consisting of moments of idleness or secret rancour.

'I'm surprised the sound of the children didn't wake me up. They were there, weren't they?'

'Nothing surprising about it, they didn't make a sound. What did you take?'

'Morpheum 7.5. A sleeping pill. I took two of them. I

have to be careful, zopiclone's an absolute bitch. It works ok, but it's still a bitch and a half!'

'Side-effects?'

'The usual things: swelling and prickling of the fingers and toes, hypersensitivity to light, noise and any physical contact, sometimes hallucinations as well. But it can be worse than that. Extreme aggression, uncontrollable rages, delirious notions and paranoid psychosis. All accompanied by terrible memory problems. You forget events as soon as they occur. Six months ago I heard of a guy on morpheum who had killed his wife by smashing her head on the edge of the kitchen sink. After that the guy went out to have a quiet smoke on the patio, went upstairs and washed and went to bed with a book. Irritated, after two hours, that his wife wasn't coming to bed, he finally found her in the kitchen in a pool of blood with her face caved in. He immediately phoned the police to come and get him. They found him prostrate over one of the kitchen chairs with his wife's body at his feet, completely unable to understand what had happened to her.'

'That's terrible.'

By way of diversion, knowing Jean-Paul's confirmed appetite for this kind of tragic story, I had picked up a local paper that someone had left on the table. The weather page didn't suggest that things were going to get any better for at least two days. A long period of rain was opening up before us.

Jean-Paul went over to the window, lighting a cigarette. He watched the last children passing in front of him on their way to the bus, which we couldn't see from where we were standing. There was something supernatural about his calm appearance, his stillness, while I could hear the sound of birds, confused by the rain, crashing into the windows. He seemed to have lost the energy that had been propelling him onwards since he woke up. He stood there, coffee and cigarette in the same hand, looking suddenly gaunt, dazed and exhausted.

'What's happening?'

He pointed towards a spot in the distance.

'There's someone coming towards us with his face covered in blood. He's staggering, he's still a long way off . . . I think it's the driver.'

I nearly knocked my coffee over. I went and joined Jean-Paul. The scene looked almost unreal. The driver was walking towards us, clutching his head in both hands, and seemed to be making a superhuman effort not to fall over. It looked like a matter of life or death as far as he was concerned. My eyes followed his erratic trajectory, and then I glanced towards Jean-Paul, who appeared to be mesmerised.

The light outside was starting to fade. It was a few minutes past noon, and the grey sky of Normandy was already turning a shimmering black. The wind couldn't blow away the rain, a fine, solid rain that hurtled down in sudden pockets like the impetuous whirl of a flock of swallows. It flew at the service station windows and climbed horizontally up the car park, sweeping the asphalt at an oblique angle. From where we were standing, we could hear a faint whistle from the trees and bushes. Time stopped abruptly as though there had been some sort of breakdown in our continuity.

A heavy silence fell on Jean-Paul and me, we were filled with a palpable, irrepressible fear. A tight fist clenched my heart. We dashed off towards the driver. I automatically glanced to the right to see where the children were.

The bus had gone.

In the shop doorway we came to a standstill. I felt myself growing more and more pale by the moment. Jean-Paul's motionlessness was impressive. I felt cold and hot at the same time, I felt dry and damp, heavy and light, lost and fully conscious. Then I began to split in two, in a bid to test the degree of reality of the scene. When that didn't help I finally decided to look frankly at Jean-Paul, hoping for perspicacity, an instruction manual to deal with the situation. He started coughing in a terrifying way that reminded me of Françoise Morin. From ten metres away you could hear the mucus drumming inside his lungs.

'There you are,' he said to me, rubbing his ribs. 'We should have seen this coming.'

The driver almost fell into my arms. I put one knee on the ground and tried to hold his back against my chest, gripping him under the arms with his head in the hollow of my shoulder. For a few seconds we stayed in that position, waiting for a little calm and peace to descend upon us. He was bleeding copiously. His scalp was cut open at the base of the occipital and the parietal bones. His shoulders looked broader to me, and his head actually seemed to have been split down the middle. He must have been struck in several places, with a view to neutralising him.

'What's happened?' I asked gently.

'The children hit me from behind. They took me far from bus to smoke cigarette with me under trees, shelter from rain . . . I said, "Cigarettes forbidden, you too young!"

but they said that you, man with beard' (he nodded towards Jean-Paul) 'often allow them to smoke . . .'

Jean-Paul looked elsewhere, vexed.

'Can you describe them?'

'A tall fair-haired boy, behind me with girlfriend on journey. Another one, tall too but very brown hair shaved short with scar under right eye . . .'

Dimitri Corto and Sylvain Ginzburger. Jean-Paul turned abruptly towards us, waving his arms. His whole body begged me to go and call the police. Seeing that I wasn't moving, he waved to me and dashed towards the service station.

'And then?'

'I fainted . . . a bit . . . they ran towards bus . . . I saw them, a girl was making big signs with arms, they were in a hurry to go . . .'

'Were all the children on the bus?'

'Yes, they were all there, I think.'

It had all happened very quickly.

We had heard nothing because of the music and the suspended state that we were in. The sound of the lorries on the nearby road had covered the noise of the bus. Dimitri had switched on the engine and closed the doors, leaving the adults outside. I looked at my watch. The children had already been gone for a few minutes. Dimitri's intense concentration on the driver's behaviour from the beginning of the journey was easily explained. The weight of his bleeding body in my arms connected me with the precise nature of events. It was as though I were, second by second, becoming aware of the whole process, of the connections between things.

Alerted by Jean-Paul, the cashier finally noticed us. She

314

arrived, crazed, beside herself, followed by the two deaf-mutes who were coming to the driver's aid. The girl crouched on her heels and stared at me in surprise. I was trembling, and couldn't say a word. Unfamiliar sensations ran through my chest, making it shiver. Everything that was happening seemed suddenly familiar, an impression of dreams and unreality, almost of relief. In my mind's eye I saw the image of Capadis in the playground, shedding his blood with all those eyes on him.

The rain went on falling, making the surfaces increasingly shiny in the pale light. The tension eased. I waited only for the arrival of the police and an ambulance, I didn't even know in which order. All I needed right now was the sound of a voice.

'What's happened to him?' asked the girl in a strident voice.

'He's been hit.'

'My God . . . who by?'

'By some children you saw a moment ago.'

'That's not possible,' she said, wringing her hands. 'Let me, I've done a First Aid course.'

She held the deaf-mutes aside with her arm, and took the driver off my hands. He was losing more and more blood now. In the girl's arms, he folded into the brace position recommended in case of a plane crash, head forward, arms clutching his knees. He assumed that position with incredible ease for someone who had been wounded in the head, his joints relaxing like those of a child or a mime artist. As I watched him crumple I felt my whole body shaking. I put my hands in my pockets to avoid the temptation of wiping his blood on my shirt and trousers. A little further off, the lorries made a rumbling noise.

315

The patch of purple spread on the asphalt, mingling with rainwater. The man's pain was acute and profound. Foam pearled at the corners of his mouth. I fervently hoped he wouldn't die before the emergency services arrived. I realised that I was more worried about him than I was about the children. All of a sudden the rain stopped. Jean-Paul arrived, unusually vibrant. He must have been feeling strong and generous.

'They'll be here any minute,' he said breathlessly, his body leaning forward, his hands on his knees and his eyes filled with compassionate gaiety, 'they're in the neighbourhood . . . They're going to take us both on board and take us to Étretat to intercept the children. The ambulance will be here later . . .'

The sky was starting to brighten in the east. There was nothing left to do but listen to the roar of the lorries and cars. For a moment I had a sense that we were all immersed in something silvery, a strangely sweet light. There was nothing more to do but wait, wait for the moment when the sirens would start howling in the suddenly clear sky.

Epilogue

La Bleymardière, 16 May 1995

Léo,

The psychologist at the centre – who is also responsible for my mental 'rehabilitation' – didn't tell me until
yesterday evening that you were here three days ago with
Nora. I asked him why it had taken him so long to keep
me informed. He told me it was an elementary precau-
tion designed to keep me at a distance, for the time being,
from all external concerns. That, he added, risked
damaging the conducive environment that has been placed
around me while I've been here. I've been wondering
since yesterday evening what he meant by 'conducive
environment'.

His name is Monsieur Fervent, and he is one of those
people who always study the ceiling when you're talking
to them. You can never quite tell whether he's really interested in the problems of the people who come to him,
and that's not a negligible factor in the seductive effect
that he seems to have on most of his patients. He's about

forty, he's quite tall, and he has a voice of surprising distinction, very persuasive. I'm sure you'll like him.

I guess it must have been Jean-Paul who gave you my address at La Bleymardière, because I didn't want any visitors. Even our parents have been kept away, as well as my colleagues and the college administrators. The school has been closed for a week. I'm not supposed to talk about it, but Jean-Paul and I were obliged to spend a week here after the 'accident', long enough for the media to forget we existed. When Catherine came to pick him up I decided to spend a bit longer at the clinic. It's important that you don't talk to anyone about what I've just told you, not even Nora.

During that first week, Jean-Paul was in a room in a building opposite mine. We were never able to communicate, at any point, the existence of each of us being hidden from the other. On several occasions I asked some nurses what had happened to my colleague. They were very evasive for the first three days and then, at my insistence, they finally told me he was in another section. At any rate, we had nothing to say to each other: it was *our* fault, and each of us knew it. If we had been more vigilant, the children would still be alive.

He phoned me last night. From the sound of his voice and the way he told me about meeting up with Catherine, I had a sense that they were getting along much better. He even seemed to have lost that tone of vague regret, that undertone suggesting individual responsibility. The tragedy seemed to have recharged him spiritually. He spoke with enthusiasm and gratitude about everything that had happened. At the end of our conversation, his voice almost betrayed a desire to see something terrifying, like the things we had just experienced, looming up once more.

I guess you must have come to see me, of course, but also to hear me talk about what happened to the children, and to provide more details. Unfortunately there's nothing I can tell you that wasn't in the papers. In fact I've been so dulled with sleeping pills that I have a bit of trouble remembering the actual events. My mind has lost all sense of chronology, so much so that the days I have spent here appear in a blur, as devoid of outlines as a childhood memory. When I make an effort to transport myself back, my brain makes me feel like a fly climbing on the stone face of a statue, able to grasp only one aspect of it at any one time.

Do you think you might be content with my version of the facts, however imprecise they might be? The bus driver was picked up in the car park, and an ambulance immediately took him to a hospital in Rouen. It seems that his life is not in danger despite all the blows he took to the head. The psychologist confirmed that. He'll have some lasting effects: speech difficulties, partial facial paralysis and defective lateralisation. The psychologist added that, according to the X-rays and the multiple contusions they have shown all over his body, they beat him up with the deliberate intention of killing him. But I think that's been part of his strategy with me since the beginning: to make the kids repellent to me so that I don't feel too guilty.

The policemen who picked us up then took us to the cliff of Aval, from which the bus had hurled itself an hour previously. The sea was calm and it wasn't raining. The fire service was there, and divers were bringing the bodies on to the beach one by one, and lining them up in plastic bags. We knew very quickly that there wouldn't be a single survivor. While the bodies were being fetched out, Jean-Paul and I were left on our own in the police van, silent, prostrate, introverted.

That's the only truth I know. I'm not really interested in the rest. A newspaper said that we didn't seem to be affected by the horror of what had happened, that we hadn't really shown any sign of torment. The truth is that we were devastated because we hadn't been able to stop these things happening, but, for my part, I felt happy on the children's behalf because *I was sure that this was what they had wanted from the start*. That's what I can tell you about my feelings.

Since this morning, since the end of breakfast, if you can imagine that, the man in the bed next to me – a music teacher the same age as me – hasn't stopped talking about the 'accident'. He has told me what he would have done in my place, his reactions when the bus set off unexpectedly, without turning his head in my direction by a single insulting centimetre. Commenting on my mistakes, he has constantly returned to my naivety about the children, particularly if one was aware of the facts that accumulated in their disfavour over a period of ten years.

I should say that this fellow, who clearly imagines he has his wits about him, has been here for three months following an ordinary act of aggression that happened at the beginning of one of his classes. A year-ten pupil, whom he had known since year seven, had stabbed him in the stomach with a hunting-knife, quite gratuitously, for no particular reason. He still hasn't worked out why, and the detachment that he has developed since the event has served only to remove him more and more each day from any reason he might have had to go back to work.

Over the course of my career I have often noticed that the most demonstrative of my colleagues were the ones who had the greatest difficulty in establishing contact with the children. It's one way for them to exculpate themselves, to persuade themselves that they can once again begin to define the foundations of their competence, away from that uncontrollable force that calls them into question every time they take a class. Their discourse seems to embody what they need at any given moment in order to know themselves again and ease the tension of being permanently ridiculed. It's very touching, in a way.

I sometimes hear him crying at night. He can't imagine a life outside education. His existence, from childhood, has centred around this vocation. When he was a little boy, he told me, his parents gave him a portable whiteboard with felt pens and a special sponge. His family always had lots of guests at the weekend. He would come downstairs with all his material, close the drawing-room door before the affectionate eyes of all those present, and improvise a lesson on any subject he came up with: shells, plate tectonics, the diplodocus or the socialisation of chimpanzees. He had prepared everything in advance. His mother came to see him in his bedroom an hour beforehand, to find out the day's subject. It was his consolation for putting up with his little classmates laughing at him all week every time he opened his mouth. I reflected that resentment had basically been the soundtrack of his life, but that his vocation had been the only coherent thing he had ever suggested. How many of us are in the same situation?

He looks very unhappy, but there's nothing I can do for him. I don't have the same passionate connection with the job. I've never managed to confess to my colleagues that I presented myself for the examination solely because the statistics were very favourable in those days. It's a touchy subject, telling people that the thing they've devoted their lives to doesn't matter much to you. The impression of imposture that you give could be very dangerous later on.

I'm thinking of quitting the education service, and handing in my resignation at the start of term in September. I can't imagine starting another year at the school, especially after what's happened. As the character in an English novel that I'm reading at the moment says, 'There's probably nothing harder than seeming sincere when your heart is broken.' And sincerity, as problematic as the word may appear to you, is also the basis of teaching. You can't pretend for long.

Could you have a think, Léo, about what else I could do? Your suggestions will be precious to me as I start my new life. I hope I'll be able to claim unemployment benefit, which would enable me to finish my thesis and go into higher education. It strikes me that conditions there are more peaceable than they are at the College, and that I could go on living by recentring myself on essential things. The monotony of a village library would suit me, too. I could make sure that the days and years were all alike. I would need, you see, a silent but amiable context, something that would serve both as a day centre and a lost-property office.

That would give me the sense of security that time is finally closing again, as though I were already inwardly preparing myself for the pitiful and serene abandon of old age. I remember that when we were younger that sort of talk used to horrify you, but if I'm still mentioning these things, it's because they definitively indicate the way I am living. At the age of thirty-two, I'm not going to change. I also nurture the hope that the way your old brother imagines his future life might still be of interest to you.

Since I can't imagine how my life will continue from here, I imagine yours now with Nora. She's both patient and active, which is very rare. I couldn't imagine a better person for you. I expect she'll have spoken to you about our phone conversation just before our little outing. Tell her I still love her voice as much as ever: she articulates so clearly that she gives you the impression her face is going to appear in the receiver at any moment, and come close to yours. She seemed very concerned that I should come to your rescheduled birthday party. Sorry, Léo, but I won't be there: I have a centrally heated room and some reading material and I feel calm for the first time in years. For me, to be calm is almost to be happy.

I wonder what became of Jean-Patrick? He's been very worried about you lately. You seem to have given him cause for concern, and he's the kind of man who fears real problems more than he fears death. I doubt that he would have mentioned our conversation to you, or has he simply not had time? By and large, I led him to believe that you were like those middle-class children who grow up into well-paid and influential senior executives. They often have excellent conversational skills, they dress in a very original way, mixing designer labels and things from charity shops, they know loads of things about the most recondite subjects, but at any moment they can completely abandon their own personalities to become easy prey for any fake adventurers who want to drag them off the straight and narrow. I hope you're not too annoyed with that description. It's more or less all I had time to say to him. Let me know if I've done the right thing.

Write to me, the address is on the back of the envelope, but I'm not coming straight away. Wait a little bit.

Your brother

Pierre

PS: One last anecdote that you won't have learned from the papers because it was Jean-Paul who told it to me yesterday on the phone. There was nearly one survivor by default, because one of the pupils wasn't able to go on the trip for health reasons. The pupil in question, Brice Toutain, fell seriously ill the day before the trip, a bronchial pneumonia that he had already had for several weeks. He had missed lots of classes, and after learning that there was no way of getting out of the trip he kept chilling his body by exposing it to lethal temperatures. He died the very day of the event. His mother came into his room at half past one before going back to work, and his little body was already cold. The doctor who examined him recorded on the death certificate that his death occurred at one o'clock. That was the precise time when the last witnesses say they saw the bus crashing through the barriers to fly towards the sea.

www.randomhouse.co.uk/vintage